Before she **what** the men were there inside the room.

She wanted to scream, to flee, but she knew the slightest movement could be her undoing. She shook and her eyes filled with tears. But she discovered that if she concentrated on each breath, her lips tightly sealed, no sounds would escape. Crouched beneath the desk, she pressed her hands and feet against the floor to keep them from knocking against anything.

The two men spoke casually to each other, almost lightheartedly, in contrast to the deadly terror she felt. Though she struggled to comprehend what they were saying, she couldn't decipher all the words. She thought about reaching for the dictionary that lay by her side, but that was too risky. The Germans had turned on the lights and were walking from desk to desk, apparently looking for something. *Oh, God, what if they are looking for the supply log?* She considered putting it back in the drawer, but instantly realized how foolish that would be. *They'll find me anyway, if they approach this desk, and I can't make a move without giving myself away.*

Every second was agony, as if death might come at any moment. But she admitted to herself that a swift demise would be easy compared to her fate if discovered. She would face humiliation, torture, and then finally, mercifully, death. The thought made her throat constrict painfully, as if a noose were being tightened around it. *Was this what Marco felt when he died?* Fear evolved into despondency. *Just breathe...slowly, deeply...focus only on that—don't think about anything else. Concentrate only on breathing.*

In the Arms
of
the Enemy

by

Lisbeth Eng

This is a work of fiction. Names, characters, places, and incidents are either the product of the author's imagination or are used fictitiously, and any resemblance to actual persons living or dead, business establishments, events, or locales, is entirely coincidental.

In the Arms of the Enemy

Cover Art by *Rae Monet*

The Wild Rose Press
PO Box 706
Adams Basin, NY 14410-0706
Visit us at www.thewildrosepress.com

Publishing History
First Vintage Rose Edition, 2010
Print ISBN 1-60154-829-X

Published in the United States of America

This book is dedicated with sincere appreciation to

Kenny Eng
Jennifer Butch
Michael Powazinik
Lise Horton

and all my friends at the New York City Chapter of
Romance Writers of America.

Prologue

The Veneto, Italy
October 1943

Above the heads of the crowd a noose dangled from the hastily built gallows. Willing herself not to faint, Isabella pushed through her fellow townspeople toward the squad of German soldiers. A stern-faced officer headed the rank at the foot of the grisly wooden structure that loomed against the backdrop of the rustic piazza. Her pulse throbbed against her temples and her breath came in quick, stabbing gasps. *I can't fall apart now—it's my only chance to save him!* She had to reach the man who held Marco's life in his hands.

"That's him!" She turned to Leonardo. "The commander of the battalion. I've got to get to him."

"The bastard who wouldn't even let us see our own brother?" Leonardo's face was red with fury. "You think he'll listen to you now?"

"I've got to try. At least he speaks Italian."

She squeezed through the villagers with a glance here and there at their averted faces. *They can't bear to look at me.* These were her neighbors, some she'd known her whole life. A few seemed embarrassed, as if ashamed that a morbid curiosity, and not only the decree of the occupying authorities, had compelled them to attend.

The door of the town hall flew open just as she broke through the crowd, and a swarm of field-gray uniforms surged forward. Then she saw him, her precious baby brother, dragged toward the gallows by two brutish soldiers. His shirt was bloody, his face disfigured by blows.

"Wait, please!" In one more step she reached the commander and grabbed his sleeve. "He...he didn't mean any harm. It was only a scuffle. He wasn't trying to cause any trouble. He's only nineteen..."

"You're the sister, aren't you?" the man spat out. His pale eyes bored into hers. "If you don't let go of me this instant, you'll be next."

She released her grasp but shifted her body to block his way. Her voice lowered to a whisper. "I'll do anything you want. Anything. Please don't do this."

The commander looked her up and down, as if considering the offer. He straightened, and the grim line of his mouth tightened into a sneer. "This is how we deal with rebellion. Your brother instigated a riot."

"A riot? It was a barroom brawl! I'm sorry your lieutenant was injured, but it was just a broken nose. And they only argued over a girl. The lieutenant said something rude and Marco tried to defend her. They were both drunk, and then others joined in. It got out of hand, that's all. But Marco didn't mean to hurt anyone. Punish him, yes, but please, *please* don't kill him!"

"You Italians don't understand anything about order and discipline. No wonder your Army surrendered and needed our Führer to save them. Your brother is a troublemaker, and we don't abide troublemakers. An example must be made. Now get out of my way."

He brushed past, throwing her off balance, but as she stumbled she felt someone clasp her arm. *Thank God...Leonardo.* But a second later, sheer terror jolted her body as the soldiers forced Marco up onto a chair and fixed the noose around his neck.

"Marco!" she cried out even as the chair was kicked away.

The scene before her, too appalling to comprehend, had the surreal horror of a nightmare. She turned from the hideous sight, dizzy, nauseous, nearly swooning. At last she relinquished all effort to stand, and sank to her knees, her body racked with sobs. Leonardo knelt beside her and enfolded her in his arms as she buried her face against his chest.

****

A deathly silence hung in the chill night air. The crowd had dispersed, but Isabella and Leonardo remained in the piazza, keeping vigil near their brother's suspended body for the full twelve hours the Germans had ordered it to hang.

Isabella held her position on the rough pavement just a few feet from the gallows. With Leonardo's wool jacket draped loosely around her slumping shoulders, she sat on the ground, legs tucked beneath her skirt. She had turned her body away from Marco rather than toward him, as if to defend him from further violence. Thus she could be near him, yet avoid the heartbreaking sight.

"Isabella, why don't you let me take you home?" Leonardo pleaded. "There's nothing you can do here."

"No."

German soldiers stood guard near by, unmoved by her misery, while a bitter hatred swelled within her. *I swear to you, Marco, I'll get our revenge.*

Chapter 1

Verona, Italy
September 1944

Isabella lifted her chin and forced a brave smile as she passed through the massive oak doors of the imposing palazzo. *I can do this.* As she followed Silvia into the grand salon, she glanced at the high vaulted ceiling, reminiscent of the cathedral she'd attended as a child. Tapestries in jewel tones of garnet and emerald—like stained glass windows—adorned the formidable granite walls, and bronze chandeliers hung like censers from above.

"Here we are, Giorgio!" Silvia announced. "Isabella, I must introduce you to my friend Giorgio Carducci. He's a very important man in the government."

"Ciao, bella!" He came toward them. To calm her anxiety, Isabella drew a quick, inconspicuous breath and then smiled and extended her hand. He was impeccably dressed in evening attire, ornamented with a neat but showy row of medals and ribbons. As he leaned forward to take her hand in his stout and sweaty one and bring it to his lips, the reek of cigars and whiskey assailed her.

"Isabella and I went to convent school together. Can you believe it, Giorgio, me in a convent?" Silvia said with a laugh as she pulled a cigarette from her purse.

Giorgio lit it and turned to Isabella. "And you,

signorina?"

"No, grazie."

"Ah, you don't smoke? You look like a nice girl. You probably don't have any of your friend Silvia's naughty habits, eh?"

"Only a few," Isabella responded with a coy smile. She scanned the room. There were ladies in silken gowns and glittering gems, gentlemen in formal black suits or stately dress uniforms, and waiters meandering silently among them, their trays laden with champagne and caviar. The doors to the balcony were open and she already longed to step outside for a touch of cool, clean air. It was a perfect September evening, the soft rosy sunset fading into a sapphire ocean of night.

"This is her first time in Palazzo Fabriano. Poor Isabella doesn't get out very much," Silvia said with a trace of feigned sympathy and an exaggerated frown. "I ran into her just the other day near the Basilica di Sant' Anastasia. We went to Piazza dei Signori and talked for hours, just like schoolgirls! How many years has it been, cara mia?"

"Too many, Silvia. Would you mind if I took a step out on the balcony? I'd like to see the courtyard while there is still a little light. Please excuse me, signore. It was a pleasure to meet you."

Isabella wasn't used to such elegant surroundings and took care not to slip on the polished marble floor in her borrowed shoes. *If I fall I'll never pull this off, and I'd probably rip Silvia's dress in the process.* She almost laughed at the thought, but it was apprehension, not amusement, she felt.

On the stone terrace, she leaned against the outer wall and drew a long breath. The view of the exquisite gardens below did nothing to ease her tension. *Perhaps a little food would help.* As she turned and looked up, hoping to spot a nearby waiter, she realized she was being observed. He was an officer, tall and dark-haired, probably in his late twenties. She noted from the insignia on his tunic that he was a captain in the German Army.

"Buona sera, signorina," he said with a courteous smile, and tipped his glass in her direction.

To Isabella, the soft tone of his German-accented Italian seemed at odds with the severity of his Wehrmacht uniform. "Buona sera," she responded, then quickly turned away. Was it revulsion for the enemy or simply shyness that induced her retreat to the salon? *I'll need to overcome both if I'm to succeed tonight.*

She made her way back to where Silvia stood with a throng of admiring gentlemen. *If only I were a little more like her. She's so relaxed, so confident around men.* Silvia's delicate features and fair coloring attracted attention; her golden hair and blue eyes suggested the Germanic ancestry of many northern Italians. But it was her vibrant personality and flirtatious charm that drew people to her. In contrast, Isabella felt self-conscious at lavish parties. A simple country girl, she considered herself rather ordinary, though she'd been told many times she was pretty.

"Would you like to dance, Fräulein?" asked one of the officers in Silvia's entourage.

Isabella's understanding of German was limited, but his nod toward the dance floor and expectant expression made the invitation clear. Despite her hatred for the Nazis, she had resolved to be amiable and compliant. This was the only way to insinuate herself into their circle and accomplish her goal. She took a deep breath and smiled as she took his hand.

He's dashing in his dress uniform, and what a fine dancer he is, if only he didn't have quite so forceful a grip on my hand. His leer made her wish the dance would soon end, and when it did, she muttered to him in broken German that she needed to refresh herself in the powder room.

In the women's lounge, Isabella rested a few moments on a velvet sofa. *Can I really go through with this?* She looked at herself in the mirror. Did she see a young woman bold enough to infiltrate the enemy, brave enough to risk her life for a cause? Or merely the naïve girl she had always believed herself to be?

Isabella closed her eyes for a moment, striving to garner her will. Then she stood and, with one last glance in the mirror, smoothed her hair and rehearsed a winsome smile. *I can't hide in here all night if my goal is to make the acquaintance of a Nazi or a Fascist,* she concluded, and braced herself to reenter the salon.

"I was beginning to wonder what had happened to you."

Isabella was startled to see her dancing partner standing just outside the door, waiting impatiently. A look of command blazed in his eyes, which roved the plunging neckline of her gown and boldly lingered at her breasts.

"I hope I didn't frighten you away," he said with a smirk as he led her back toward the salon. "You are very pretty, Fräulein. What is your name?"

She took him in with a furtive glimpse. From his crystal blue eyes and blond hair to the embroidered eagle and swastika adorning his tunic, he epitomized the fearsome Aryan warrior. *He must have been the perfect Hitler Youth.*

"My name? Oh, Isabella Ricci," she responded demurely.

"And mine is Lieutenant Wilhelm Rauch. There is a very interesting painting in another salon down the hall. May I show it to you, Isabella?"

"If you speak a little more slowly maybe I

7

understand better. My German is not so good, I think. Parla italiano?"

"Ah, sì, sì," he said, laughing. "Vieni con me stasera...a casa mia?"

She wondered at his brazen suggestion. *Does he really expect me to go home with him tonight?* She dared a direct response as they proceeded down the hallway. "I think you are a little too forward, sir," she told him in Italian.

"Bitte...I don't understand," he said, a bit humbled. "I must confess. I don't speak Italian. I don't even know what I said to you just now," he replied innocently, though his smile suggested otherwise. "Hmm...now I can't remember where that picture is...maybe in here."

He brought her into a darkened room, far from the crowded salon. Before her eyes could adjust to the dim lighting, she found herself pushed up against a wall. The Iron Cross dangling from his collar scratched the tender skin of her throat as he leaned into her and forced her mouth open with a probing tongue. Tepid breath teased her neck, while groping hands slithered down her black taffeta gown. His fingers grazed a nipple, then ventured downward, nearly reaching her thigh. She felt crushed beneath his weight and instinctively tried to push him off. Then recalling her mission, she endeavored to repress her feelings of disgust.

"Please..." She struggled to remember his name. "Lieutenant...uh...Wilhelm...not here."

"Where then?" he asked with annoyance. "Well, I suppose I could try to find a private room."

And then what? Oh, no. I need time to think. "I like better," she told him. "You go find, yes?"

"All right." He sighed, as if her request were the impertinent demand of a subordinate. "This may take a bit of work. Will you wait for me in the other room?"

8

"Yes, Wilhelm," she said, repeating his name in an effort to imprint it in her brain. He took her arm, not too gently, and walked with her back to the main salon before he headed off to arrange accommodations.

Isabella gratefully accepted a glass of champagne from the nearest waiter. Then, overcome by a wave of agitation, she looked around for a quiet place to retreat and recover her poise. An empty chair in an alcove near the immense marble fireplace beckoned, and once there she gulped the entire glass in an effort to steady her nerves and relax the tight-corded muscles of her throat.

An internal battle raged as she weighed her aversion to Wilhelm against the store of information he might provide. *Didn't I know this is how it would be? Can I presume to ingratiate myself with these brutes without at least appearing to favor their company? And beyond that...what will he expect from me?* She scarcely wanted to admit that she already knew the answer to that last question. Her motive for this scheme of deception, her loathing for the occupying Germans, was the very reason she must attempt to charm them. She thought all Nazis were frightful and this one particularly odious. *But if I've any hope of achieving my aim, I must abide their attentions. Now then, am I enough of an actress to pull it off?*

After ten minutes of stern dictates to her wavering emotions, she regained her composure and joined the other guests, determined to stay calm long enough to quiet her stomach with some food. The buffet table held an elaborate display of carved beef and game, oysters and escargots, and she perused it in search of something she could eat without making a mess of herself.

"Difficult decision, signorina?" She turned and found herself face to face with the dark-haired captain encountered on the balcony earlier. "It all looks so lovely, doesn't it? Why don't you try the venison? It's very good."

"Maybe I'm not so hungry after all," she responded as she glanced around nervously for Wilhelm.

"Is something wrong?" he asked. "Come, sit down; you look a little pale." He took her by the elbow and guided her toward a divan, then asked her to rest while he got her something to drink.

"Please, just water, danke," she said in German as she sat down. He returned a moment later with a glass of water and sat beside her.

"I see you speak a little German. Not many girls here do."

"Only a few words, Captain. Your Italian is much better," she said with a tentative smile. "Thank you for the water."

"My pleasure. You don't look comfortable, signorina. Perhaps you are not so happy to be here? Oh, I don't mean to embarrass you. I'd rather not be here myself. At least that's how I felt until a few moments ago." His smile widened and she noticed his deep blue eyes for the first time.

"A few moments ago? What changed your mind?" she replied, trying to appear more relaxed than she felt.

"Ah, cara signorina, you are very sweet. Would you like to take a walk with me outside? I know where we can find a quiet spot to talk. I think a little fresh air will do you good."

She wondered how long it might be before Wilhelm came looking for her. *Well, this Nazi can't be any worse than the last one, and a captain should prove more valuable than a lieutenant.* Strangely, something in his manner reassured her. He seemed pleasant enough, almost benign. Perhaps this task wouldn't be impossible after all, as long as she remained on her guard.

"All right. But I must tell my friend Silvia or she will be worried about me."

"Silvia Matteo is your friend? You don't seem at all like her."

"What do you mean by that? You really don't know me, signore, do you?"

"You are right, of course. Please forgive me. I just meant that you seem more reserved. Signorina Matteo is very...how shall I say...lively, you know?"

"I'm not quite dead yet," Isabella murmured, and the trace of a smile broke across her lips.

On their way to the door, Isabella stopped to inform her friend that she would be stepping outside for a brief tour of the grounds with her new escort.

"Brava, Isabella, he's a handsome one," whispered Silvia as she eyed the captain, who remained several feet beyond. "I'm sure the gentleman can bring you home later. I don't know exactly where I'll be, but you have your key, no? Have fun, carina." With a tilt of her head Silvia indicated her approval and returned to her own flirtations.

****

Low bushes edged the gravel path on the far side of the palazzo overlooking the darkened city below. Isabella caught the subtle fragrance of an herb or flower she couldn't identify. The distant lights of the party and a nearly full moon illuminated just enough for her to make out his features.

"Are you cold, signorina?" he asked as he laid a warm hand on her bare upper arm. He unbuttoned his tunic and placed it over her shoulders. "You know, I don't even know your name. I am Günter Schumann. And you...?"

"My name is Isabella Ricci, signore. Have you been in Italy long?"

"I was stationed in Rome for about a year. I've been in Verona only a few months; it is very beautiful. The hills remind me a little of my village in Bavaria. Here we are." He indicated a stone bench a few steps ahead and waited for her to sit down before joining her.

"The view is lovely from here. You seem to know the palazzo well."

"Not really. I've been invited on a few occasions. Usually I try to escape the din inside for a walk around the grounds. I can still hear the music out here, but I feel much more relaxed. Not so much smiling to do, I think."

"Is smiling so difficult for you, Captain Schumann?"

"Certainly not at this particular moment. And please call me Günter."

"All right, Günter. So why is smiling so onerous for you on other occasions?" She searched his eyes for any hint of insincerity and found none she could discern. *Well, he's a man, and a Nazi at that. Surely he must know how to deceive.*

"I guess I'm a bit introverted, you see," he said with a sigh. "I really don't like these parties so much. They're not my favorite kind of entertainment."

"And what would that be?"

"I like music, but not to dance. I'm not very good at that. Chamber music is my favorite—Haydn, Brahms—gentle, yet stirring. My mother had hopes I would study with Meister Kolditz in Vienna, but I'm afraid I didn't have her talent."

Isabella sensed a note of sadness in his voice. She imagined a long forgotten dream, an existence he could still remember before joining the Army of the Third Reich. Was it possible he could have been an ordinary boy once, the object of a mother's love?

"No talent for music, then? So what are your

talents?" *A talent for brutalizing innocent civilians, no doubt.* But she reminded herself that she must not betray her contempt.

"Well, I'm proficient in languages: Italian, English, French, Latin. I was pursuing a degree in linguistics, but then the war came..." His voice trailed off. "It's getting late, Isabella. I'd better get you home before your parents start to worry."

"My parents? I'm staying in town with Silvia and I doubt she'll be pacing the floor wondering about me. She knows I'm in good hands, doesn't she?"

"Of course," he replied with a smile. "May I arrange a ride for you? I'm sorry I can't come along, but I'm due to check in with my commanding officer." He stood and offered his hand. "I will see that you get home safely."

Though it wasn't very late, Isabella consented. *At least I can elude that horrid Wilhelm.*

Günter signaled for a car as they arrived at the front of the palazzo. "Klaus here will take good care of you. I'm afraid I will need this back." He removed his tunic from her shoulders. "Do you have a wrap inside?" She shook her head. "There's a blanket here in the back seat." He waited at the open door of the black limousine as she settled in. "When can I see you again, Isabella?" he asked as he leaned in toward her.

"I can meet you tomorrow afternoon, if you like."

"I would like that very much. Do you know Caffè Gavi on Via Cattaneo?" She nodded. "Why don't we meet there tomorrow, say about five o'clock?"

"All right," she replied, her brown eyes locked on his azure ones. His eyes shone as he kissed her hand.

"Sleep well, bella signorina. Until tomorrow, then."

Chapter 2

The diffused light of morning gleamed off the limestone and chalky-white granite buildings surrounding Piazza delle Erbe. Farmers from the countryside filled the marketplace, hawking their fresh eggs and cheese while weary housewives searched for the rare bargain to put a little more food into their screaming babies' mouths. Isabella made her purchases as she worked her way toward the far side of the cobblestone square. There, a few of the idle wealthy sat in the open-air caffè, sipping their espressos or flicking their cigarette ashes onto the ground. Isabella spotted Massimo leaning against a column in a shaded corner of the piazza, his cap low over his eyes. He looked annoyed.

"You are late, Isabella." He didn't bother to look up as she approached. "I've been waiting all morning."

"I'm sorry. You know that I stayed at Silvia's last night. I didn't think she'd understand if I departed at dawn."

"I see," he replied with a frown. "So how did it go at the palazzo? Did you learn anything, meet anyone important?"

"I met Giorgio, um...ah, yes, Carducci. Silvia said he is an important Fascist."

Massimo shook his head and let out an irritated groan. Isabella knew he had only a slight interest in Mussolini's minions, who held little power. Their Duce, deposed by his own government and reinstalled by the Nazis, had been reduced to a puppet despot under Hitler's control.

"And I met a German officer," she continued, "a Captain Schumann."

"A captain? You don't aim very high, Isabella. But I guess that's not bad for your first attempt. Tell me about this captain. What unit is he in?"

"I don't know, but I'm meeting him later today. He seems to like me."

"Find out where he is stationed and who is his commander. Don't spend too much time on him if he's useless to us."

"Well, I don't want to make him suspicious by asking too many questions about his military duties. I'll find out more as I gain his confidence. Don't rush this, carino. You know the risks."

"Perhaps you'll like to bed him first?"

Isabella glared at him before responding. "That's a very nice thing to say to the woman you supposedly love. Maybe you should find someone else for this assignment."

His voice softened. "I'm sorry, carina. I don't mean to be harsh. You know that I love you very much, don't you?"

"Of course I do. But this isn't easy, Massimo. I mean...I've never done anything like this before."

Massimo lifted her chin with his hand and smiled. "I'm confident you'll do your job well. How long are you staying with Silvia?"

"She didn't say. I can probably stay for a few more days. But I'd rather come home."

"Let's wait and see what develops. Just keep me informed, step by step."

She looked deep into his piercing black eyes. "I miss you." She caressed his face, admiring the masculine set of his jaw, shadowed by a dark, closely trimmed beard.

"You'd better go now. I'll meet you here

tomorrow morning; try to make it by seven. And be careful, Isabella."

"Of course." After a tender kiss, she withdrew into the shadows of the columns and slipped away.

****

Despite Massimo's expression of confidence, Isabella remained uneasy, immersed in circumstances far beyond her control. She was determined to conquer the fits of self-doubt and prove she was up to the task, though at this point it wasn't clear what that task would entail. *Where will my acquaintance with the German captain lead? What will he expect from me?*

She and Massimo hadn't resolved all the contingencies of her foray into the world of the Fascists and Nazis. Though her mission required involvement with another man, they hadn't discussed the uncomfortable implications. The possibility of an intimate encounter hung in the air between them, unsettled yet understood.

Isabella strolled up the narrow, twisting streets to Silvia's apartment and by the time she reached it had cast these thoughts from her mind. *All that matters is our goal.* She reflected on the previous night, on the pompous crowd dancing, laughing, drinking, oblivious to the suffering of the world beyond the thick stone walls of the palazzo. *How long can they remain sheltered from the ravages upon our country, trying to preserve the illusion of their frivolous life?* Ruthless German occupation with its atrocities inflicted upon Italian citizens— political repression, deportations, summary executions, mass slaughter—had spurred her hatred for the Nazis and their Italian collaborators. Marco's murder had convinced her to defy them.

Isabella climbed the steps to Silvia's cozy apartment and let herself in with her key. Silvia sat in her dressing gown at the kitchen table, sipping strong black coffee and holding her head with one hand.

"Oh, my head! Why does the Lord punish me so for having a good time? Still, if all goes as planned, it will be worth it."

"What plan is that?"

"I've thrown out a net to catch Federico di Balduccio, that new charmer I met last night. He is wealthy, and I believe he has connections with Il Duce. It's been too long since I've had a new boy to play with." Silvia giggled. "But you, my dear, seem to have hooked a fine catch yourself. You're meeting that handsome Captain Schumann later today, are you not?"

"I'm meeting him at five o'clock. Do you know him, Silvia?"

"Not really, only by reputation. The word is he's a bit shy, but a real gentleman and honorable, if you can believe that!"

He seems to know about your reputation, too. "Is it so hard to believe a man can have honor, or is it because he's a German?"

"Oh, I've nothing against the Germans—some of them make great lovers! But it's rare to find an honest man of any nationality."

"Maybe you're looking in the wrong places." Isabella smiled, poured herself some coffee and sat down across from Silvia. *Massimo is an honorable man, but I must not mention him to Silvia.*

"Did you pick up anything at the market, Isabella?"

"Just some potatoes and a few eggs," Isabella replied, producing a small sack.

"Let's scrape together some lunch for ourselves. There's some bread that's not too stale, and some cheese in the icebox. Be a dear and start cooking, would you? My head is still aching."

****

It was nearly three when Isabella heard a knock.

"Just a minute," Silvia yelled as she walked to the door. She opened it and admitted a young German soldier holding an envelope in his hand. Isabella recognized Klaus, the man who had driven her home the previous night. After handing the envelope to Silvia, he nodded politely, turned deftly on his heel and departed.

"It's for you, Isabella," Silvia said in spirited anticipation as she passed her the missive. "Come on, let's see what it is!"

Isabella carefully broke the seal, unfolded the note and read aloud:

Cara Signorina Ricci,

Please accept my sincerest apologies but I won't be able to meet you at five o'clock today as we planned. I am in conference all day and can't get away until much later. I hope you are free tonight and can join me at Villa Bagliotti for a private concert. I've enclosed the invitation and will send a car for you at seven. I'll probably be rather late, but please enjoy the concert until I arrive. I am looking forward to seeing you again.

Günter Schumann

Isabella searched the envelope again and discovered the invitation. "Gala Concert featuring the Vorholz Chamber Orchestra with artists from the Teatro alla Scala; Villa Bagliotti, eight o'clock," she read. "I've never been to an event like this before. I've no idea what to wear!"

"Oh, don't worry about that. We'll find something for you." Silvia took Isabella by the hand and led her to the bedroom. "Let me turn you into a vision that captain of yours won't soon forget!"

Isabella sat on the bed as she was instructed

while Silvia opened her closet to reveal an array of luxurious garments. *Luckily for me, we're nearly the same size.*

"What about this?" Silvia asked as she modeled a long red beaded gown against herself. Isabella's eyes widened in awe. "Or maybe the black one?" Silvia offered, producing a classic column of satin with rhinestones encircling the neckline and sleeves. "This was from Giorgio, the gentleman you met last night." Isabella sat speechless. "What is it? You don't like either one?"

"Oh, no, Silvia, they're absolutely gorgeous! But...I would feel so...I don't know...not like myself. Maybe something a little simpler?"

"Here, why don't you have a look for yourself?" Silvia waved her hand toward the closet.

Isabella approached the wondrous collection and began to finger her way through. Then she stopped and withdrew a sleeveless sheath in the palest hue of green. It was completely devoid of decoration and tailored simply with two subtle darts at the waist. "May I try this?" she asked.

"Of course, Isabella. You *do* have style, my dear, and I think the figure for that one, too!"

Isabella undressed, slipped the gown over her head and asked Silvia to zip up the back. At the full-length mirror in the corner of the room she twirled around in both directions. The silken fabric, in a shade evoking the first breath of spring, felt feather-soft against her skin. "Maybe it's a little too big here," she said indicating the waist. "What do you think?"

Silvia examined the fit with the skill of a seamstress, and pinched an inch or two of fabric in the back. "I can take this in with a few simple stitches. It will only be about twenty minutes of work. Then it will be just right!"

Isabella's smile broadened as she admired the

way it clung to her slender body. "I do like this one."

"Now I really am jealous. That dress looks better on you than it ever did on me. I love the way that color brings out your dark hair and eyes. I think it was made for you! But you need something to make it a bit fancier for Villa Bagliotti. That estate makes the palazzo look like an old ruin! I know what..." Silvia headed back to the closet and brought down a large box from the highest shelf. It held a heavenly mink stole lined in brocaded silk, embroidered with Silvia's initials in gold thread. "Giancarlo gave this to me on our first anniversary. Ha! To think that I actually courted the same man for a whole year!"

"Oh, I couldn't. It's really magnificent! But I think it's a little too warm out for mink."

"Well, it's cool at night; you'll need a wrap...and maybe some gloves." Silvia searched through her drawers and tossed possibilities onto the bed. "Here they are. These gloves will work, I think."

Before Isabella turned to see the gloves her glance caught on something intriguing hung on a hook behind the closet door—a large rectangle of gossamer silver tulle edged with iridescent sequins. She wrapped it around her shoulders and displayed it for Silvia's approval.

"Yes, why not? And with these gloves and the silver shoes I wore last night, your ensemble will be complete." Silvia retrieved the shoes from beneath her bed and laid them on the floor in front of Isabella.

"They're a little tight. Maybe I should wear the ones I wore last night," Isabella said as she slipped them on.

"Don't even think of wearing black shoes with that outfit! The silver ones will be fine. You can kick them off later in the evening when everyone is too drunk to notice." Isabella tried on the long white gloves that came to just above her elbows. "Go, look in the mirror."

Isabella couldn't help but smile as she gazed at the elegant young woman who stared back at her. "I hardly recognize myself!" But her smile faded as she recalled the purpose of her glamorous attire. *Tonight my seduction of the enemy will begin.*

"Now let me just pin the back so I can sew it for you." Silvia withdrew her sewing kit from the bottom drawer of the dresser. "Ah, yes!" she said as she pulled out another box, a black velvet one, from the same drawer. She opened it and removed a pearl necklace and placed it around Isabella's neck. "That's it. Perfect! And I've the earrings to match." She finished pinning the dress and began to put the other items back. "Take that off and help me clean up this mess."

"Of course, Silvia." Isabella took a last glimpse in the mirror, then turned to Silvia and gave her a gentle kiss on the cheek. "You've been so sweet to me. Thank you, my dear friend."

Chapter 3

At half past six Isabella paced the floor in the tight silver shoes. Silvia had worked her hair into a twist at the nape of her neck, leaving a few loose strands to dangle and "excite the captain's interest." She'd insisted that Isabella wear just a hint of rouge and lip color. Isabella had protested, not wanting to look like "a painted woman," but it was barely noticeable, just as Silvia had assured. *I look so sophisticated even Massimo wouldn't recognize me! Perhaps I can pull off this charade after all.*

"Isabella! You are making me very uneasy. And I'm not even the one attending the gala! Would you please sit down and relax? You mustn't look so anxious. In fact, you should make the driver wait for you at least ten minutes when he arrives. One would think you've never had a rendezvous with a man before. You have, haven't you?"

Isabella sighed as she sat down in a chair. "Yes, I'm not as innocent as you imagine. I've just never been to this type of affair. Last night was the most fashionable event I've ever attended."

"I think it's something else," Silvia added with a glint in her eye. "I think this Captain Schumann will become someone very special to you. I noticed the way he was looking at you. I'd say he's already smitten. And maybe you feel it, too, but don't recognize it yet."

"Oh, Silvia, you can't possibly know that. We've only just met. Don't read so much into it." *What you*

22

don't know, Silvia, is that he already is someone very special to me. He's the Nazi who will, with some luck, unwittingly lead me to the information the Resistance needs. "So, tell me what Villa Bagliotti is like. You said it's more extravagant than the palazzo. I find that difficult to imagine."

"Well, it's smaller than the palazzo, but much more elegant. The palazzo seems so ancient and forbidding to me, like a medieval fortress, all stone and marble, with only a few tapestries to brighten it. I'd expect to find some dusty skeletons in the cellar there. But the villa is truly luxurious. It's decorated with gorgeous velvets and silks and the most exquisite antiques. I imagine Madame de Pompadour would have entertained in a place like that. Only the cream of society ever gets invited there, you know. I've only been once!" Silvia laughed. "The captain must have better connections than I'd have guessed."

"I think I'm more nervous now than ever!" Isabella giggled.

A knock announced the arrival of Isabella's car. She jumped to open the door, then looked back at Silvia, remembering her advice to make the driver wait. She opened it anyway. *I don't need to impress Klaus, and I'd just as well get the evening started now.*

"Here, don't forget your purse," Silvia said as she joined Isabella at the door. "Have a great time, carina, and *relax*," she whispered. Silvia watched from the window as Isabella turned and waved, then slipped into the back seat of the limousine.

****

A forty-minute drive brought them to an estate atop a verdant hill outside the city. From the main road it was another five minutes along a private drive lined with meticulously tended lawns and stately cypress trees. Ahead stood a breathtaking

Palladian mansion with a majestic façade of
Corinthian columns and neo-classical flourishes.

She presented her invitation at the door and
was shown to a large salon filled with perhaps a
hundred crimson velvet chairs, carefully spaced. In
front were several more chairs, as well as music
stands and instruments. The soaring walls, covered
in gold damask, were crowned by a delicately carved
gilt cornice, while the arched ceiling was painted in
subtle shades of pale blue, with touches of white and
gray, creating the illusion of a fair summer sky. *It's
just like the art books I loved at school.* The war and
the needs of her family had long deferred her dream
to study art history.

It was almost eight o'clock, and the many chairs
were filling rapidly, so she took a seat near the back.
The assemblage was different somehow from the
revelers at the previous night's festivities, but in
what way she couldn't quite decide. The room was
nearly full when an elderly gentleman rose to greet
the audience and introduce the musicians who had
entered from a side door.

They began with a Bach concerto, as she noted
from the program, and she looked around to observe
the other patrons. It finally struck her what was
different about this group compared to the carefree
spirits at the palazzo. These were mostly older
people, certainly well to do and elegantly dressed but
quiet and serious as they enjoyed the serene music.
*I'm afraid, Silvia, you'll be wrong in your prediction.
I think these people would notice if I kicked off my
shoes!*

Isabella closed her eyes and tried to relax and
allow herself to be swept away by the gentle strains.
A pair of opera selections followed the concerto: a
soprano solo from *Don Giovanni* and a duet from *La
Traviata*. Isabella delighted in the stirring melodies,
the extraordinary range and fluidity of the voices.

After two more chamber pieces the first half of the program was nearly over.

Isabella was so rapt by the music that she barely noticed when Günter arrived and sat down beside her at the end of the second piece. As the applause died down he reached over, touched her arm and smiled to greet her. She looked at him shyly and returned the smile, trying to mask her apprehension for the role she must play.

A corpulent mezzo-soprano stepped before the audience and delivered a bittersweet German love song with such passion that Isabella felt a twinge of emotion. She glanced over at Günter, who also seemed affected by the rendition. *Perhaps he's thinking of his homeland.*

When the song ended, the audience rose and moved in a leisurely way toward doors that led to an adjoining salon. Following the others, Günter offered his arm and escorted Isabella into a room softly lit with crystal chandeliers.

"You look lovely tonight," he said. "I'm sorry I'm so late. I hope the program has pleased you so far."

"Yes, it's been wonderful. I don't know much about classical music, but I admit I am really enchanted by it. That last piece, the one in German—it was very moving. I couldn't understand all of the words. What was it about?"

"Actually, it's a traditional ballad about star-crossed lovers who die in each other's arms. I've heard it many times and it always makes me a little melancholy. Not so much because it's a sad story but because it reminds me of my mother. She used to sing it sometimes."

"Does it make you sad to think about your mother?"

"Only sometimes. Most of my memories are very fond. She died when I was twenty-one, a year before the war started."

"I'm so sorry, Günter. You must miss her very much."

"Yes, I do. I miss my whole family now that I'm so far from home. But let's not talk about such things. I want you to enjoy yourself tonight. Would you like a glass of champagne?" he asked.

"Yes, please. How long is the intermission? Do we have time to sit down?" Her feet were beginning to hurt now.

"Of course. There are two seats right over there." He indicated two wing chairs a few steps away. "Please sit. I'll get us some champagne." He motioned to a waiter holding a tray of glasses.

"Are you hungry?" he asked.

"No, not right now. Maybe a little later. How about you?"

"No, I'm fine. Well, more than fine, I should say. I have lovely music to listen to, excellent champagne to drink and, most happily, a beautiful companion with whom to share it all."

He's really quite the charmer, isn't he—such cloying sweetness could make me lose whatever appetite I have.

A few minutes later, the guests were called back into the other room for the conclusion of the concert. The second half was shorter than the first and included a Vivaldi concerto, a quartet from *La Boheme*, and a haunting tenor solo from *Lohengrin*. The final piece, Pachelbel's "Canon in D Major," left Isabella with such a feeling of serenity that she nearly forgot the purpose of her mission.

"Thank you so much for inviting me, Günter. I enjoyed the concert immensely," Isabella said as they walked back to the reception salon.

"I'm so happy you liked it. You must be very hungry by now. Shall we have something to eat here, or would you prefer to go elsewhere?"

"What I would really like to do is take off my

shoes—my feet are throbbing!" Her hand flew to her mouth. "Oh, dear, I shouldn't have said that."

A warm smile lit Günter's face. "It's all right, Isabella. I'll think of something." He guided her to a plush settee in the entrance hall and told her not to move until he came back. He disappeared, returning a few minutes later to escort her to the car that waited right outside. "Make yourself comfortable. I'll be right back." In a whisper he urged her to remove the offending shoes.

When will he ask me to take off the rest of my clothes? she wondered, as she once again questioned the wisdom of this venture.

To Isabella it seemed only a few moments before he returned with a package wrapped in brown paper and gave Klaus some instructions in German before joining her in the back seat.

As they drove off he asked, "Do you feel better now?" He looked down at her bare feet and smiled.

"Yes, but I'm a little embarrassed."

"Let me try to make you feel more comfortable," he said as, to Isabella's amazement, he removed his own shoes.

Some ten minutes later they pulled off the main road onto a gravel one and parked beside an open field. Günter said a few words to Klaus, who stepped out of the car and walked off out of sight.

So, this is where he brings women to seduce them. She steeled herself, remembering how imperative it was that she secure his trust. She had determined that the best chance of getting information was to encourage his attentions but not give in to his desires all at once. Better to entice him little by little, to keep him coming back for more. If she allowed him to take her now, he might then toss her aside before she had an opportunity to uncover any intelligence.

But now she felt completely at his mercy, alone

with him in this forsaken spot, miles from anyone else except his subordinate. *What if he forces himself on me? Well, I've no one to blame but myself for getting into this. I'll use my wits to fend him off, if need be.*

Günter unwrapped the brown paper package and asked her, "Mozzarella and tomato, ham, or salami and provolone?"

"Excuse me?" Isabella was dumbfounded. Then she realized that the package contained three large wedges of crusty bread, stuffed with various delicacies. "Oh, you want to eat," she said trying not to look startled.

"Well, I would have preferred taking you to a restaurant for a late supper, but I didn't think you'd like to dine barefooted in public. I'm afraid this is the best I could come up with on such short notice."

Isabella couldn't help but laugh. "I'll have a little of the mozzarella, thank you." She took the sandwich along with the linen napkin he offered. "Don't tell me you stole this from the villa!"

"I believe as invited guests we are entitled to the food. The napkins are borrowed. I'll have Klaus return them tomorrow."

"I don't suppose you managed to borrow a bottle of wine by any chance?" she inquired with a broad smile.

"No, I'm sorry. I promise I'll be better prepared for our next picnic. Forgive me for asking, but I hope those awful shoes are borrowed. I'd hate to think you would own something that tortures you so."

"All right, I confess. Everything I'm wearing is borrowed—and last night, too. I'm just a poor country girl and don't own anything so dazzling. I'll be sorry when I have to return these, I must admit!" She indicated the strand of pearls around her neck.

"I'd never have guessed. Finery suits you so well. But I'm sure you'd look lovely in anything you

28

wore."

When they had finished their meal, Günter asked, "Would you like to go back now? It's getting rather late."

"Yes, maybe we'd better."

Günter whistled for Klaus. On the drive back to Silvia's apartment, with more smiles and laughs exchanged, Isabella felt much more at ease with Günter. *He's actually rather sweet, and his charm is natural and sincere.* But then she glanced at the swastika on his uniform and dismissed these thoughts from her mind. *As pleasant as he may seem, I must not forget that he is still the enemy.*

Günter walked her to the door. "May I meet you on Sunday afternoon?"

"Yes, that would be nice."

"Shall I pick you up here about three?"

"All right."

He leaned over and kissed her on the cheek. "I can hardly wait until then. Thank you for a delightful evening, Isabella."

"Thank you, Günter. Good night."

Chapter 4

"So, you really haven't learned anything about him, except that he studied linguistics and is well versed in Bach and Wagner! That bit of information will be very useful to our allies. This isn't a game, Isabella," Massimo said.

"You think I don't know that? I would be more than happy to end it right here, if you prefer. I'm sure you can find someone else to interrogate him more effectively."

Massimo scowled but assuaged his tone. "Well, you are seeing him later today, anyway. If you can at least find out what his duties are, then I can judge whether there's anything to be gained from him. I'll drive you back into town around two o'clock. You're to meet him at Silvia's at three?"

"Yes, hopefully her new lover will be gone by then," Isabella replied with a frown. "I'd better go and see if anyone needs help in the kitchen."

There were eighteen in their group, most inhabiting the modest farm about twenty miles outside the city. They raised chickens and goats to keep the place running, and to provide a cover for their activities. There were few women besides Isabella, just the wives and girlfriends of the squadron leaders. She and Massimo shared a tiny one-room cabin on the edge of the property between the pasture and the woods. It had no running water or electricity and only a fireplace to heat it. In the beginning she had been enchanted by its romance.

Even in the dead of winter, his body kept her warm and happy at night. Now, after nearly a year, she regretted not having taken a room in the main house, especially on those nights when she had to slip off into the woods for a call of nature. *Still, it's our refuge, and someday we'll have a home and family of our own.*

As she walked toward the main house she thought of the other women in their group. *Would any of them take on this mission?* She knew they were loyal to the cause but satisfied to lend their aid in ways that helped sustain their men: preparing the meals, doing the cleaning and washing, tending the animals and selling farm products at market.

Isabella entered the kitchen by the back door and saw Vittoria and Carla busily rolling dough, and Luisa standing by the stove, stirring a huge pot of stew. "Can I help with the cooking?" Isabella offered.

"Oh, no, my dear," Luisa replied. "I hear you have important work to do later today. Why don't you just go inside and relax. We can handle the women's work in here." Luisa's patronizing manner and the embarrassed look on Carla's face as Vittoria whispered to her made it clear to Isabella that they had been talking about her, and their judgment was almost certainly critical. *I suppose they think the task I've been assigned is beneath them. And I doubt their men would even ask them to do what Massimo has asked of me.*

The sitting room was filled with men, smoking and talking in animated tones about the current partisan operation to cut German communication lines. When Isabella passed, they stopped momentarily, then resumed as she continued through and out the front door. She found a seat for herself on the front steps and petted their adopted mongrel pup that greeted her with a shower of wet kisses. Gazing up at the soaring mountains in the distance, she suddenly felt quite alone.

For many years now, Isabella had witnessed fellow Italians beaten down by Fascist tyranny. Friends and acquaintances who protested were imprisoned or deported. Some fled the country— socialists, liberals, Jews—in dread of Mussolini's regime. Before enlisting in this squadron, she had participated in demonstrations and distributed leaflets, always taking care to avoid arrest.

Then, when the German Army seized control of northern Italy, civilians were subjected to even more terrifying repression. Torture and executions increased mercilessly, crushing any hint of dissension. After Marco's hanging, Isabella's revulsion deepened, and she could no longer resist her craving to fight the oppressors.

Massimo had assured her that she was the only woman in their circle daring enough to carry out his scheme. *Perhaps he's just using me. He'll surely rise in the ranks if our plan succeeds. But I know he loves me.* Massimo was the anchor in her life—guiding, protecting and caring for her. How consoling he'd been when Marco died; the shared grief had brought them together, and ignited her zeal to defend her country. But she had no female companion in whom she could confide. She had little in common with the other women here, and shuddered at the thought of telling her mother or sisters of her mission to beguile a German officer. *Mamma would be appalled and entreat me to come home immediately!* Her family, though sympathetic to the cause, had been terrified when she told them she'd decided to live with Massimo and the other partisans. They knew that, if discovered by the Germans, the penalty for aiding the Resistance was death.

****

Later that day, as she waited for Massimo in front of the farmhouse, Isabella heard someone approach her. She turned to see Carla standing there, brushing flour from her apron.

"I know Luisa can be very hurtful sometimes, but she doesn't dislike you. None of us could do what you are doing."

"Yes, you're all too moral and pious," Isabella replied with a bit of sarcasm.

"No, that's not what I mean. You're risking your life. I admire you for that."

"We're all risking our lives, Carla."

"But meeting that German officer...and spying... I think you are very brave, Isabella. I just wanted to tell you, that's all."

"Thank you," Isabella responded. Carla touched Isabella's arm and smiled before she went back to the house.

****

Massimo let Isabella out of the truck two blocks from Silvia's apartment just before three o'clock. Explaining his presence to Silvia would be an unnecessary complication.

"I'll see you tomorrow in the usual place, Isabella. Be careful."

"Of course, carino. Wish me luck."

She walked to the apartment and knocked on the door. Silvia greeted her joyfully.

"You just missed Federico. We had a fabulous time. He's so charming! Last night he took me to the most expensive restaurant in Verona, and it didn't take much effort to induce him to stay for the night. In fact, I practically had to fight him off!" Her wicked smile told Isabella that she hadn't put up a vigorous resistance.

"Perhaps you're falling in love."

"I don't know; I don't remember what that feels like. He's invited me to his villa next weekend. That means you and Günter can stay here if you like."

"Oh...I don't know," Isabella replied, suddenly

apprehensive. "Let's see how things go between now and then. I've only just met him a few days ago."

"I don't know how you can resist him. He's extremely handsome. If you were not my friend you'd have reason to worry that I might steal him!" Silvia said with a laugh. "But I would never do that to you, my dear. Anyway, Federico has me quite distracted at the moment."

Just then, there was a knock at the door and Silvia hurried to open it, with a sly wink to Isabella.

"Please come in, Captain Schumann," Silvia offered.

For a moment, Isabella was taken by surprise at his appearance. He was wearing a casual sweater, trousers and a short leather jacket. She hadn't pictured him in anything besides a uniform.

"You must be Signorina Matteo. It's a pleasure to meet you," he said, and extended his hand. "Hello, Isabella. I'm so happy to see you again." He smiled at her brightly, with an approving glance at her low-cut dress. "You look very pretty today."

"We'd better get going, Günter. I'll see you later then, Silvia." For some reason, Isabella felt an urgency to leave. She took his arm and gently pulled him toward the door.

"Good afternoon, signorina, it was nice meeting you," Günter said as they left. Once outside, Isabella relaxed.

"I'm sorry to rush you, but sometimes Silvia makes me a little uneasy," she whispered. "Maybe I'm afraid she'll say something to embarrass me in front of you—unintentionally, of course." She thought of Silvia's comments about his good looks and her suggestion that Isabella stay with him in the apartment. She sensed that Günter would feel embarrassed, too. Although she didn't know him well yet, Isabella could see in Günter a reserved and gentlemanly manner. *Didn't he admit his shyness*

34

when we first met?

"What would your friend say to embarrass you?"

"Oh, I don't know. As I believe you noted at the palazzo, she and I are very different. But she's been kind and generous to me, so let's talk about something else, all right?"

"Good idea. I'd rather learn more about you, anyway." Günter stopped in front of a motorcycle with sidecar. "May I help you get in?" he asked as she stared at the machine nervously. "You've never ridden in one of these, I suppose? Trust me, it's perfectly safe," he added with a smile.

"I was expecting to see Klaus."

"Even Klaus is entitled to a day off now and then. Actually, he's not even my driver."

"Really? He seems to show up quite often."

"He's a good lad; he'll do anything for me. You see I covered for him once, some indiscretion in the back seat of the colonel's car with an attractive young girl. I didn't report him, and he's been grateful to me ever since."

"I hope you're not taking undue advantage of him, Günter," she said jokingly as he helped her into the sidecar.

****

Isabella's apprehension changed to exhilaration as they flew out of the city toward the foothills and rural countryside. She was glad she'd brought a scarf, which she tightened around her head to keep her hair in some semblance of order. She was amazed at the speed Günter dared to reach and guessed that he enjoyed the feeling of freedom. The roar of the motor and the rush of the wind made conversation impossible, so she contented herself with the bucolic scenery—rolling foothills, green pastures dotted with cows and goats, a few small farmhouses and tiny villages.

He slowed near the top of a hill and pulled off

the road onto a grassy field, where he helped her from the sidecar and grabbed a canvas bag and a blanket stowed in the back compartment. "This is a lovely spot, I think. You can see Verona in the distance, there." He pointed beyond the hills toward the city.

"Yes. It's so peaceful here."

He laid out the blanket beneath an ancient oak tree at the far side of the field and invited her to sit down. Out of the bag he pulled a bottle of wine, along with two cups and a corkscrew. He poured some for each of them and offered a toast. "To the most beautiful lady in the Veneto and her most fortunate companion."

She took a sip and laughed. "What exquisite crystal, sir!" she said as she lifted the plain white ceramic cup.

"The finest the officers' mess has to offer, my lady. Do you like the Bardolino, Isabella?"

"It's wonderful. The finest of the officers' mess?"

"No, it's from the colonel's private stock, and not the finest, I'll admit. He won't miss this bottle. But if I'd borrowed from his premium collection I'd be risking my neck!" Günter withdrew a few more items from the bag: a loaf of fresh bread, prosciutto, cheese, some grapes and apples and small box of chocolates. He removed one from the box and held it before her lips.

She demurely opened her mouth to accept it. Then she lay back on the blanket, savoring the rich flavor and creamy texture of the sweet indulgence. "I can't remember when I've tasted anything so luscious. I think you could easily spoil me."

"Nothing would give me more pleasure." He leaned over and brushed the hair out of her eyes with his hand. She tensed slightly at his touch. Seeming to sense her discomfort he drew back. "Would you like something to eat?" he offered. "The prosciutto is excellent."

"I'm not very hungry right now, but I'd like some more wine, please," she said as she sat up and held out her cup.

He refilled both of their cups. "Do you come from Verona, Isabella?"

"I grew up on a farm outside the city. My family still lives there. When I was ten I was sent to convent school in Verona and stayed there until I was eighteen. Our parish priest had recommended me as beneficiary of an endowment. Every year, a wealthy spinster in our village sponsors a promising student from a local family. My family wasn't poor, but they could never have afforded to send me away to school."

"So you still live on the farm with your family?"

"Yes. My brother drove me into the city today. I'll stay at Silvia's tonight. If I can find a job in Verona, I'd like to find a place to stay. I think I prefer city life."

"I grew up in a small village, too. But my family doesn't have a farm. My father owns a small shop in town. My brother Otto went off to war before me, and I had to leave my studies in Munich to return and help my father. Then my brother..." He stopped and looked off toward the distant horizon.

"What is it, Günter? What happened to your brother?"

"He was killed in Poland in '39. I was drafted soon after that."

"I'm so sorry." *How strangely our lives paralleled. We've both lost a parent, a brother, both abandoned our studies to help our families.* "Is your father alone now?"

"No, I've two younger sisters. Maria is married and lives in Stuttgart. She visits him as often as she can. My youngest sister, Else, still lives at home and helps my father at the store. She'd be eighteen now, a young woman already." There was a trace of sad reflection in his voice. "It's been so long since I've seen any of them." He looked at her and smiled, as if trying to cast off his pensive mood. "Do you have a large family?"

"I have two sisters and three brothers. They...uh...we live with our mother. My father died seven years ago. I too had to put off my dream of studying—for me it was art history in Florence—to stay home and work the farm. It seems you and I have much in common." She dared not mention her fourth brother Marco. How could she risk telling Günter that he had been murdered by the Nazis?

"Perhaps we were destined to meet, Isabella."

He turned toward her, took her face in his hand and kissed her softly on the lips. She had felt the moment coming and prepared for it, reminding herself that she needed to put him at ease. Venturing further, he slid his arm around her waist. His fingers glided along her spine, up to the nape of her neck, then wove into her hair. His mouth captured hers, his lips warm and moist. Her breath caught in her throat and for a moment she pulled away. Then summoning her nerve, she sought to reassure him that his interest was returned. She nestled close but avoided his eyes, trying to imagine it was Massimo she embraced.

Günter felt strong and lean in her arms. He lightly caressed her back and traced the length of her neck with kisses. Her body tingled. *It must be the wine.* He clasped her shoulders and looked into her eyes. She held his gaze for a few seconds, but then looked down.

"You're so beautiful," he murmured and gently cupped her chin. "I haven't felt anything like this in a very long time."

He reached over to the box of chocolates and held another one to her lips. She accepted, and as she consumed it, studied his face. *He is very handsome*, she thought, noting his lovely blue eyes offset by dark brown hair, a strong chin and finely sculpted, masculine features. Then he lay back on the blanket, seemingly content just to be in her presence, as if their brief embrace had sated him.

"Günter," she said casually, "what do you do in the Army?" She had tried to conceive a subtle way to ask about his duties, but could think of nothing but a direct approach. She knew how angry Massimo would be if she returned without any information.

"I'm surprised that would interest you."

"I'm just curious, that's all. Women don't usually get to hear about these things. I wonder what it's like."

"My role is rather unglamorous, I'm afraid. I serve under Colonel von Haeften's command in the administrative branch of Army Group C. Our unit oversees the transport of supplies for the Italian campaign. I was lucky that my friend Major Gerhardt brought me along as his aide when he transferred here from Rome. Before that I relayed supply data to headquarters from the front, and that was as close to combat as I cared to be," he said with a smile. "Now it's mostly paperwork—preparing reports, logging supply shipments. They must have concluded that I was a better clerk than soldier, so I've been safely behind a desk since my transfer. And because I'm fluent in several languages, they use me as a translator for our group and for the General Staff. Sometimes when the colonel or other senior officers meet with Italian officials, I accompany them to interpret. I suppose that's the most interesting part of my job."

"You must meet a lot of important people. I think that would be fascinating."

"Not really, but at least it keeps me away from the front. If you'd imagined a fearless warrior, you may be disappointed," he replied with a laugh.

"I'm sure you'd be very brave in battle, but I'm glad you're not on the front lines."

"Don't tell my commander, but that makes two of us," he said as he pulled her toward him on the blanket. She lay next to him, resting her head on his shoulder as he stroked her hair. "I'm so grateful we met that night at the palazzo. With you beside me like this...the whole world could just fade away and I'd be quite content to stay here forever."

She sat up and looked at him. "It would get a bit cold up here by October." She smiled as she touched his cheek. His skin felt smooth and soft, so unlike Massimo's rough-bearded visage exuding boldness and virility. There was something appealing about Günter's clean-shaven face; it suggested a candid and affable nature. *What incongruous qualities for a Nazi officer.*

"I didn't prepare as well as I should have. I forgot to pack a tent and stove. And I'm afraid we don't have enough food to last until October, though I could try to hunt some rabbits for us."

"That's all right, Günter. Perhaps we can find someplace a little closer to civilization to be alone together."

"I hope so. I'm not very good at hunting rabbits."

****

It was already dark when they arrived back at Silvia's apartment.

"Would you like to come in?" Isabella offered. She felt too comfortable now with Günter to allow any comments from Silvia to bother her.

"No, maybe another time. I should really get back to quarters. I would like to take you out for a real dinner. So far I've fed you only bread and cheese! Perhaps we can meet on Thursday evening. I'll be at headquarters late every other night this week. I do wish I could see you sooner, but there is this war going on," Günter said with a wistful smile. "How shall I contact you?"

"You can leave a message here at Silvia's. I'll check with her by Wednesday. But how can I reach you?"

"I'm stationed at Palazzo Maggiore on Via Scaligeri. You can leave a note for me with the guard on duty. But don't include anything too personal; it's likely to be read before I get it."

"All right, I'll save my *personal* remarks for when we meet," she said coyly.

"I look forward to it," he said as he took her in his arms and kissed her. She allowed her body to respond to his embrace, pushing aside the uneasy thoughts that had begun to plague her conscience. *What will I do when his desire grows to something more?*

Chapter 5

Isabella waited for Massimo on the front steps of the farmhouse. It was mid-afternoon Saturday and she was anxious to get back to Verona to prepare dinner for Günter. She thought about the charming trattoria, not far from Silvia's place, where she and Günter had dined on Thursday.

"Do you come here often?" she'd asked him at the restaurant, wondering how many other Italian women he'd entertained during his Army's occupation of her country.

"No, I've never been here before. In fact, I rarely eat out at all. The food in the officers' mess isn't the best, but it's free and I get to spend time with my friends. Though I must say that the company here is much lovelier," he replied, taking her hand in his across the table.

Throughout the evening he was attentive and respectful, and despite her misgivings, she had to admit she enjoyed his company. They had discussed many things: art, music, literature, philosophy; she marveled at the breadth of his knowledge and liberal education. Isabella realized that Günter's love for music mirrored hers for art. They both revered man's ability to create works of exceeding beauty that could transcend even the brutality of war.

After dinner, they walked back to the apartment, where he briefly chatted with her and Silvia, much to Silvia's delight. Isabella had invited him to come back on Saturday night so she could treat him to a home-cooked meal. Nervous though she was, she'd decided to accept Silvia's offer to stay in the apartment for the weekend while Silvia joined Federico at his villa.

Finally, Massimo pulled up in the truck and got out to help her with her packages. She brought bags of farm-grown vegetables, homemade bread and a fresh-killed chicken, along with a small suitcase of her personal items.

"I hope you'll get a little more out of him this time, considering he's eating into our food stocks," Massimo said as he lifted the bags into the back of the truck. "So, is he spending the night with you?" Fixed by his penetrating gaze, she felt cornered like captured prey.

"I...I don't know. If he's going to tell me anything I've got to get him to trust me. And if he expects... Well, I'll just have to see where things go. We both knew this was a possibility from the start. But if you're going to be jealous, I won't go through with it."

"I'd gladly give my life for the cause of freedom, Isabella. To share my woman with this barbarian, that must surely be less of a sacrifice. I can bear it if you can. Just don't enjoy it too much!" His attempt to put her at ease with a smile was betrayed by the menacing look in his eyes.

"We'd better get going," she said as she slid into the seat next to him and closed the door of the truck.

Despite his gruffness, Isabella could never remain angry with Massimo for long. She realized that he was accustomed to vying with other men in politics and warfare and would sometimes forget that women craved more delicate attention. She had known Massimo most of her life. The childhood friend of her eldest brother Leonardo, he was a frequent guest in her family's home, and as a teen, she'd developed a girlish infatuation. He was bolder and more confident than any man she'd met, and she was attracted by his rough-hewn, handsome features and physically powerful frame. Though he was sometimes insensitive, and seldom romantic, Isabella never doubted he loved her, and in the end she always forgave him. She knew he possessed a compassionate heart beneath his hardened façade.

****

"Are you sure I can't help you with the packages?" Massimo asked as he stopped the truck a few blocks from Silvia's building.

"I don't think Silvia has left yet. It would be better if she didn't see you."

"I'm sorry if I was difficult with you back there. I suppose this isn't easy for either of us."

"No, Massimo, it isn't."

"I'll meet you here Monday morning, then. I love you very much, Isabella." He grasped her hand tightly and kissed her.

"I love you, too."

She struggled with the bags but managed to get to the apartment and open the door, nearly dropping everything as she entered.

"Your brother couldn't even help you with these bags?" Silvia asked, and helped carry the food into the kitchen. "He has never come in when he's brought you here. Is he afraid of me or something?"

"He was in a hurry. I'm sure he'll come in next time." Isabella made a mental note that she must introduce Massimo the next time he came; otherwise Silvia might become suspicious. Isabella couldn't recollect whether Silvia had ever met her family. *If so, it would have been many years ago, and Silvia won't remember. I can introduce him as Leonardo. They're about the same age.*

"So much food, Isabella! Are you planning on feeding the entire German Army?"

"Some of it's for you. You've been so generous to

me. It's the least I could do."

"You don't have to do that. I haven't had a friend like you for a very long time. I enjoy having you stay here and keep me company," Silvia replied as she carried Isabella's suitcase to the bedroom.

Isabella organized her ingredients, then heated a small amount of olive oil in a large pot to start her preparation.

"Do you have a cleaver, Silvia?" she yelled as she looked at the chicken.

"It's in the cabinet next to the stove."

As Isabella toiled in the kitchen, Silvia busied herself with packing necessities for her weekend at the villa. When she finished, she joined Isabella, making herself comfortable at the kitchen table as she watched Isabella with fascination. Silvia seemed to pride herself on her domestic ineptitude, as if it signified good breeding.

"This reminds me a little of my childhood, you know. I'd sit in the kitchen as the cook prepared our meals. She used to give me treats while I watched."

"You can nibble on some carrots if you like. In fact, you might as well start peeling them while you're sitting there."

Silvia reluctantly picked up a paring knife and began to work at the vegetables. "I hope there's a reward in this for me, helping to prepare a meal for that handsome man of yours."

"Your reward will be enjoying your own dashing beau in his luxurious villa!"

"I'm getting that anyway, even if I don't peel your carrots!" She laughed. "You can't trick me that easily, Isabella."

****

At about six o'clock, a car horn sounded outside. A sleek, silver Mercedes-Benz had stopped in front of the building.

Silvia peeked out the window. "Ah, my chariot

awaits! I don't know when I'll be back, hopefully not for several days. Stay here as long as you like, my dear." She grabbed her bag and rushed off, blowing a kiss to Isabella.

"Have a wonderful time, Silvia."

Isabella checked on her dinner, cleaned up the kitchen, set the table with Silvia's modest china and flatware, and searched for candlesticks. She found a pair of pretty crystal ones along with two white candles. After one last look in the simmering pot on the stove, she withdrew to the bedroom to freshen herself.

At precisely seven, there was a knock at the door. *These Germans certainly are punctual*, she thought, as she took one last look around and let Günter in.

"Good evening, darling." Günter greeted her with a kiss, then presented a bottle of wine and a bouquet of fresh flowers.

"Oh, they're lovely, Günter. Let me find something to put them in. I'll keep the wine in the icebox until we're ready to eat. Just make yourself comfortable in here," she said, indicating the sitting room. "I'll check on our dinner."

As she stood before the stove, he came up behind her, grabbed her around the waist and began kissing her neck. "Are you hungry?" she asked.

"Ravenous." He turned her around, took her in his arms and kissed her passionately on the lips.

"Well then, leave me be so I can finish our dinner. Now go wait in there and I'll call you when it's ready." She gently pushed him away and watched as he retreated into the other room. She felt her stomach quiver, then took a deep breath and returned to her cooking. *This may be the night I must summon my courage and submit to his desire. It's all for the cause.*

****

"How I do miss home cooking, Isabella. That was the best meal I've had in ages. Perhaps even better than my mother's, God rest her soul. Certainly better than my sister Maria's!" he said, laughing. "I could easily get used to this," he added, and took her hands in his.

"Would you like some more wine, Günter?"

"Yes, just a little. But here, let me serve you." He filled her glass then poured the remainder in his. "Why don't we relax in the other room? I'll clean this up later."

"No, you're my guest. I'll do the cleaning up." She took his arm and his wine glass and led him to the most comfortable chair in the sitting room. "Here's a newspaper for you to read. I'll just be a few minutes."

Back in the kitchen, she looked at the mountain of dishes and sighed. *Maybe I should let him help me*, she thought for a moment, and then started the tedious job herself. About ten minutes later, Günter returned to the kitchen.

"Here's one more glass to wash," he said, placing his empty wine glass into the sink. "You've hardly touched yours." He picked up her glass from the table and offered it to her.

"My hands are full of soap. Just leave it there; I'll get to it."

He took a towel from the counter and dried her hands. "Your guest is getting lonely waiting for you. Come and keep me company."

"All right, I'll finish this later," she said as he led her into the other room.

She sat beside him on the sofa. Focusing on his graceful features and vivid blue eyes, she tried to banish her fears. He cupped her cheek, and his ardent kiss parted her lips. Slowly, he unbuttoned her blouse and slipped it off her shoulders. He fondled her breasts with his fingertips, then began a progression of kisses, starting at her neck and inching downward. His touch was wondrously gentle, yet persistent. A shiver rippled through her as his moist breath warmed her tingling flesh, and a faint, involuntary gasp escaped her lips. The tremors in her stomach began to quell, eclipsed by a throbbing lower down. Lifting his head, he gazed into her eyes as he held her face in his hands. He softly kissed her, then gathered her into his arms and carried her to the bedroom.

Every sinew in her body trembled with trepidation and expectancy. Had she meant it to go this far? Could she possibly stop it now? Did she want to? Arousal and discretion battled in Isabella's brain.

Günter laid her on the bed, then hastily unbuttoned his tunic and shirt, revealing smooth, taut skin and a lean, athletic build. Undeniably drawn to his manly frame, she reached out to stroke the firm muscles of his shoulders and chest. He knelt beside her on the bed, lavishing a profusion of kisses upon her slender body, from her ripening nipples to the velvety flesh of her belly. Gliding his hand beneath her panties, he awakened a searing hunger deep within her core. Frenzy mounted, and clothing was recklessly tossed aside. As he enveloped her lips with his eager mouth, she felt the urgency of his thighs against hers, and deliciously melted into his embrace. Isabella's apprehension and guilt were conquered by an irrepressible fervor as she willingly yielded to his tender lovemaking, abandoning her reserve and allowing her body to respond naturally to sensual pleasures. An intense, soulful moan escaped as she reached the peak of rapture. Seconds later he followed with explosive ecstasy and breathlessly collapsed beside her. Neither spoke as they savored the elation of fulfilled desire.

Günter nestled against the curve of Isabella's

back as she lay on her side, and lightly caressed her shoulder and arm with his fingertips. He kissed the nape of her neck, then wrapped his arm snugly around her. She remained awake, listening, as his breathing slowed to the tranquil pace of slumber.

****

After hours of restlessness Isabella rose, careful not to awaken her lover. Half the night had passed, but her tortured ambivalence hindered her sleep. She could not deny she had relished their carnal gratification, but her conscience struggled to rationalize the significance. Massimo's warning echoed in her head: "Just don't enjoy it too much!" Did the delight she took in this comely Nazi brand her a whore? If her affectionate feelings for Günter were genuine, was she then being faithless to Massimo, while attempting to be faithful to their cause? After finding her dressing gown in the dark, she tried to dismiss these plaguing questions as she crept to the kitchen. *If I can't rest, at least I'll make use of the time to finish washing the dishes.*

In an hour, the kitchen was immaculate again and exhaustion began to take hold of Isabella. She stumbled into the sitting room and lay down on the sofa. For some reason, she couldn't bring herself to return to Günter in the bedroom. A combination of guilt and anxiety, mingled with a tinge of dread, kept her from him. *Günter's so gentle—surely I've no need to fear him. But this won't end happily for either of us.* For a moment she longed for her own bed, not the one she shared with Massimo in the little cabin but the one in her parents' home. She recalled those naïve, blissful days before Günter, before Massimo, when her greatest burden was having to awaken before sunrise to milk the cows. Eventually, sleep overtook her as images of boundless green pastures and sun-streaked hilltops wafted through her brain.

****

The rosy blush of first light awakened Günter from the most peaceful sleep since leaving his Bavarian homeland five years before. His eyes still clouded with sleep, he reached over to feel for Isabella beside him. He found himself alone in the bed, and wondered for a moment if it had all been a dream. He looked around at the unfamiliar room and knew that he had not imagined the pleasurable events of the previous night. He arose, pulled on his trousers and went to find her. He stood quietly at the doorway of the sitting room and watched Isabella who seemed, in his eyes, a sleeping angel. Slowly, he approached her and crouched beside the sofa. She had just begun to stir when he awakened her with a kiss.

"Good morning, darling," he said softly. "Are you all right? I was a little concerned when I didn't find you beside me this morning."

"Oh, good morning, Günter. I...I guess I'm not used to sleeping with you. I mean, well..." she said, flustered.

"It's all right. Hopefully, you'll have many more opportunities to get used to sleeping with me." He stroked her hair. "It was wonderful last night."

He gazed at her, entranced by the honeyed glow of her skin and her warm brown eyes fringed with dark sable lashes. Her lips, full and red, looked ripe for another kiss. But she suddenly rose and tied her dressing gown tightly around her waist.

"Let me show you where you can wash up." She led him to the bathroom and gave him a few necessities. "I'll put some coffee on."

As Günter washed, he wondered at her reticence, hoping he had not upset her by being too forward. But he recalled her willingness the previous night and reassured himself that his affection was not unwelcome. He smiled as he remembered their first meeting, and the startled look on her face when he approached her at the palazzo. It was partly her shyness that made her so appealing to him. There was a freshness, an innocence that set her apart from most of the women to whom he'd been introduced as an officer of the awesome German Army. They were too eager to become amorous with him, and he always doubted their sincerity. *There are enough gallant officers with more medals and ribbons than I have to keep those shallow sorts happy.* In Isabella, he hoped he had found the cherished companion whose charm, intellect and beauty promised enduring joy for as long as he dared imagine.

****

They relaxed over a simple breakfast of warm rolls and coffee. Günter held her hand at every opportunity, as if he feared she would flutter away like a sylph.

"What shall we do today?" he asked. "Do you usually start your Sundays with Mass?"

"I'm not so religious, but we can go if you like. I don't think there's a Protestant church in Verona, though."

"I'm Roman Catholic, Isabella. Aren't you?"

"Well...yes I am. For some reason I thought most Germans were Protestant."

"There are many Catholics in Germany, especially in the south where I come from. Maybe we are quieter than the Protestants—we keep a low profile. That must be why you never noticed us before," he said with a laugh.

"Are you making fun of me, Günter?"

"I would never do that, my dear! I don't go every week, but sometimes I like the service at Santa Maria degli Angeli. The old priest there is kind, and I enjoy listening to the choir."

"Then we'll go. That is, if our sin-filled souls can

pass through the doors."

"I can't imagine a trace of sin in your angelic heart."

"What we did last night—was that not sinful?"

He looked at her sincerely. "I believe what comes of love cannot be sinful. We have done nothing to feel guilty about."

Perhaps you *haven't, Günter*, she thought.

****

On their way to Santa Maria's, Isabella teasingly pointed out to Günter that he hadn't shaved and was wearing the same clothes as the prior day for his "Sunday Best."

He wanted to return to his quarters to change. "It's only a few blocks away."

"It's all right, Günter, you look fine. Besides, the detour will make us late for Mass."

After the service, she had the opportunity to see where he lived and worked. Verona was the center for German military administration in Italy, headquartered at Palazzo Maggiore, several blocks from the church. It was a large but ordinary city building, not nearly as impressive as Palazzo Fabriano. Günter reluctantly took her inside for a quick tour, telling the guard on duty that she was the daughter of a high-ranking Fascist Party official.

"No unauthorized personnel are allowed in this building, Isabella."

"So, I'm the only female to ever set foot here?" she asked him innocently.

"Only the domestic staff, and occasionally the wife of an Italian dignitary, have been here, as far as I know. The Army does its entertaining outside the city at Palazzo Fabriano." Then he winked and added in a whisper, "Rumor has it the field marshal keeps his mistress there, too."

As they left the building, he pointed out the officers' barracks, a hotel around the corner from headquarters, which she could view only from the outside.

"Women are strictly prohibited," Günter warned her.

"So where do your fellow officers carry on their trysts?"

"Their sweethearts must all have friends like Silvia!" he said, laughing.

They spent most of the afternoon walking hand in hand through the city. Both were familiar with Verona, but exploring it together renewed the beauty and romance of the ancient city. They strolled along the banks of the twisting Adige River, whose chilly waters flowed down from the pre-Alps. Verona's narrow streets led unpredictably into irregularly shaped piazzas, lined with the colorful umbrellas of al fresco caffès and ornamented with Baroque fountains or statues of the dukes and despots of the Veneto. Many of the buildings they passed displayed evidence of Allied bombardment, but for Günter and Isabella that scarcely diminished the city's charm.

The layout of Verona had not been planned; rather, it had evolved organically over the millennia. Soaring Gothic spires, graceful Renaissance palazzos, and picturesque red-roofed villas seemed to spring like exquisite blossoms in an untended garden.

Isabella pointed out the Convento di Santa Caterina where she and Silvia had been schoolgirls together.

"That's where I learned a little bit of German, Herr Schumann. If that frightful Austrian nun, Sister Josef, hadn't been so mean and unpleasant I might be fluent today!"

Günter laughed. "I'm sure I'm not as mean as Sister Josef, and I'd be happy to give you private lessons...for a small fee, of course. Erste Lektion,

Liebchen. That means 'first lesson, sweetheart.' Ich liebe dich—'I love you.' And now for my fee...ein Kuss." He took her in his arms and kissed her. "Now don't forget what you've learned, Fräulein Ricci. There will be a test later."

Chapter 6

How strange to awaken in an empty apartment. Isabella could recollect no other time in her life when she had spent a night so entirely alone. Her childhood home, the dormitory at convent school, the cabin with Massimo, even this apartment had always been shared by at least one other, in another room if not in the bed beside her. There was no one to greet "Good morning," no one to race to the bathroom. The silence unsettled her. She rose and went to look at the clock in the kitchen. It was past seven already, so she put on a pot of coffee and scurried to the bathroom to wash.

As she sat drinking her coffee, she thought of the leisurely Sunday she and Günter had spent together the previous day. She smiled, recalling how much they'd enjoyed each other's company. It had been a very long time since she and Massimo had passed such a carefree and pleasurable time together.

Oh, no, he's waiting for me. Isabella had become so lost in reverie that she'd completely forgotten about Massimo. She knew how irritated he would be if she were late. Glancing at the clock, she saw that it was nearly eight, the time he'd told her to meet him. She hurriedly cleaned up the kitchen and ran to the bedroom to dress.

When she reached Massimo's truck, she hesitated a second before climbing in. He scrutinized her face, inspecting her with narrowed eyes and a suspicious gaze.

Ignoring the rigidity of his posture, she leaned in to greet him with a kiss. He gripped her shoulder, holding her at arm's length for a moment, then pulled her toward him. He claimed her lips with a fierce kiss as his tongue plunged inside, ravishing her mouth.

She gasped when he released her. She suppressed the impulse to wipe the moisture from her lips with the back of her hand. "Did you miss me, Massimo?"

"I hope you had a productive weekend. Did you learn anything?"

Isabella was tempted to report that she'd learned how to say "I love you" in German but knew Massimo would not find that amusing. "Well...I got to see the inside of German military headquarters, accessible to authorized personnel only," she replied and waited for his reaction.

With a slight nod, he grunted his approval. "Not bad, Isabella." From Massimo, that was a mountain of praise.

****

Isabella spent the next few days at the farm, busying herself with preparations for the coming harvest. She stayed close by Massimo's side. She'd missed his reassuring presence. Not since the loss of her father so many years before had she enjoyed the sense of security that Massimo provided. But she was also aware of the conflicts beginning to encircle her, and she hoped to use this brief time away from Verona to attempt to sort them out.

When she'd first embarked on her espionage mission, she hadn't considered the possibility of feeling real affection for her target. Her main worry had been overcoming the utter revulsion of submitting to the enemy, an ordeal she'd willingly agreed to suffer. The virtue of their cause, her love and devotion to Massimo, and the hunger to avenge Marco's death had been compelling enough to convince her. Though she'd acknowledged Günter's charm and good looks from the start, she hadn't anticipated the immense pleasure of his company. It made her task both easier and more difficult. She resolved to walk the very fine line between enjoying Günter's friendship and allowing herself to develop a tender attachment. *He might even be falling in love with me, but I'll take care to avoid that snare myself.*

****

One morning after feeding the chickens, Isabella entered the farmhouse and was surprised to see her younger sister Laura waiting in the main room.

"What's wrong?" Isabella asked. "Is Mamma sick?"

Before Laura could respond, Massimo entered. He seemed not to notice Isabella, and turned instead to Laura. "Come, let me show you around." Holding out his hand, he indicated that Laura should follow.

"Massimo..."

"Oh, Isabella, I didn't see you come in. I was just going to show your sister our operation."

Isabella went swiftly to Massimo and pulled him aside. "What is going on?" she whispered. "Why is she here?"

"I can hear you, Isabella. Don't talk about me as if I'm not in the room. I'm not a child."

"All right, then. Why are you here?"

"I've come to join up. I told Massimo I want to be part of the Resistance."

Uncertain where to direct her anger, Isabella furiously turned from one to the other. She settled on Massimo, nearly ten years older than Laura, and therefore the more responsible.

"You take my sister home this minute!"

Lifting her chin in defiance, Laura faced Isabella. "You're not in charge of me. I'm twenty-two years old and *I'll* decide what to do with my life!"

"I'm not going to let you risk it here!"

"But you are."

"Yes, and one daughter in the Resistance is more than Mamma can stand now. Go home, Laura."

"You can't make me."

"Madonna mia!" Isabella threw up her hands in disgust and walked out the front door, slamming it behind her.

After an hour or so, Isabella had calmed down enough to approach Massimo about Laura. She searched the compound and found him in the barn, joined by a few of the other men as they inventoried the modest arsenal of weapons hidden in the rafters.

"Massimo, I want to speak with you."

She noted the mocking grins of the other men as Massimo took her by the arm and led her outside.

"What?" he asked impatiently.

"Why did you bring my sister here?"

"The last time I visited your family she told me she wanted to sign up. She approached *me*, Isabella. I didn't recruit her. If anything, you're the one who convinced her to come."

"That's a lie! I *never* suggested such a thing—I never would! Do you think I would want to put my sister's life in danger?"

"She admires you. She wants to be like you." He paused, then added quietly, "She lost a brother, too."

With a sudden pang of guilt Isabella turned away. She had never meant for anyone in her family to follow her example. She could abide the idea of losing her own life ·but to lose another loved one... *I won't allow Laura to chance it.*

"Please, just take her home. I don't know what I'd do if anything happened to her." Gazing intently into Massimo's eyes she pleaded with him to understand.

"She should decide for herself," he countered.

58

"She's a grown woman."

"Barely. You know how willful and childish she can be. But you should know better. And Leonardo? I can't believe *he* would approve. He'll be fuming when he finds out she's here. If nothing else, Massimo, do this for me."

"All right. For you."

****

The three rode in silence from the partisan base to the Ricci home. Laura sat between Massimo and Isabella in the front seat of the truck, her arms crossed and her eyes glaring the entire time.

When they arrived at the house, Leonardo was standing at the open front door. His aspect was grim.

"You've brought her back, I see," Leonardo said coolly to Massimo. "I heard the truck pull up." Then he turned to Laura. "Do you have any idea how worried we've been? You think you can just disappear like that? Leave a note that you've 'gone off to fight the Nazis'? And you, did you help him sneak her out?" he asked, glancing at Isabella.

At that moment, their mother rushed into the room. "You thoughtless girl!" she cried. "How could you leave us like this? Haven't I lost enough? Haven't I suffered enough? Lord in Heaven, my children will put me in the grave!"

Laura rolled her eyes. "Oh, Mamma, don't be so dramatic."

"Don't talk to your mother like that!" Leonardo scolded.

"And I don't want to hear anything from you, either," Laura rejoined, then turned and raced up the stairs, her mother hurrying after her.

"Leonardo..." Massimo offered his hand to his friend, who didn't reciprocate. "I'd, uh...I'd stay, but I have some things that I need to take care of. I'll pick up Isabella a little later."

Leonardo said nothing.

Astounded, Isabella turned to Massimo. "What?"

"I'll pick you up a little later, Isabella." He was outside and starting his truck before Isabella could even think how to respond.

So he's left me alone to deal with Leonardo. Massimo, the model of courage when facing down the Nazis, is too much of a coward to face Leonardo's wrath.

She now saw that her other two brothers were sitting in the living room waiting for her, but the women of the family were nowhere in sight. Isabella was about to face the tribunal of her three brothers, even Giovanni, her junior. Clearly the men ruled the house, but she was determined not to give them the upper hand. *If the Nazis ever capture me,* she considered wryly, *this should prove good training for their interrogation.*

"Sit down, Isabella." Leonardo's words were an order, not a request. She refused to comply. "How dare you encourage Laura to join you? It's bad enough that you're off trying to get yourself killed and living with Massimo in that shack!" Isabella's eyes widened. "Yes, I know all about that."

"How? Did Massimo tell you?"

"He didn't have to. I have my sources."

So, I'm not the only spy in the family. "And what upsets you more, Leonardo, the fact that I'm a partisan or the fact that I'm living with Massimo?"

"Think of the example you're setting for your little sister! I understand why you joined up after what happened to Marco, but to live like a..."

"Puttana?" Then turning to Enzo and Giovanni she hollered, "And you two, why don't you just get out of here? Unless you have something intelligent to contribute!"

With a tilt of his head Leonardo signaled to the other men that they should leave.

"Isabella," he said when they left, "if it were any other man than Massimo I'd..."

"You'd what? Kill him for making your sister a whore?"

"God, Isabella, where did you learn to talk like that? Is this what they teach in convent school?"

"Look, Leonardo, I'm tired of you trying to control me. And as far as Laura...? I didn't know anything about her joining the squadron. I was as shocked as you were and insisted that Massimo bring her home." Isabella was already weary of the senseless quarrel and tried to convey a conciliatory tone. "I know you're only trying to protect us like Papa would have. But you've got to let me live my own life."

Leonardo's anger seemed to dissipate. He reached for his sister's arm, inviting her to sit beside him on the sofa.

"When you decided to go off to join the Resistance I was so afraid for you." He took her hand in his. "I'm proud of you. But I've got to be honest. I don't like the fact that you're living with Massimo. When Marco died, I was overwhelmed. Looking after Mamma, trying to keep everything going when we were all falling to pieces. I couldn't have gotten through it without Massimo's help. I'll always be grateful to him for that. He's my closest friend and I love him like a brother. I just wish he would have married you first."

"He'll marry me someday. I know he will. With the war now it's hard to think about the future. We're just trying to hold onto a little bit of happiness while we can."

Leonardo shook his head sadly. "I should have joined instead of you. But with the farm to run..."

"I know, Leonardo."

He touched her cheek. "Promise me you won't put yourself at more risk than necessary, that you

61

won't volunteer for any dangerous missions. Massimo said that you were helping the other women with household chores. I hope that's all you're doing."

"I'm not going to promise you that. But whatever job I take on for the Resistance I'll be as careful as I can."

"You've always been so damned stubborn."

"Thank you, Leonardo. I work very hard at it," she replied with a smile.

"Impertinent, too. Well, I just hope Mamma can convince Laura to stay home."

"If she doesn't, I will."

In the Arms of the Enemy

Chapter 7

It was not too early, Isabella hoped, to disturb Silvia. Pausing at the door to the apartment, she saw that Silvia had removed the red ribbon from the knob. *Good, Federico's not here.*

Using the key Silvia had lent her, she unlocked the door and let herself in.

"Silvia, are you home?"

In a pink satin dressing gown, blond curls pinned atop her head, Silvia dashed out of the kitchen to greet her. She drew Isabella into a warm embrace.

"Cara mia! How are you? You're here early. Well, I suppose eight o'clock isn't early for you, but it is for me!" she said with a laugh. "Come into the kitchen; I've just made coffee."

Isabella followed her friend and sat down at the table. Silvia yawned, pushing back a stray lock of hair, then filled two espresso cups from the pot on the stove. "Federico just left a little while ago." Silvia winked. "I guess you noticed that I removed our little signal. That ribbon was a clever idea."

"Well, I wouldn't want to interrupt anything. I mean..." Isabella replied as her cheeks heated.

"Now you mustn't be embarrassed," Silvia reassured. "You're an innocent country lass, not a decadent city girl like me. But I promise not to corrupt you too much!"

"Silvia," Isabella began hesitantly, "I've a favor to ask you."

"Of course, Isabella, anything."

"I'd like to stay in Verona, but I need to find a job. Do you know anyone who's connected with German headquarters?" Massimo had urged Isabella to exploit Silvia's contacts to get her a job at Palazzo Maggiore. He'd heard that the Germans sometimes offered domestic positions there to local Italian women.

"I know why you want to work there," Silvia replied with an impish grin. "To keep an eye on Günter! Well, I can certainly ask around. And if you do find work you're welcome to move in with me, if you don't mind helping out with the expenses. I'll be away at Federico's most weekends anyway, so you and Günter can have the place to yourselves. In fact, I'm going this Saturday and won't be back until Tuesday, so the apartment is yours. What do you think of that?"

"I think that sounds wonderful!"

****

In anticipation of her possible new living arrangement, Isabella brought a few personal items and a suitcase of clothes on her return to Verona Saturday morning. She'd convinced Massimo that he should come in and meet Silvia this time, instead of dropping her off several blocks away as had become their routine.

"She already thinks there is something strange about you. The last time you wouldn't even help me carry my bags into the apartment."

"That was your idea, Isabella. I offered to help you," Massimo protested.

"Yes, that's true. It was Leonardo who was in such a hurry he couldn't help me. Now remember, you're my eldest brother Leonardo."

"Yes, my darling sister," he said peevishly as he carried her bags up the stairs to the apartment.

Isabella opened the door with her key. "We've

arrived, Silvia. My brother Leonardo is with me."

"We're in here, Isabella," Silvia responded from the kitchen. "Come see who's dropped in on me this morning."

Isabella coaxed Massimo into the kitchen. "Günter!" she exclaimed. "I didn't expect to see you until much later."

Günter stood and pulled out a chair for Isabella. He gently squeezed her shoulder as she sat, and extended his hand to Massimo.

"Silvia, Günter, this is my eldest brother, Leonardo. He was kind enough to help me bring up my belongings."

"Please have a seat, Leonardo. Would you like some coffee?" Silvia offered.

"No, I'd better be heading back now. Thank you." Massimo turned to leave.

"It was nice to meet you, Leonardo," Günter said as he rose to shake Massimo's hand.

"Yes, very nice to meet you," echoed Silvia.

"Likewise, I'm sure," replied Massimo brusquely. "Please excuse me."

Isabella followed Massimo to the door. "You could be a little more sociable," she whispered.

"I didn't expect to see your lover here. Just be grateful I didn't take a swing at him," Massimo grumbled.

"Let's not get started on that again. I'll meet you in the piazza Tuesday morning. Maybe by then I'll have news of my new employment."

"Good-bye, Isabella." As he bent over to kiss her, she quickly turned her cheek to him.

"Good-bye, Leonardo. Take care of Mamma while I'm away."

Isabella opened the door and awaited Massimo's departure. With a frown and a glare, he descended the stairs. She shook her head and sighed, then returned to the kitchen to join the others.

"I don't think your brother likes us very much," Silvia said as she poured a cup of coffee for Isabella and refilled Günter's and her own.

"I'd guess it was me that he disliked, Silvia. Does he know about us?" Günter asked Isabella.

"I think he has an idea about it. Don't take it personally, Günter. He's my eldest brother. He's just being protective of me. I'm sure you'd feel the same way in his place. How would you react if you met your little sister's lover unprepared?"

"Else? She's only a child. Well, I suppose she's eighteen now." Günter thought for several seconds as a look of uneasiness clouded his face. "Anyone who touches my sister will have to deal with me! Yes, I see what you mean, Isabella," he said with a laugh.

"Why are you here so early?"

"Darling, I had just stopped by to leave you a message about tonight when Silvia invited me to stay for coffee. I hope I haven't caused any problem for you with your brother."

"If there's a problem it's his, not mine. I don't really care what he thinks; I intend to do as I please."

"Still, I'd hate to start off on the wrong foot with your family."

"Don't worry. When you meet my family I'm sure they will be very fond of you." *If they ever get over the fact that you're a Nazi.*

****

Günter and Isabella enjoyed dinner that evening at the trattoria, followed by a romantic moonlit stroll along the river. It was nearly October, and they wanted to savor one of the last temperate nights before the cold alpine winds forced them indoors for the winter. Even so, there was a chill in the air and Isabella clung to Günter, who wrapped his arm snugly around her as they walked. They stopped for a moment as Günter enfolded her in his arms.

"Are you getting cold, sweetheart?" he asked.

"Yes, a little. Perhaps we should start back now."

They quickened their pace and headed in the direction of Silvia's building. Günter removed his tunic and placed it over Isabella's shoulders, just as he had done that first night at the palazzo.

"Shall I make some coffee for you?" Isabella offered when they arrived back at the apartment.

"No, thank you, Isabella. But make a pot if you'd like some."

"I'd better not. It might keep me awake tonight. Although I would like something to take the chill off."

"Why don't you give me a chance to warm you up?" he said with a gleam in his eye and an amorous smile as he held out his hand to lead her to the bedroom.

****

That night, Isabella slept more placidly than she had on their first night together. She awakened with the sunrise and looked over to see Günter slumbering on his stomach, his naked body half uncovered beside her. As the golden light of dawn illuminated the room, she admired the expanse of his skin over ripples of taut muscles, his strong arms embracing the pillow beneath his head. She combed her fingers through his fine, dark hair, and then carefully traced his spine from his broad shoulders down to the arch of his lower back with one venturesome finger. He awakened with a contented smile, then moved closer and held her face in his hands.

"You make me so happy. I love you, Isabella."

"Günter...I..." She hesitated.

Before she could utter another word, he placed his finger gently over her lips. "You needn't say a word, my love. Lie there just as you are, beautiful and serene as an angel." He caressed her face and gazed at her in adoring silence for several moments.

Isabella's heart melted at his tender words. *Massimo has never spoken to me like this.* But she dismissed the comparison, attributing their differences to education and temperament, and not to depth of feeling. *Surely Günter cannot love me more than Massimo does.* But Günter's love was very real to her now, and she couldn't help but be moved by his ardor.

He planted delicate kisses on her forehead, cheeks, neck and lips. His fingers sought the soft, warm contours of her body as hers explored the firm muscles of his buttocks and thighs. As he eased his body on top of hers, their affection ignited into smoldering passion. She delighted in the sweetness of their lovemaking, sensing a blissful sympathy she didn't fully comprehend.

They spent half of Sunday in bed together, laughing and talking intimately, alternating between playful and serious moments, taking pleasure in each other's beautiful, youthful, energetic physiques.

At about noon, Günter regretfully announced that he would have to return to headquarters earlier than usual. "The colonel wants to meet with the staff this afternoon, Liebchen. I'm sorry but I will need to head back soon. I should have told you yesterday, but I didn't want to spoil our wonderful time together."

Isabella frowned but then stroked his cheek. "I'll be so lonely here without you, Günter, but I suppose the colonel has first claim to you."

"Not to my heart."

"When will I see you again?"

"I don't know. I'll contact you in the next day or two. Things are heating up at the front. The Allies are pressing toward Bologna and things soon may become very difficult. I won't have much leave time, I'm afraid," he said with a tinge of apprehension.

This reminder of the war roused Isabella from their cozy love nest, and brought her back to the purpose of these encounters with her handsome German lover. Like Günter, she too was recalled to duty.

****

Tuesday morning, Isabella was just getting ready to meet Massimo in the piazza when she heard Silvia enter the apartment.

"Ciao, Isabella!"

"Oh, Silvia, I was just on my way out, and I'm glad you got back before I had to leave. How was your weekend with Federico?"

"It was fabulous! And you'll never guess what I've discovered!" Silvia said in a conspiratorial tone. "Of all my connections, it's Federico who's paved the way for your new job at German headquarters."

"Really?" Isabella tingled with excitement. *Perhaps my mission can begin after all.* "What did you find out?" she asked as calmly as she could manage.

"Well, it turns out Umberto, Federico's plant manager at the winery, has a cousin who works for the Germans—Signora Vettori, head housekeeper at Palazzo Maggiore. Federico's already arranged an interview! And don't worry about references and background checks and all that. With his position in the government no one would dare question his recommendation."

"That's great, Silvia. I must thank Federico."

"Maybe he should thank you."

"What do you mean?"

"He's quite the entrepreneur, charming the signora into giving you an interview, but also pursuing a little business for himself."

"What kind of business?"

"The Germans are rather fond of Italian wine, it seems. Federico and the housekeeper have worked out a deal: a market for the familial vintage to keep the Germans happy and a little extra money in the signora's pocket. So everyone gets something out of the arrangement."

And I get a chance to spy on the Germans, Isabella thought with keen anticipation, mingled with a touch of fear.

****

Isabella appeared, as instructed, at the service entrance on the south side of the palazzo at seven o'clock Wednesday morning. She explained to the guard that she had an appointment with Signora Vettori and was escorted to the kitchen. The middle-aged woman greeted her hastily as she intermittently shouted orders to her staff.

"Please excuse me, Signorina Ricci, but I must make sure that the senior staff have their breakfast served precisely as they like it. These Germans are very demanding."

"I'm sure they are, signora. Is it always so busy here?"

"Well, we get a break about ten, before lunch preparation begins, and again at mid-afternoon. But there is always enough work to keep everyone occupied. Now tell me, have you any experience cooking for large numbers, say up to fifty or so?"

"I've worked at a farm and cooked for as many as twenty at a time. I'm sure I can handle the larger number."

"And what about housework and laundry? What is your experience in those areas?"

"Again, I've kept house at the farm, and I think you'll find me an able worker."

"I could use a girl to fill in all around, you see. You can start in the kitchen, but I'll need to send you upstairs as a chambermaid on occasion, when the other girls don't show up. It's very difficult to get good help. These girls are so flighty and unreliable. They should consider themselves fortunate to have any kind of work these days."

"Oh, I agree with you."

"Do you speak any German?"

"Yes, a little."

"Good, you can help serve the meals then. When can you start, Signorina Ricci?"

"Right away, signora. And please call me Isabella."

"All right. Why don't I start you on the early shift and see how you do with breakfast and lunch? Can you be here tomorrow at six o'clock?"

"Yes, of course. I would be happy to start then. Thank you."

"If you can handle the work tomorrow, we'll sit down and discuss your wages and hours then. Is that acceptable, Isabella?"

"Yes, that would be fine. I'll see you tomorrow at six. Thank you again, Signora Vettori."

Chapter 8

Isabella arrived at the palazzo a few minutes before six o'clock the next day. She was given a uniform and a quick tour of the premises before being put to work in the kitchen, helping to prepare breakfast for the General Staff. After the meal was served, she washed dishes and cleaned up. At about ten, Signora Vettori asked Claudia to bring Isabella along to serve coffee in the conference room for Colonel von Haeften's daily staff meeting.

"You're certainly pretty enough," the signora said. "The officers like that, you know. Sometimes they misbehave, but you've got to indulge them a little. It makes some of the girls uncomfortable, but let's see how you do. Military men are not always gentlemen, but most of them don't mean any harm."

Colonel von Haeften—that's Günter's commanding officer. He was sure to be in that meeting, and Isabella had not even told him of her intention to seek employment there. She worried about Günter's reaction to seeing her. *Well, he must find out sooner or later. It might as well be now.*

Claudia showed Isabella to the conference room several minutes before the meeting was to start. No one was in the room, so they were able to set up before the staff arrived. Claudia told Isabella that they must wait until the colonel entered before they could leave, in case he wanted anything. They stood on the side, out of the way, as men began to trickle in. Isabella's heart pounded as she surveyed every face. Günter arrived and took his seat without even noticing her. Isabella tried to position herself behind Claudia in case Günter looked over in their direction. When the colonel arrived, Claudia approached him and asked if he needed anything else. Günter happened to look up at that moment and saw Isabella. He stared at her, a baffled look on his face. She gave him a nervous half-smile, looked down and slinked out of the room following Claudia.

"Are you with us, Captain Schumann?" the colonel asked. A few of Günter's fellow officers chuckled.

"I'm sorry. What was that, sir?"

"The fuel consumption report? Do you have it, Captain?"

Günter shuffled through his papers. "Uh...I think I left that on my desk. I'll get it right away, sir." Before waiting for a response, Günter rushed out of the room after Isabella.

He caught up with her and grabbed her arm, just before she reached the stairs. "Isabella!" he uttered in a whisper. "What are you doing here?" Claudia gave her a curious look.

"Claudia, I'll be down to the kitchen in a minute. Go ahead, I remember how to get there." As Claudia walked away Isabella turned to Günter. "I'm sorry I didn't get a chance to tell you, Günter, but I just started today. You'd better get back to your meeting before the colonel gets angry. And I'll probably lose this job on my first day if I don't get down to the kitchen right now."

"But why are you working here?"

"Well, I do need the work. Can we talk about this later?" She gently touched his arm, afraid she'd upset him.

"All right, when can I see you?"

"Come to the apartment tonight. We'll talk then, I promise."

"I can try to be over there by nine. I can't make it any earlier."

"I'll see you then," she whispered and gave him a quick kiss on the cheek before scurrying off.

Isabella hurried down to the kitchen, hoping to catch Claudia before the girl had a chance to talk with Signora Vettori. She was relieved to find Claudia alone.

"Please don't say anything to the signora. It just happens that I'm acquainted with Captain Schumann, but I don't want to get into trouble for speaking to him. I really do need this job." *Can I trust her?*

"All right, Isabella, but you'd better be careful. The signora wants us to be amiable to the Germans, but not *too* amiable, if you know what I mean." She smiled and then whispered to Isabella, "I've noticed that one before. He's very good-looking. Is he your beau?"

Isabella blushed a little as she replied, "Well, yes, I suppose you could say that. I met him at Palazzo Fabriano. But please don't tell anyone."

"Palazzo Fabriano? Were you working there?"

"No, I went to a party with an old friend who socializes with some of the officers. I happened to meet Günter—I mean Captain Schumann—there." Claudia was younger than Isabella, probably only eighteen or nineteen. The girl seemed in awe, perhaps seeing Isabella, though only twenty-five herself, as a sophisticated older woman who mingled with German officers. Isabella decided it would be advantageous to have a friend at Palazzo Maggiore, and feigned an interest in the girl's personal affairs.

"What about you, Claudia, do you have a beau?"

"Oh, no," she said shyly. "My father would thrash me if I let a boy even kiss me!"

"Well, you'll have plenty of time for boys later. Men can be more trouble than they're worth, believe me!" They shared a laugh as Signora Vettori came in.

"What's all this chatter in here? You girls had better get back to work!" she scolded. "It's time to get started on lunch. Claudia, show Isabella what to do."

"Yes, signora," Claudia replied with a furtive smile to Isabella.

****

Isabella anxiously awaited Günter's arrival at the apartment. Silvia was out dining with Federico, and Isabella hoped she would have a chance to speak with Günter before they returned. It was half past nine already, and she was growing a little concerned that perhaps he would not come. She worried that he was angry with her or suspicious of her motives for seeking employment in the very place where he worked.

Another fifteen minutes passed before she heard a knock at the door.

"Who is it?" she asked. It was too late to open the door without knowing who was there, especially since she was alone.

"It's Günter."

She opened the door apprehensively. "Come in, Günter. I was getting a little worried about you. Please come and sit down."

"I'm sorry I'm so late. The colonel had many things to discuss with us tonight."

"Is anything wrong? With the war, I mean. Has something happened?" *Massimo would be proud of me if I gained information so casually.*

"No, nothing unusual. I really can't talk about it anyway," he said as he sat down on the sofa. "Is Silvia here?"

"No, she's out with Federico. Have you eaten yet? Can I get you anything?"

"I ate at the palazzo. We worked through supper. But yes, there is something you can get me."

He smiled and beckoned her to sit beside him. "I haven't given you a proper greeting." He kissed her and ran his fingers through her hair, brushing it away from her face. "Now tell me, sweetheart, why are you working at the palazzo?"

"Don't you remember I told you I wanted to find a job and stay in Verona? Silvia and I have decided to share this apartment and the expenses. She plans to spend the weekends at Federico's villa, so that means you and I can have the place to ourselves. I thought that would please you. I hope you're not angry with me."

"Of course I'm not angry with you. Why would you think that?" His voice conveyed a mixture of affection and concern.

"You seemed upset when you saw me today. Did I get you in trouble with the colonel?"

"Don't worry, Isabella. I was just startled, that's all. But how did you manage to get a job at German headquarters?"

"Silvia has many connections. I thought it would be wonderful to be so close to you, although I was already warned to be discreet about our relationship. And with all the appealing young girls who work there...well, this way I can keep an eye on you, too. I hope you don't mind."

"I would like to think that you trust me."

"I do trust you, Günter. But you're a man, aren't you?"

"I think I am. If you'd like me to prove it..." His smile was roguish. "You needn't worry about me. I only have eyes for one woman." He slipped his arm around her waist and drew her toward him. Her body heated as he kissed her, letting his hands wander downward from her quivering breasts to her waist, then pausing at her thighs. "I wish Silvia and Federico were not returning tonight."

"Tomorrow is Friday. Perhaps Silvia will leave

for Federico's by the evening. Then we can be alone."

"I can hardly wait, darling."

****

To Isabella's surprise, Silvia had not yet returned by the time she had to leave for work the next morning. *She probably spent the night at Federico's.* Isabella left a note for her, telling her that she hoped everything was all right and that she would be back there about half past four in the afternoon. She wondered whether Silvia would indeed leave for her weekend with Federico that evening, instead of waiting until Saturday. Isabella realized with self-reproach that she was looking forward to being alone with Günter again. Every time she caught herself thinking of him fondly, even romantically, she felt a twinge of guilt. *This isn't meant for my enjoyment.* To cool her ardor, she forced herself to refresh her loathing for the Nazis, remembering that Günter was one of them. Recollecting Marco's murder was enough to blunt her passion.

****

When Isabella had last seen Massimo, they'd devised a system for exchanging messages, since Isabella was to spend most of her time now in Verona. One of their compatriots had a cousin who worked at a bakery in the city. Either one could leave messages there for the other. Massimo accompanied Vittoria and Luisa, who went to Verona three times a week to sell farm products at the market in Piazza delle Erbe. If Isabella happened to be working the later shift at Palazzo Maggiore on one of those days, she could find him at the piazza early in the morning. By the end of the second week of her employment, she was able to meet Massimo for the first time in almost two weeks.

She left the apartment just before sunrise to seek him out at the piazza. She left Günter asleep in their bed, a note on the kitchen table that she had gone to the market to buy fresh fare for their breakfast. The streets of Verona were silent as the unfolding dawn tinted the ancient cobblestones a golden blush. As she neared the piazza, the bustle of activity and the noise of commercial trucks began to assail her ears. Merchants and farmers were setting up stalls, arranging their goods and crops, while butchers and fishmongers in bloodstained aprons poured out trays of chopped ice onto tables to preserve their precious commodities. She spotted her comrades on the far side of the piazza, loading their stalls with fresh eggs and goat cheese from the dairy, and turnips, carrots and squash from the fields.

"Ciao, amici!" she greeted.

Vittoria and Luisa offered sisterly embraces as Massimo looked on, his face displaying a strange fusion of affection and edginess, as if he were pleased, but uneasy, to see her.

"I've missed you, carino," she murmured as he enfolded her in his stalwart arms.

"Me, too," he said in a low voice. "Let's go for a ride," he added with an almost imperceptible grin.

"Where?"

"Nowhere in particular. I'd like to talk to you alone, that's all."

"All right, but I can't be gone for too long. Günter will be leaving for the palazzo in another hour, and he'll be worried if I'm not back by then."

Massimo sighed audibly and looked at Isabella with a tinge of anger. "Let him be worried. I don't want to hear about *him* right now, anyway. I haven't seen you for nearly two weeks. I just want to spend a little time with you."

"Please don't be jealous, carino. You know you're my only love, don't you?"

"Come with me now and show me," he said as he

took her hand and led her to his truck which was parked several yards away. Grasping his intimation, Isabella felt an ambivalence she didn't quite understand.

They drove out of Verona and into the countryside. After about fifteen minutes, Isabella began to feel anxious. "Where are we going, Massimo? You know I have to work today at the palazzo. If I lose my job..."

"What time do you have to be there?" he interrupted.

"Not until eleven, but Günter..."

"Would you shut up about him, already?"

Isabella remained silent for the rest of the ride, until Massimo turned off from the main road, down a dirt path to a remote meadow. He stopped the truck, turned to her and bombarded her with questions.

"So, what can you tell me about Palazzo Maggiore? Have you discovered where they keep their documents? Where is the war room? And what is your boyfriend up to over there?"

"I'm just starting to get a feel for the place. I'm usually banished to the kitchen; there's no vital information there. I've been upstairs only a few times. Günter's unit is on the second floor. He and the rest of Colonel von Haeften's staff oversee the transport of weapons, ammunition and equipment for Army Group C. I'm trying to get Günter to show me around, but I have to be careful. We could both get into trouble if we're seen together too often. The field marshal and General Staff meet on the fourth floor, though I think the war room is in the basement, in the north wing of the building. I'm guessing that because the stairs down to that area are always guarded and I've seen the senior officers go down there. Why else would they go to the basement?"

"Good thinking," Massimo said with an approving nod. "Does the kitchen lead down to the basement?"

"Yes."

"Can you get to the war room from there?"

"I don't think so. It's in a separate section of the building. But I have an idea about how to access some of the other offices when no one is around. The lower floors of the building, including Günter's unit, all but shut down at night after nine. Usually the staff has returned to quarters by then, and no one stays in the lower section apart from three guards: one at the front entrance, one near the stairs to the basement in the north wing, and one on the third floor. All entrances are locked except for the front. When I've been on the late shift, I've managed to stall long enough to note this."

"Good, carina, very good. But can you stay there past nine without drawing suspicion?"

"Most of the staff, including the domestics, leave by the front entrance. If I make it my practice to leave by the back door, I could fake my departure for the evening. Otherwise, the guard at the entrance will expect to see me leave after my shift. There's a heavy metal door leading to the back alley, a few steps down from the kitchen, and the stairs to the basement are right there. It's locked from the inside. I could make my farewells, let the door slam shut— presumably behind me—then sneak down to the basement instead. If I hide there until most of the staff is gone for the night, I can go back upstairs, being careful to avoid the three guards. They're toward the front, so using the back stairs, I should be undetected."

"Brava, Isabella! You've thought this out well. When can you do a trial run?"

"I'll have to find out when my next late shift is. I'll try for sometime next week. Don't you think we should be getting back to the city now?"

"I didn't bring you all the way out here just to discuss business. I've something else in mind." He slid toward her on the front seat of the truck and, pulling her into his arms, kissed her passionately. As their fervor rose, he unbuckled his belt and drew down his trousers while slipping his other hand beneath her skirt and hastily removing her panties, ripping them in the process. He pushed her up against the passenger door as he thrust himself inside her. Wild with desire, he plunged into her with ever-mounting speed and ferocity until he climaxed with one last forceful surge.

"Ah, carina, I've been so hungry for you!" he said breathlessly.

The encounter concluded so quickly that Isabella barely had time to comprehend what had happened. Though her ardor was aroused, the act lacked completeness and left her yearning for more. Her back ached, and she realized that the metal handle of the door had rammed into her repeatedly. She dared not mention this to Massimo, lest she dampen his enjoyment. Snuggling up beside him, she rested her head again his brawny chest.

"I miss you so much, Massimo. I long for our little cabin on the farm," she said looking up into his fiery jet-black eyes.

He smiled and kissed her affectionately. "We will be there together very soon, my love." Then he started the truck and headed back for Verona.

Chapter 9

The following Monday, Günter arrived in the conference room several minutes before Colonel von Haeften's daily briefing. He found Isabella atop a stepladder, intent on reaching a cobweb above the tall window with her feather duster. She didn't hear him enter, so he crept up behind her, grabbed her by the waist and said sternly in German, "Fräulein, it seems you missed a spot right there!" She nearly fell off the ladder, but Günter had her in his arms and gently lowered her down.

"Günter! You scared me half to death. I could have fallen and broken my neck!" she chided, then smiled and struck him lightly on the arm with the feather duster.

"I'm sorry, but you looked so fetching up there in your little maid's uniform." He took the duster from her hand. "I can think of some interesting ways to use this," he said with a mischievous smile as he pulled her toward him and kissed her.

Isabella stroked his jaw with her fingertip. "You'd better let me go, Günter. You don't want to get me fired now, do you?"

"All right, go on then. I'll see you later." Günter gave her a soft tap on the rear with the duster before handing it back to her.

His smile dropped when he noticed Major Gerhardt standing in the doorway with his arms crossed, shaking his head and frowning.

"Please excuse me, mein Herr," Isabella

stammered as she squeezed past the major and hurried out.

"How long have you been standing there, Max?" Günter asked with more than a touch of embarrassment.

"Long enough. You'd better be careful, Günter. These Italian girls always want something from us."

"Isabella's not like that. Perhaps you are a little jealous, my friend," he responded with a smile.

"So it's true love, then?" Gerhardt asked sarcastically.

"I suppose you're too cynical to believe in such things. But I absolutely adore her, and I know she feels the same way."

"The colonel would not be pleased, I'm sure of that. Just keep your guard up and don't be so trusting. We're at war, remember? Most Italians would happily cut our throats if given the opportunity."

Günter dismissed the major's warning with a shake of his head, grinning at the thought that Max's slight frame, diminutive mustache, and air of self-importance made him a feeble parody of the Führer.

Günter sometimes wondered why he and Max were good friends—their worldviews and personalities so differed. But he found Max's pessimism almost amusing and enjoyed their lively debates.

Günter recalled an afternoon months earlier, shortly after their transfer from Rome to Verona. He and Max had sat under the broad red-and-white canopy of an outdoor caffè, enjoying the shady refuge from the intense Italian sun. They often relaxed in Piazza dei Signori when off-duty, lazily watching the civilians and soldiers who passed by. If an attractive young lady happened to be sitting near them, Max would invariably try to entice her, usually without success.

Günter's smile to the waitress quickly drew her to their table. In fluent Italian, he engaged her in a brief, genial conversation, then ordered an icy granita for himself and an espresso for Max.

"Were you asking her for a date, Günter?"

"Actually, we were discussing the weather. You know, Max, if you want to meet a nice girl here you should try to learn a little Italian."

"We can't all be linguists like you. Anyway, it's not conversation that interests me," Max grumbled.

"You're very testy today. I don't know why you should be in such a foul mood. Here we are in beautiful Italy, far from the front..."

"Thanks to my connections," Max interrupted. "If it weren't for me you'd still be at the front, that is if you'd managed to avoid being captured or killed."

"And for that, my friend, I'll always be in your debt!" Günter replied with a laugh.

****

The next morning, as Isabella waited for Massimo in the piazza, she mulled over their scheme. He'd asked her to case Palazzo Maggiore that night, after most of the staff had gone home. This would be her first late shift since they'd discussed her plan of hiding in the basement, and he wanted her to begin the operation as soon as possible.

Suddenly she jumped as someone grabbed her arm.

"Massimo, you scared me," she said as she turned to see that he'd come up behind her.

"If you scare that easily then I have a lot to worry about," he replied with a frown. "Are you ready for tonight?"

"Yes, I suppose I am. But it won't be pleasant to spend the whole night in the basement," Isabella said with a sigh. "And I'm not sure how I'm going to explain to Silvia where I've been. If I'm gone all night she might be suspicious."

"Maybe you can tell her you're visiting Schumann at his quarters."

"No, that won't work. I've already told her that women aren't allowed at the barracks. We'll have to think up another story." She paused a few moments and tapped her finger on her lip. "What if I say that I need to visit my mother? I can tell her Mamma's been sick and Leonardo will meet me after my shift and take me home, just for the night. Then he'll bring me back to Verona the next morning. What do you think?"

"It might work. Are you going to tell Schumann the same thing?"

"Yes, I'll have to. Then you'll pick me up here tomorrow morning at five. I can't stay in the basement any later. Some of my co-workers arrive early and if they find me down there... Well, I don't even want to think about that!"

"Why don't you just go back to the apartment then?"

"At five in the morning? I don't think Silvia will believe that Leonardo would drop me off so early. My shift doesn't start until eleven. No, you'll just have to meet me here."

"At five?"

"Yes, Massimo, at five." She fought her rising irritation. "Look, I'm the one who has to spend the night in the basement. I doubt I'll get any sleep. It's the least you can do."

He exhaled heavily. "Very well, Isabella."

****

Shortly after Isabella had begun working at German headquarters, she and Günter decided to meet once a day, taking a ten-minute cigarette break at a predetermined time in the alley behind the palazzo. Neither of them were habitual smokers, but

Günter would occasionally light a cigarette, and began the practice of enjoying one to disguise his clandestine meetings with Isabella. Günter's hours at the palazzo had increased of late and this was often their only time together except for weekends and rare evenings during the week. On this day, their meeting was set for three-thirty in the afternoon.

Isabella waited for him in the alleyway. She had been anxious all day and feared revealing her agitation and rousing his suspicions. Finally he arrived and approached her.

"It's just torture to spend only ten minutes a day with you," he said as he held her tenderly in his arms. "I can't believe it's only Tuesday and we won't be together until Friday at the earliest."

"We're together now."

"You know what I mean, don't you?" he asked with an amorous smile.

"Is that the only thing you men think about?"

"Of course it isn't. I enjoy every moment we have together. Don't you know you mean everything to me? Our relationship is much more than purely a physical one."

She looked into his eyes, remembering her hurried encounter with Massimo just a few days earlier. Though Günter was as fervent as Massimo, she doubted he would enjoy such impetuous lovemaking. She realized that for Günter, her pleasure was as important as his own. *If only Massimo could take a few lessons from Günter*, she thought with irony. As she put her arms around him and held him close, she reminded herself that tonight her deception would begin in earnest. *It is all for the cause.*

"Günter, my brother is picking me up here tonight. My mother hasn't been well, and I really want to see her. He'll bring me back in the morning.

I wanted to tell you in case you were thinking of stopping by the apartment tonight."

"I'm sorry about your mother. I hope it's nothing serious."

"I don't think so, but I do want to see her. I'd rather go tonight than miss seeing you this weekend."

"But you won't have much time to spend with her. Aren't you working until nine tonight? It will be nearly ten o'clock before you see her."

Isabella was now afraid he doubted her story. "Perhaps it's not the best time to visit, but I just feel I can't wait any longer. You understand, don't you?"

"Of course. I'm sure your mother will be fine, but if you're concerned you should see her as soon as possible. Can't you arrange for a day off tomorrow?"

"No, I don't think I've been working here long enough to ask for that. We'd better get back to work now, don't you think?"

"Ah, but I haven't even had my cigarette yet," he said with a smile.

"Then you can stay out here and enjoy one if you like. I'm going back to work." She began to turn away when he grabbed her gently by the arm.

"Don't I get a good-bye kiss?" He took her in his arms and kissed her lovingly. "Can you meet me here tomorrow at the same time?" She nodded. "Please give your mother my best wishes, will you?"

"Thank you, Günter, I will."

****

As nine o'clock drew nearer, Isabella's anxiety increased to an almost unbearable level. She had already begun her practice of leaving by the back door, after calling out "Good evening" to her co-workers. She was careful to ensure that they would hear but not see her leave. This night, she would allow the door to close after taking her leave, and then she would silently descend the stairs to the

87

basement. When she arrived at the palazzo that morning, she'd concealed a flashlight beneath her coat and hidden it in the basement. She had also prepared a hiding place for herself near the furnace and collected a few blankets from the palazzo to provide her some comfort during the long night. She hoped to get some sleep so she could manage to get through the next day of work.

Her heart pounded as she executed her plan and made her way down to the basement. Fear and uneasiness nearly overwhelmed her as thoughts of backing out raced through her brain. She settled near the furnace and waited until all sounds above her ceased.

After about forty minutes, she grabbed her flashlight and crept up the stairs to the kitchen. The lights in the hallways were left on, so the flashlight was not yet needed. She silently inched her way up the back stairs to the second floor and, removing her shoes, proceeded to Colonel von Haeften's suite.

To her dismay, she found the doors to the offices locked. Her heart nearly stopped beating when she heard footsteps above her. She desperately tried every door until she found one that opened. It was one of the conference rooms and she darted in and hid in a corner.

After a few minutes, the footsteps stopped. *The guard on the third floor must have been pacing and is now back at his post.*

It took her several minutes to recover her nerve and venture out into the hallway. Again she tried all the doors but found only one other conference room accessible and neither adjoined any other rooms. *The third floor's too dangerous.*

I'll go back to the basement and explore it more thoroughly. She tried to reach the area where she believed the war room was located, in the north wing of the building. That, too, appeared to be inaccessible, separated from the rest of the basement by solid walls. *The Germans have mapped out their headquarters well.*

The only other parts of the building to survey were the few offices on the first floor. She came up to the kitchen again and slowly advanced toward the front of the palazzo, staying clear of the guard at the front entrance. She found that those offices, too, were locked. Disappointed, she returned to her basement lair and tried to sleep.

Isabella hardly slept that night, and rose at half past four to meet Massimo. The streets were dark and foreboding, and she was chilled by the damp night air. Shivering, she hastened toward the piazza, passing rows of houses painted in muted shades of saffron, wheat and terracotta. Some were adorned with the remnants of faded frescos; others revealed exposed brick beneath crumbling plaster façades. When she reached the deserted marketplace, her only companions were pigeons, huddled in niches where stones had fallen away from ancient walls. Their soft cooing, like lovers' whispers, penetrated the early morning silence.

As the sky lightened, farmers and merchants began to arrive, and finally Massimo pulled up in his truck. He kissed her as she settled into the front seat beside him, then drove to the same isolated meadow where they had gone before.

"How did it go, carina?"

"Not so well, I'm afraid. Though there are only three guards on duty at night, the place is scrupulously secured. All of the offices are locked and the war room is completely inaccessible."

"Then you'll have to get the keys somehow. What about the housekeeper, Signora Vettori? Where does she keep hers?"

"She carries them with her all the time. She probably even sleeps with them."

"Wait a minute...of course! Your boyfriend, does he sleep with his keys, too?"

"Well, no. At least not when he's with me."

"And where does he keep them then?"

"I suppose they would be in one of the pockets of his uniform, probably his trousers. But if I stole his keys in the middle of the night don't you think he would notice? He'd surely suspect me when he discovers they're missing."

"Then you'll have to return them before that, after making copies, of course."

"And how am I to do that?"

Massimo thought for a few moments. "I'll give you wax plates so you can make impressions of them. I can then have duplicates made for you. He'll never even realize that you 'borrowed' them. It shouldn't take you long to make the impressions, only a few minutes, I would think."

"And do you know how to make usable keys from wax impressions?"

"I don't, but I'm sure I can find someone who does. When are you to spend the night with him next?"

"It will either be Friday or Saturday, depending on when Silvia leaves for Federico's. Could you get me the plates by then?"

"I should be able to. Can you meet me in the piazza on Friday morning?"

"Yes, I'm on the late shift the rest of the week."

"Good." He began to caress her feverishly, covering her face and neck with kisses, and then reaching beneath her blouse to fondle her breasts. Her passion was awakened but she remembered the discomfort of their last encounter.

"Can't we go someplace else?" she asked. "This truck is so...restricting. It's only about six o'clock now. We could drive out to the farm and indulge ourselves in the luxury of our own bed. You'd still have time to drive me back to Verona by eleven."

"The farm is in the other direction, Isabella."

"Please, Massimo. It would be so much more enjoyable for both of us," she entreated.

"All right, carina," he said with a slight smile as he started the truck and headed for the farm.

****

Isabella met Massimo as planned in the piazza early Friday morning. Vittoria and Luisa were also there, arranging their goods for sale at the market. When Isabella climbed into the truck, Massimo showed her five large wax plates.

"You know what to do with these, right?"

"Yes. I'll impress each key, front and back. I think you've given me enough plates here for fifty keys! I doubt Günter has as many as that."

"When can you return them to me?"

"I start late on Monday. I'll meet you in the piazza as usual."

"Very good, carina. Now, shall we take a ride back to the farm?" he asked with a smile.

"No, not today, Massimo. I should really go back to the apartment so I can figure out where to hide these plates."

"That shouldn't take long. We have plenty of time."

"Well...it wouldn't be a good idea right now." She hesitated. "You know that we have to be careful. It's not a safe time of the month." That wasn't the truth; for some reason, she did not wish to be intimate with him at that moment but didn't know how to explain it to him. She was afraid to upset him.

"I see," he replied with displeasure. "But you're still seeing *him* this weekend?"

"Yes, that's the plan. He'll still stay with me even if we don't...well, you know. I should be able to make the impressions."

His voice brusque with irritation, Massimo said,

"All right, Isabella. I'll take you back to the apartment now."

****

Silvia decided to have Federico come for her early on Friday, so Isabella and Günter could begin their weekend together that night. They arranged to meet at nine o'clock in the alleyway behind the palazzo. Günter left by the front entrance as he always did, then walked around to meet her. As soon as he saw her he hurried to embrace her.

"I'm so happy we can be together tonight."

"So am I, Günter."

"Would you like to get something to eat? We can go to the trattoria near the apartment, then go home and be alone together at last."

"That sounds wonderful."

Throughout dinner, Günter held her hand whenever he could and barely took his eyes off her the entire time. *There's no denying he's truly in love with me.* She hadn't seen that ardor in Massimo's eyes in a very long time. Yes, Massimo had a fierce desire for her, but in Günter's eyes she saw something more; there was an enchantment, a passion that transcended corporeal delight. He was a doting and generous lover whose tenderness and devotion suggested the abiding love of a lifelong union.

****

Later that night, after making love with Isabella, Günter fell into a tranquil sleep. She lay awake, thinking about her assignment of securing wax impressions of his keys. When she was sure he was sleeping soundly, she quietly withdrew from their bed and warily picked up the trousers that he had tossed onto a chair. They were heavy and she could tell immediately that the keys were in the front pocket. She backed out of the bedroom, glancing over toward Günter to make certain he was still asleep. She inched her way to the bathroom and closed the door behind her. Her heart beat wildly. *What if he awakens before I finish my task?* She pulled the wax plates from where she had hidden them in the cabinet below the sink, then removed the key ring from the trouser pocket. She opened it and began to make impressions, one by one, until all eleven keys were copied front and back. Then she meticulously put the ring back together, making sure that the keys were in exactly the same order in which she had found them. She retraced her steps, replacing the trousers and climbing back into bed beside Günter. He barely stirred, completely ignorant of her ruse.

Though she mutely sighed with relief, Isabella felt a deep sadness overtake her. *So now I've betrayed him,* she thought with remorse. *But it's all for the cause...* How many times had she repeated these words, like a magical incantation that could absolve any transgression? *He's a Nazi—I must never forget that. Haven't they committed enough atrocities to justify this simple act of deceit?* Many soldiers are faced with abhorrent duties, and that's what she was, a soldier fighting the double oppression of domestic tyranny and brutal foreign occupation. Devious acts, which in peacetime could not be condoned, must be exploited in war.

Chapter 10

After a restless night, Isabella awoke at dawn and nestled beside Günter in their bed. He drew her close into his arms as she rested her head on his bare chest. They lay there silently for several moments, enjoying the warmth and smoothness of each other's skin.

"Good morning, sweetheart." He caressed her face and kissed her. "Did you sleep well?"

"Not so well, but at least I don't have to be in until eleven. I think I'll take my time getting up this morning and indulge in a couple of hours of extra sleep."

"You should do that, my dear. I'm afraid I don't have that luxury, though. The colonel wants us in early today. In fact, I'd better get ready quickly." He kissed her again, then got up and headed for the bathroom.

Isabella embraced his pillow, taking in the faint, pleasant scent of his body and the trace of heat left behind on the sheets where he had lain. She felt a pall of melancholy envelop her as she reflected on the deceitful undertaking she had begun. *I cannot be falling in love with him. It isn't possible.* Yet she couldn't deny her fondness for him, and she regretted that she had chosen such a kind and loving man as her target. She resolved to spare him any unnecessary pain, just as she resolved to keep her affections in check and not surrender her heart.

****

At nine o'clock that evening, they met behind the palazzo.

"Shall we go to our usual place tonight for supper, Isabella?"

They were becoming regular customers at the trattoria near the apartment, where the proprietor and waiters already knew them by name. It was not uncommon for a German officer to escort a young Italian woman, but some who frequently saw Isabella and Günter together remarked on the bond between them.

"I'm very tired tonight, Günter. Would you mind if we just headed home instead? Perhaps we can scrape something together with what we have in the apartment. I'm not really hungry anyway."

"Of course, darling. You said you didn't sleep well last night. We'll have a bite to eat and go to bed early. Tomorrow is Sunday. We get to spend the whole day together!"

Isabella slept better that night and woke up refreshed, happy for a day off from her tedious but exhausting duties at the palazzo. She rose early and began to prepare breakfast. She was standing by the stove, putting on a fresh pot of coffee when Günter entered the kitchen.

"Good morning, sweetheart." He came up behind her and wrapped his arms around her. "What would you like to do today?"

"Do you know what would be nice? Let's take a ride and have a picnic up in the hills. It's the middle of October already, and soon it will be too cold to enjoy the fresh air. Can you borrow one of those motorcycles with the silly seats attached to them?"

"Why not? And it's called a sidecar," he whispered in her ear. She looked at him with feigned annoyance for having corrected her, but he kissed her on the cheek and she instantly forgave him.

"Would you pick up some food and wine from the

palazzo while you're there? The kitchen staff will let you take anything you want."

"I suppose that's because I speak Italian to them. Not many officers do."

"Oh, it's not just that. All the women there are in love with you. The other day Claudia and Lina were going on endlessly about how charming and handsome you are. It makes it very difficult for me to work there, you know," she teased. "They're all jealous."

"Well, I'll try not to be so charming and handsome then," he replied with a smile.

****

As they sped out of the city and into the countryside, Isabella remembered that first motorcycle ride soon after they'd met, and the tender moments they shared that day.

Günter pulled off the road near the top of a hill and brought the motorcycle to a stop a few yards from the same oak tree where they had first kissed.

"I remember this spot," Isabella said as she helped him lay out a blanket beneath the tree. "Let's make this our own special place. You could carve our initials in this tree."

"It's a beautiful old tree, Isabella. I wouldn't want to injure it. What would make you think of doing something like that?"

"It's supposed to be a romantic gesture. I think I read it in a book once. Just a way to mark our territory, I guess."

"Well, I suppose it's not as bad as the way dogs mark their territory. I could do that if you want me to; it probably wouldn't hurt the tree as much," he said, laughing.

"There you go again, making fun at my expense."

"No, Liebchen," he protested sweetly. "If it would please you I'd cut down this tree with my pocketknife." Günter took out the small knife and looked for the right spot on the tree to "mark their territory." He found an area where the bark had partially peeled away and deftly scratched an I and a G into the wood. "How does that look?"

She examined his craftsmanship and conferred her approval. *How gentle he is, even with the oak tree. He certainly doesn't epitomize my notion of a Nazi.*

"Would you open the wine, please, Günter?"

She watched him and admired the manly beauty of his face, the way his eyes crinkled up when he smiled, accentuating their azure brilliance, and the boyish innocence of his demeanor. *Oh, this is silly. I'm acting like a schoolgirl. But he is undeniably handsome...* She forced herself to think about Massimo then, as if she feared his German rival might overshadow him in her heart. She closed her eyes and envisioned his stalwart frame and masculine bearing, exuding the power and authority of a natural leader. He was larger than Günter and stronger. She shuddered to think of Günter's fate if the two of them ever came to blows.

"Here you are, my dear," Günter said as he offered her a cup of wine.

She was startled by his voice, having just conjured up his unfortunate state after an imagined brawl with Massimo.

"Isabella, you're as white as a ghost! You look as though you've been awakened from a bad dream. Are you all right?"

"Yes, I'm fine." She was embarrassed to realize how far she'd allowed her imagination to wander.

"What were you thinking about just now?" he asked.

"Oh, nothing, really." She was sure he wouldn't want to hear about his humiliating defeat at the hands of his robust opponent. "Do you know what

97

would make this scene perfect?"

"Let me see...we have the glorious landscape at our feet, an excellent bottle of wine, an assortment of wonderful things to eat, and most important, the happiest couple in the Veneto. No, I can't think of anything we are missing. Well, except one thing—an end to the war."

"That would be the best thing of all, but that wasn't what I was thinking of, and I'm afraid that's not in our control. I was thinking of music. Didn't you tell me that your mother was a talented singer and that she wanted you to study music in Vienna?"

"Yes, that's true. I suppose we could borrow Silvia's Victrola."

"I was thinking of live music, Günter. Don't you sing or play an instrument? Why don't you serenade me?"

"I play the piano a little, but it would be difficult to bring one up here in the sidecar. I used to sing in church as a boy soprano, but that was many, many years ago. My voice was never the same after I reached adolescence."

"Well of course it wasn't the same. A six-foot-tall Army officer with a coloratura voice would be quite disconcerting."

Günter was beside himself with laughter at the thought. "I barely manage to command any respect at headquarters now. Imagine how that would affect my military career!"

"If you used to sing in church I'm sure you still have a fine voice. Why don't you sing for me?"

"What, now? You know I'd do anything to please you, Isabella, but well...it's a little embarrassing. And I haven't practiced or anything..."

"Oh, please! It would make me so happy. And I promise not to laugh even if you're dreadful. There isn't anyone else around for miles. Please, Günter." She playfully mustered all her powers of female persuasion.

"Very well, then," he said with a sigh. "But I expect a big reward for this. What shall I sing for you?"

"Anything!" she said with delight. "How about something in German?"

"I was planning on that. It's hard enough to sing *a cappella* without any practice. I'll stick with my native tongue. Now let me think of something suitable, but not too difficult, of course." He paused a few moments, seemingly absorbed in thought. "I've an idea." He stood, took a few steps and cleared his throat. Then he turned back, grabbed the wine and took a long gulp straight from the bottle. "I need some fortification. All right, I will try a little Mozart for you."

Isabella sat in gleeful expectation as Günter took some deep breaths, cleared his throat again, and tried to warm up his vocal cords. *He's so endearing when he's nervous.*

He drew a long breath then began the lilting melody:

Ein Mädchen oder Weibchen
Wünscht Papageno sich!
O so ein sanftes Täubchen
Wär' Seligkeit für mich!

Wird keine mir Liebe gewähren,
So muss mich die Flamme verzehren!
Doch küsst mich ein weiblicher Mund,
So bin ich schon wieder gesund!

He was a little shaky at first but sounded more confident as he continued. Isabella was captivated by the sweetness of his lyric baritone and applauded enthusiastically.

"Bravo, Günter, Bravissimo! Oh, Günter, you

have such a lovely voice. You could sing at the opera house in Milan!"

"No, I don't think so." He flushed, but beamed with pleasure. "I'm glad you liked it."

"It was wonderful! May I have the translation?"

"Translation? That wasn't part of the bargain. What about my reward?"

"Come here." She beckoned him to sit beside her. She took his face in her hands and gave him a long, passionate kiss. "I love you, Günter," she whispered. The words had escaped her lips before she had time to reflect. She realized it was the first time she had uttered them.

"I love you, too, darling," he said as he took her hand and pressed it to his lips.

"Why don't you lie down now? Just stretch out on the blanket and relax." She stroked his soft, dark hair while he closed his eyes in contentment. "Now, would you please translate for me?"

"It's from Mozart's *Die Zauberflöte*. Papageno laments that all he wants is a sweetheart or wife because 'such a soft little dove would be bliss.' If no one will love him then he will be consumed by flame. But a woman's kiss would immediately restore him to health."

Isabella leaned over and kissed him. "Are you restored now, Papageno?"

"I've never felt better!"

****

Isabella rose before dawn the next morning to meet Massimo in the piazza and deliver the wax plates imprinted with Günter's keys. Günter was still asleep as she dressed and left the apartment.

Waiting for Massimo, Isabella was preoccupied with her declaration of love to Günter the previous day. *Am I growing too attached to him? I'll never fulfill my mission if I let myself fall in love.* She considered the significance of her words, trying to assign a meaning that her conscience could abide. She dismissed her utterance as an inconsequential impulse, not an indication of genuine devotion. *It is only infatuation. He is certainly attractive and charming enough to captivate any woman. It is a passing caprice, nothing more. My true love is Massimo.*

When Massimo appeared with his truck, she climbed in and closed the door behind her. He suggested they drive to the farm to discuss their strategy.

"Here are the plates. These should suffice."

He examined them closely and indicated his approval with a nod. "I've found someone to make the keys; it will take a few days. I hope you are ready for the next step, Isabella."

"I hope so, too. I admit that I'm nervous about it, though." She knew that her mission involved deadly risk, but she tried not to dwell on it. She had decided long ago that she wouldn't tolerate the despotism that was poisoning her country. After Marco's murder, she'd vowed to actively fight the oppression, and willingly risk her life for the partisan cause.

"Are you sure you can go through with it?"

"I know that I must. It's too late to turn back."

"Take care and keep your wits about you. If you are caught they will torture you to give us all up. Do not allow that to happen!"

She was startled by his vehemence and affronted that he would think she could inform on her comrades. "Do you think I would do that? Don't you trust me?"

"I trust your loyalty but fear you may break under pressure."

Her body tensed, as she imagined what horrors the Nazis might inflict. "I won't let you down."

"All right, Isabella. I want you to look for information about supply routes, troop movements and ammunition shipments. These may come by rail or by truck. The action at the front will slow as winter sets in, but that's when they'll regroup and rearm. The Allies need to know where they're amassing their forces. Have you been studying up on your German?"

"A little. I can read it fairly well, but I have trouble understanding the spoken language, especially when they converse quickly."

"It's the reading that's important for now. Remember, you must only copy documents. Do not take anything with you and be sure to leave the premises just as you find them. Otherwise it will arouse suspicion."

"I know that. I'm not an idiot!" Isabella had grown weary of talk. "Can we end this discussion now, please? I've missed you so much, Massimo. Why don't we visit our cabin for a little while?" she suggested with a winsome smile.

"Of course, carina."

****

After an amorous encounter, Isabella cuddled close to Massimo in their bed, savoring the heat from his body. She caressed his powerful torso, gliding her fingers through the thick black hair of his muscular chest. For her, there was no safer place than in Massimo's arms.

It was Massimo who had taught her the pleasures of lovemaking, though he was not her first sexual partner. She recalled with amusement the awkward affections of the teenaged suitor with whom she'd had clumsy adventures in the barn at her family's farm. For Isabella, it had been a mixture of coercion and curiosity, but she hesitantly complied, believing that this adolescent ardor would end in wedded bliss. As a girl, she had been indoctrinated that carnal knowledge was reserved for holy matrimony. Yet as she matured she came to understand that her strict Catholic upbringing did not suit her. *How much can those celibate priests and chaste nuns teach me of life and love?* she had wondered, and decided to investigate these matters for herself.

Chapter 11

The German Army billeted its officers at Albergo Venezia, a large, elegant hotel near Palazzo Maggiore. Günter had the good fortune to be assigned an accommodating roommate, Captain Kurt Graf, another officer on Colonel von Haeften's staff. Kurt willingly abetted Günter's non-regulation housing arrangement, allowing Günter the luxury of spending occasional nights at Isabella's apartment. If Günter were summoned in the middle of the night, Kurt knew exactly where to find him and could dispatch a trusted enlisted man to bring him back.

Kurt and Günter shared a small but pleasant room at the hotel. The pale floral wallpaper and exquisite crystal lamps gave an inapt delicacy to the quarters of two military officers. Kurt had laughed when he'd caught Günter idly staring at the sole painting that decorated the room. The pastoral scene, depicting the demure courtship of a shepherd and a maiden, recalled the tranquil vistas of Günter's rural homeland. He pictured window boxes overflowing with red geraniums, and the white lace-trimmed curtains of quaint cottages. Memories of the blossoming hillsides and romantic castles of Bavaria offered a fleeting respite from the war. At night, Kurt and Günter would leave the shuttered windows of their room open to welcome the fresh air, and to allow the early morning hum of the awakening city to gradually rouse them from sleep.

Kurt arrived one evening at their barracks to

find Günter reclining on his bed, rereading Goethe's *The Sorrows of Young Werther*, one of the few books he had managed to retain throughout all his tours of duty. Kurt was in a particularly spirited mood and didn't hesitate to disturb his friend's quietude.

"Günter, did you hear? They captured the partisans who murdered Lieutenants Schneider and Vogel. We're going to hang those bastards tomorrow morning in Piazza Bra. It'll be quite a show. We shouldn't miss it!"

Günter looked up from his book and sighed. "Watching a man writhing at the end of a rope is not my idea of a pleasurable diversion."

"There are three men, and a woman, too."

"A woman? Even more reason for me to avoid it," Günter said in disgust.

"Well, I've never seen a hanging before. Have you?"

Günter stifled a shudder, recalling an execution he had witnessed when a captured Resistance fighter was hanged from a tree. The prisoner struggled in his death throes as Günter's comrades looked on, apparently enjoying the spectacle of the man's suffering and humiliation. "Just once. That was enough for me."

"You don't really think these people deserve any compassion, do you? Do you know how they did it? The girl, she lured Schneider to a park, told him to bring a friend along because her sister was going to be there and they would all have a great time. Schneider bragged about it before they left. Hell, it could have been me instead of Vogel if he'd asked me first! When they got to the park there was no sister, of course, just the three thugs who gunned them down in cold blood. They never had a chance. The poor guys thought they were going out to enjoy the favors of a couple of sluts but got their heads blown off instead!"

"I agree that they deserve to die for what they did, but I don't believe in public executions. And I know that the Army will make their deaths as painful and degrading as possible. There should be justice, but it doesn't have to be indecent. That just lowers us to their level."

"We're at war. We can't afford to treat these criminals with kindness. You know how the field marshal feels about this. Let the public see how we deal with insurgents. It's a deterrent."

"Then you can go watch if you like, but I've no stomach for it."

Kurt shot Günter a disapproving glance. "Now don't take this the wrong way, Günter, but sometimes I don't think you've the stomach for any of this. The war, the Army—you must be the most softhearted officer in the Wehrmacht! You've no concept at all about discipline. I don't understand how you even came to be an officer. You've always been in supply, right? I mean, with no combat experience... Your family must have a lot of pull or something."

"No, Kurt, my family doesn't have any pull. My father is a simple small-town storekeeper. And I *was* at the front, even if it was only in the supply corps."

"Look, I don't mean to offend you. But you certainly don't seem like the career soldier type. How did you become an officer, anyway?"

"The same way you did. With an act of great courage," Günter countered tersely.

****

Günter had been drafted in early 1940 and after three months of training was elevated from raw recruit to private. He attributed his assignment to the supply corps, instead of the infantry or artillery, to luck, and to a second-rate performance on the shooting range. Günter participated in Germany's invasion of France by driving trucks loaded with ammunition, equipment and provisions from the rear to frontline positions. His commanders recognized his diligence, discretion and quiet leadership, and he attained the rank of sergeant within two years of military service.

In May of 1942, Günter became the aide of a young lieutenant, Berthold Wolff, son of a high-ranking Nazi Party official. By that time, France had surrendered to the occupying German forces, and fighting was limited to repulsing partisan actions—sabotage, ambushes and sniper attacks.

Wolff was indecisive in his approach to command and Günter suspected that the lieutenant's commission in the Army was awarded not because of his martial prowess, noticeable mostly by its absence, but due to his father's close ties to the Führer. At first glance, Wolff's narrow face and round, wire-rimmed glasses gave him a studious air. But his lack of even a cursory knowledge of history, science and literature was evident to Günter whenever their conversation diverged from purely military themes.

The lieutenant was responsible for requisitioning provisions and supplies from local tradesmen. Because of Günter's proficiency in French, he served as Wolff's interpreter, in addition to his duties as driver and clerk.

On one occasion, Günter accompanied Lieutenant Wolff to a winery in the Loire Valley of German-occupied France. Günter drove them back to the garrison, their kübelwagen loaded with cases of fine wines and cognacs. Wolff had boasted that this procurement would impress the senior officers by providing a touch of refinement for their mess table.

Günter and the lieutenant were traveling along a dusty back road to deliver the shipment when an impasse obstructed their progress. A large and slow-moving herd of sheep was making its way across their path.

"Damn! I can't believe a German officer must yield way to a herd of sheep!" Wolff grumbled. "This is not to be endured!"

"I'm sorry, sir, but I don't see how we can go around them. We have the woods to our left here and that paddock on the right. It appears that we'll just have to wait." Günter bit his lip to avoid smiling at his dim-witted superior.

Wolff sat back with a huff, then crossed his arms and pouted like a child. "Then get out and tell that shepherd to move it along. I'm not going to sit here all day."

"Yes, sir." Günter got out of the car and walked toward the man and his flock. A vague, unsettled feeling came over him, but at first he couldn't discern what was wrong. Then he realized what it was: the sheep were not moving at all. In fact, the sheepdog was inhibiting their advance. *It's not the dog, but the master who stopped the herd.* Out of the corner of his eye, Günter spotted three more men coming out from behind a shed some fifty yards away. He instinctively grabbed the rifle from his shoulder and threw himself down on the ground.

"Lieutenant, get down!" Günter yelled out, just as a bullet whistled over his head.

Günter scrambled back to the kübelwagen. The lieutenant was sitting, dazed, in the passenger's seat. When Günter crouched next to him, he saw that Wolff was shaking and holding his sidearm clumsily in his trembling hand. Several more bullets rang out and one shattered the windshield. Günter grabbed his superior and half pulled, half dragged him out and to the rear of the car.

The lieutenant sat behind the car while Günter peeked over it toward their assailants, seeing nothing but sheep. Bewildered by the shots, the animals moved about erratically, too disorientated to scatter and escape the firefight.

Günter waited, his heart pounding, as sweat poured down his face, soaking the collar of his uniform. He glanced to the right and left to make sure that the enemy hadn't made their way around the living barricade of dingy white wool. When he spotted a dark form rising from behind the herd, Günter leaned around the kübelwagen and fired. The piercing cry of a wounded animal told Günter that he had missed his target.

"Sir, it's a trap. There are four of them—partisans. If you cover me I can try to get to the woods and outflank them."

Wolff looked up at Günter. His face was pale and his breath came in short, shallow gasps. "What are we going to do?" he whimpered.

Though Günter had been in the Army for two years now, this was his first combat experience. *The lieutenant is useless. I've got to stay calm, or neither of us will make it out of here alive!*

Günter hunkered down and watched, waiting for the enemy to make another move. Suddenly, inspiration came and he crawled back to the car. With considerable effort, he pushed the crates of wine out of his way and found the ammo box. He grabbed a grenade, pulled the pin and lobbed it toward the center of the herd. He ducked down and a second or two later heard a tremendous explosion, followed by the miserable wails of humans and sheep, and the doleful howls of the dog.

He looked up and saw sheep scattering in all directions, some rushing toward him and passing the car. As the blockade dispersed, Günter could see that only one of the partisans was readying a weapon; Günter quickly shot him before he could take aim. *Beginner's luck*, he thought, as the man was blown back and lay supine and motionless on the ground.

Two of the others were wounded and the fourth fled. Günter fired a few shots at the man but missed. He reached the shed and disappeared inside, emerging a second later gunning a motorcycle as he escaped.

Günter jumped to the back of the kübelwagen to check on the lieutenant, while peering toward the wounded men to make sure they weren't able to return fire. "It's all right, Lieutenant. One escaped but I got the other three. I think one is dead."

The lieutenant looked at Günter with a stunned expression. Günter grabbed his arm and pulled him to his feet.

"Come on, sir. I need your help." Günter took Wolff's pistol from his hand and holstered it for him. *Before he panics and shoots himself...or me!*

They got into the car and drove up to the wounded men. An acrid mix of black powder and raw flesh assaulted their nostrils. As Günter stepped over mutilated carcasses of sheep, he felt the bread and soup of his midday meal rise to his throat and with difficulty forced it back down. He reached the body of the man he had shot. Blood seeped from his chest, staining his olive jacket a deep brown. Vacant eyes fixed on the sun and ashen lips were frozen in wonder. There was no doubt he was dead.

A few feet off lay a young sheep. Two of its legs had been blown off and, from its slashed belly, intestines spilled out onto the ground. Günter trembled; his legs nearly gave way as the words he'd heard a thousand times at Mass resounded in his brain: *"Lamb of God, who takest away the sins of the world, have mercy on us."* He'd received his baptism of blood.

Günter gazed in sorrow at the destruction he had caused. Then he garnered his nerve and pulled a clean handkerchief from his pocket to cover the man's face.

Moving from the dead to the wounded, he called

to the lieutenant, "Grab the medical bag and some cord from the back of the car." Then remembering that he was technically not in command, he quickly added, "Please, sir."

Günter and Lieutenant Wolff collected the prisoners and their weapons. One man was bleeding from a gash in his side, ripped open by shrapnel; the other had been trampled by sheep and lay gasping on the ground, his face crushed by hooves. Günter tended to their wounds as best he could and then, after binding their hands, he and the lieutenant placed them in the back of the kübelwagen. To make room for the captives, the crates of wine and cognac had to be left behind, along with the dead man and numerous sheep carcasses. The wine and the carcasses would later be retrieved and enjoyed in the German mess hall.

As Günter drove back to the garrison, he realized that he was responsible not for one death but for three. *If those two survive their wounds, they'll be executed.* Partisans were viewed by the German Army as terrorists, not as regular combatants, and therefore not protected by military rules of engagement. Günter scrutinized his actions, trying to absolve himself from violating the Fifth Commandment. *Killing is an inevitability of war. Besides, this was self-defense.*

Hours later, Lieutenant Wolff had regained his composure and pulled Günter aside. "I'll have to make a full report on this incident. What will you say about it, Schumann?"

"The truth, sir. What else would I say?"

"Yes, of course. You performed remarkably well in the face of the enemy. I think I'll recommend you for an Iron Cross, second class."

"Thank you, sir."

"You're quite intelligent, you know, and display a fair amount of leadership potential. Have you ever thought about becoming an officer? You'd make a fine candidate."

He's not as much a fool as I'd thought. Wolff apparently recognized his own spineless performance, and its likely cost to his military career. *He'll need my cooperation to bend the story in his favor.*

"An officer? I've never really thought about it before." *Why not? A commission surely has its benefits.* "If you truly believe I'm worthy, I would be honored to be considered, Lieutenant."

"Excellent. Then you'll help me write up this report? We can work on it together. You write very well, you know. Perhaps even better than I do."

No doubt about that. "Of course, sir."

Wolff nodded. "Very good, Sergeant Schumann," he replied with a satisfied smile.

Chapter 12

After an extended weekend at Federico's villa, Silvia returned to the apartment in Verona early Tuesday morning.

"Isabella, are you here?" she called out.

"Silvia, is that you?"

"Of course, cara mia, who else? I was hoping to catch you before you left for the palazzo."

Isabella was getting dressed in the bedroom and invited her friend to come in.

"You look so chic!" Isabella declared as Silvia entered the room in a smartly tailored russet tweed suit. The three-quarter-length sleeves of the jacket were cuffed in ivory silk and the slim skirt fell just below her knees.

"You like it?" Silvia struck the pose of a fashion model as Isabella looked on in wonder.

"It's gorgeous. But you must have spent a year's worth of coupons to buy that!" Clothing was strictly rationed, thanks to wartime demands on material; even those who could afford such extravagance had to limit their consumption.

"There are certain advantages to being the mistress of a high-ranking Party official. There is nothing new coming out of Paris, of course, but I've managed to locate a few treasures. The shoes and handbag come from New York, I believe," she added in a whisper, alluding to her chocolate-brown suede pumps and clutch.

Silvia glanced over at Isabella's clothes, laid out

on the bed: a plain gray wool skirt, white button-down blouse and white ankle socks. Her well-worn brown lace-up shoes lay on the floor near the dresser. "I'll have to bring you some stockings. They are difficult to find these days, but I have a few extra pairs."

"Thank you, but the socks are fine," Isabella replied with a hint of embarrassment. Then she recalled Günter's remark after the concert at Villa Bagliotti—that she'd look lovely in anything she wore—and smiled to herself. "You're here early this morning. I hardly see you anymore since you've been spending so much time with Federico. I think he makes you very happy."

"Oh, he's wonderful!" Silvia clutched Isabella's hands excitedly. "And I have some great news to tell you. Federico has asked me to come live with him in his villa! Isn't that fabulous? Not only for me, but now you and Günter can be together here all the time."

"How marvelous for you! When will you move in?"

"Today! I'll pack my things this morning. Federico is picking me up in the afternoon. I'd like to leave a few of my belongings here, if that's all right with you."

"Of course, Silvia, anything you like."

"And I'll still pay my half of the rent. That way, if things don't work out with Federico, I can always come back."

"That's very generous of you."

"Not at all. Federico is taking very good care of me now."

He must be giving her money. Isabella had sometimes wondered how Silvia managed to get by with no obvious source of income. She thought maybe Silvia received funds from a trust—her family was wealthy—but she knew also that her friend was estranged from her parents, who disapproved of her lifestyle. *She's always been willful, even when we were at school.* Though Isabella did not condone the way her friend fed upon men, she admired her boldness in daring to live as she chose. Silvia didn't care what others thought of her and wasn't compelled to follow the dictates of convention. Isabella considered her own reliance on Massimo. He did not support her financially, but she had come to depend on him, often surrendering her own resolve to comply with his wishes.

****

When Isabella arrived for work at the palazzo that morning, she approached Signora Vettori. "Would it be possible for me to have the later shift on a regular basis? It would be better since I often meet my brother in Piazza delle Erbe early in the morning to hear news of my family. He comes in to sell produce from our farm, so I also get food from him then. I can still work the early shift when necessary, if you need me to fill in."

"I think we can try that, Isabella. We'll start tomorrow. Do you still prefer to work Monday through Saturday?"

"Yes, that would be fine."

Isabella had decided to suggest this to increase her opportunities for espionage after nine o'clock, and to be able to see Massimo almost any morning in the piazza. And since Günter often worked until nine, too, this arrangement would not diminish their time together.

She met Günter later that day for their usual cigarette break behind the palazzo. "Günter, I have important news for you. I think you will be pleased."

"Tell me, Isabella."

"Silvia came to see me this morning at the apartment. She told me that she is moving in with Federico today! That means we can have the apartment almost all the time. She will still pay half of the rent and reserve the right to come back if she tires of Federico."

"I'm very happy for her, and for us, too." He caressed her face. "I guess that means we'll be living together. Though I'll need to show up at the barracks on occasion, so they don't think I've deserted!" he said, laughing.

"Well, I assume you'll still be coming here every day. But even if you don't have to work, I do, so we can't spend *every* moment in bed together!"

"Oh, but that sounds like an excellent idea. I'll keep it in mind for when the war is over. And then we can make it legal."

"Legal?"

Günter looked at her earnestly. "I hope we'll be married someday. I would ask you now, but with the future so uncertain... You know that I love you very much, don't you?"

"Yes, Günter, I do know that." She felt her eyes water as she considered the meaning of his words. *He's completely devoted to me. If only I didn't have to break his heart...* She had intended to discuss her new hours at the palazzo but was too moved to speak without faltering. Instead, she held him close and avoided his eyes, for fear he would read the disquiet that weighed on her mind. She thought too, with regret and irony, that Massimo had never broached the subject of marriage.

After a few quiet moments, Günter told her it was time for him to return to his duties. "I'll see you tonight, then. Let's meet here at nine, to enjoy our first weeknight together!" He kissed her, then headed back into the palazzo.

Later that afternoon, Günter pulled his roommate, Kurt, aside to explain that the apartment would now be available nearly every night, and to solicit his help on a more frequent basis.

"So, you'll need me to cover for you all the time now. But what do I get in return?" Kurt asked with a smile.

"Well, if you ever decide to actually spend an *entire* night with a woman, we can rotate duty at the barracks. But considering your predilection for hasty encounters, I doubt I'll have many opportunities to return the favor." With a laugh Günter added, "You're probably afraid of a lady's reaction to seeing your face revealed in the daylight. Better to sneak off under cover of darkness."

****

Günter and Isabella left the palazzo together at nine o'clock that night and walked to their favorite trattoria for dinner. As they strolled arm in arm, Isabella noticed a diminutive, elderly woman approaching them. Dressed completely in black, her head covered with a lace shawl, she appeared to be a widow, perhaps returning home from evening Mass. The woman's glare and hostile demeanor caught Isabella's attention even before she passed and muttered a scarcely audible remark.

"Excuse me, signora," Günter said sharply as he turned back toward the woman. "What was that?"

"Don't worry about it," Isabella urged as she clung to Günter's arm. Though spoken softly and directed toward the ground, the words had sounded to Isabella like "Nazi slut."

The woman looked at them with disdain, shook her head, and spat on the ground before continuing on her way. Günter took a step toward her. His brow furrowed, he seemed intent on getting an explanation, or at least responding to the affront.

"Just let it be, Günter," Isabella implored. "Please don't make a scene." Already, a few passersby had slowed and were glancing in their direction.

Günter turned to Isabella. His expression was a

117

fusion of anger and embarrassment, but also concern. "No one should disrespect you like that. I didn't hear what she said, but I know it was rude."

"Forget it. It was nothing."

Günter put his arm protectively around her shoulder as they headed to the restaurant. *He probably heard the same words I did. He's just too polite to admit it. But whatever she said, the message is clear.*

This wasn't the first time Isabella had noted the scorn of fellow Italians aware of her involvement with Günter but not of her role in the Resistance. Most Italians despised the German invaders, though few openly opposed them for fear of retribution. She sensed the silent condemnation of some of the neighbors, storekeepers and tradesmen whom she daily encountered. Many times she wanted to proclaim that she was fighting the Germans, not befriending them—that she was a patriot, not a wanton woman—or worse, a collaborator.

With irony, she realized that it was nothing more than the threat of German reprisal that shielded her from the vengeance of her countrymen. She knew that perceived collaborators could be brutalized, even killed, by partisans or outraged citizens. But under Günter's protection, she was safe, as long as the German forces retained control. *Have I more reason to fear the Italians who don't know of my mission, or the Germans if they uncover it?*

Chapter 13

On Friday, Isabella waited in the piazza to obtain the duplicated keys from Massimo. She had long acknowledged her uneasiness but now conceded that she had considerable misgivings about proceeding with the operation. The thought of being captured terrified her, but she vowed to herself that she would accomplish her mission, despite her fears. She considered those who fought on the front lines. *If they are willing to risk their lives for our country, then I must be, too.*

When Massimo arrived, she got into the truck, and he handed her the keys. She quivered as she accepted them.

"Your hesitancy is making me very nervous. Remember what I told you. You must be vigilant and make certain you are not discovered. If you are not sure..."

"Have faith in me, Massimo," she interrupted. "I can do this."

"All right, Isabella. Our fate is in your hands," he said as he looked down at the keys she held.

****

Isabella decided not to delay the start of her espionage and asked Massimo to meet her the next morning at five. She arranged to take Saturday and Sunday off from the palazzo, telling Signora Vettori that she wished to spend the weekend with her family. This time, she *was* in fact going to visit her family, whom she hadn't seen in weeks, and then spend part of the time with Massimo at the farm.

She met Günter later that day and told him of her plans.

"I won't be able to see you tonight. My brother is meeting me after my shift to take me home to visit my mother. In fact, I won't be back until Sunday night. Signora Vettori is letting me take two days off so I can spend some time with my family. You know that my mother hasn't been well."

"What's wrong with her?"

"She's been ailing for some time." Isabella hated to lie about such a dire subject. If her mother's health ever failed, Isabella might feel that she had brought it about with her deceitfulness. "She has a weak heart." It was the first illness that came to mind; it had been the cause of her father's death.

Günter looked at her with concern. "If there's anything I can do..."

"I appreciate that. I'd better get back to work now. We can meet Sunday night, if you like. Why don't you wait for me at the apartment?"

"All right. It's a long time to be apart from you, but I'm glad you'll have a chance to spend time with your family." His expression grew pensive. "I haven't seen mine in over a year. I'll miss you very much, Liebchen."

"I'll miss you, too, Günter."

****

Isabella trembled as she hid in the basement that night, awaiting the silence that would herald the start of her mission. Finally, when she felt it was safe, she advanced upstairs to the administrative offices. She arrived at the door and anxiously tried each key until she found the one that worked. She felt a wave of trepidation, mingled with excitement, as she surveyed the office in the dim illumination of her flashlight. *Where should I begin?* she wondered, overwhelmed by the multitude of desks and file cabinets that filled the vast room. She began with the file cabinets, many of which were, surprisingly, unlocked. As far as she could tell, these contained old supply records and maintenance reports. *I suppose the Nazis don't need to secure these. They're of no use to us.*

The room was an open space, except for three doors on one side. The first was merely a closet, filled with stationery and office supplies. The next was a washroom. But she found the last one locked, and her anticipation mounted. As she entered, she saw an impressive black walnut desk, complete with a lamp for her convenience. *Good, some light.* She stepped to the window and, after making certain the shutters were closed and the drapes completely drawn, turned on the lamp and closed the door. The first thing that caught her attention was a framed picture of Hitler, directly behind the enormous desk. Upon the walls were photographs of military officers in dress uniforms and three large maps: one of Italy, another of Germany, and the third of the entire continent of Europe. There were no pins, flags or markings on the maps, so she assumed they were not used for strategic purposes but only as decoration for the sparsely furnished office. She began to explore the desk itself. There were several locked drawers, but none of her keys could open them. *So, Günter is not privy to all of the Axis secrets.* On top were a few files and letters, and an array of desk items including a gold pen in a heavy marble stand. A brass plate on the stand bore an inscription in German that she roughly translated as an honor bestowed for some military achievement and presented to Colonel von Haeften by General Keitel, chief of the High Command. There was also a portrait of a mature but striking woman, presumably the colonel's wife.

The files and papers on the desk were of little

importance to her. There was nothing that indicated movements of supplies or troops. *Where next? The desks of the higher-ranking officers should be close to the colonel's office, and he'd need ready access to his aide. That's Major Gerhardt, and since Günter is his assistant, his desk must be nearby, too.* She deduced that the desk immediately outside the colonel's office was Gerhardt's. Before inspecting it, she decided to try to locate Günter's. She glanced around at the desks in close proximity and spotted an Italian/German dictionary on top of one. As she moved nearer, she discovered some notes written in a familiar handwriting. She felt a fleeting tinge of relief as she sat in Günter's padded metal chair, as if she could sense his comforting presence. After a few moments of respite, she opened the drawers of his desk. She found an abundance of documents, translated from German to Italian and from Italian to German, encompassing a variety of subjects. There was correspondence from Mussolini's ambassador to the Reich, edicts issued to the Italian populace regarding severe penalties for aiding the Resistance, and an intercepted communiqué from a partisan agent to Allied intelligence. This last missive excited her interest, and she searched Günter's desk for pen and paper with which to copy it.

By the time the task was complete, she felt exhaustion overtake her. She estimated that several hours had passed since she'd left the basement, so she would only be able to get a few hours sleep before having to meet Massimo. *I'm too tired to accomplish anything more tonight,* she decided, and returned to her covert shelter to get some rest.

****

Major Gerhardt approached Günter at eight o'clock the following night and invited him to join some of their fellow officers for an evening out at a local tavern. Since he'd become involved with Isabella, Günter almost always turned down such invitations, preferring to spend his free time with her.

"Günter, why don't you join us tonight? Isn't your girlfriend away for the weekend?"

Despite their efforts at discretion, Günter and Isabella had been seen together several times, and it had become common knowledge among the junior staff that Günter had a sweetheart. Somehow, this information never reached the colonel's ear, or that of any officer above the rank of captain, with the exception of his friend, Max Gerhardt. Günter got on well with his comrades, who respected his privacy and counted on the same consideration from him. He was not the only junior officer to frequently spend nights away from the barracks.

"How do you know this, Max?"

"I know that you spent every night this week away from your quarters—until last night—and you're seldom alone, especially on a Friday or Saturday evening. Also, you didn't take your 'cigarette break' today."

"So, now you're a detective? I didn't realize you had spies tracking my movements," Günter said half in jest.

"Come on, Günter, you're starting to turn into an old married man long before your time! Come with us."

"Well, all right. Why not? How much harm can you boys do, anyway?"

The small group descended on an establishment in a seedier part of Verona, across the river from Palazzo Maggiore. It was crowded with Italians when they entered, but the other patrons made room for them, vacating a large booth to accommodate the six officers. Günter sensed the uneasiness among them; some left hastily when the Germans arrived.

Others departed after several rounds of beer engendered boisterous renditions of German drinking songs and raucous behavior on the part of the officers.

Two lieutenants from their party approached the bar to engage a pair of pretty Italian girls. They enlisted Günter to act as their interpreter. He reluctantly complied, noting by their demeanor that his colleagues' intentions might be less than chivalrous.

"Günter, ask them if they have any plans for the rest of the evening."

Günter translated the question and replied to the lieutenants that the ladies had no prior commitments. As his companions became more forward with their affections, Günter felt increasing discomfort and politely declined to continue as translator. He returned to the booth to find that only Major Gerhardt and Captain Graf remained.

"What happened to Ernst?" Günter inquired about the missing officer.

"I believe he went to the washroom to vomit. Too many beers," Max replied with a laugh. "Maybe you'd better go check on him, Kurt." Graf's departure left Günter alone with the major.

"So, Günter, you're all by yourself this weekend, eh? Perhaps we should try to pick up a girl for you. I know you're not used to sleeping alone."

Despite Günter's slightly intoxicated state, he was perceptive enough to note his superior's insolence. He took care to avoid an insubordinate response. "I think I can survive two days without female companionship. Maybe you're the one feeling lonely," he added with a smile.

"I've been lonely for months. Why don't you ask your girlfriend if she has a friend for me?"

"I don't think Isabella's friends would appeal to you. I sense you wouldn't fancy a modest girl."

"Why would her friends be like that? Your Isabella is one hot little..."

"I think you've had a bit too much to drink," Günter interrupted before Gerhardt could complete the insult. "I'm sure you don't realize what you're saying."

"I know what I'm saying." His slurred speech belied this assertion. "Romance blooms in Italy, Günter! Buy an Italian girl a small trinket or a cheap dinner and she's yours for the taking."

Günter was seething but struggled to contain his fury, lest he risk serious charges for striking a superior officer. However much he yearned to defend Isabella's honor, and that of all the Italian women Max had callously insulted, Günter realized the wisest move would be to leave.

"I'm getting very tired, Max. I think I'll return to quarters now." Without awaiting a response, Günter abruptly stood, threw some money on the table, and walked out of the tavern onto the silent streets of Verona.

Chapter 14

"Very good work, Isabella! This could be useful to us." Massimo had examined her notes, which suggested what the Germans might know about partisan operations. "It appears to be from a Garibaldi operative to an agent with the American Office of Strategic Services. It gives us a clue to what the Communists are up to and how much the Nazis know of their plans."

Isabella knew that Massimo distrusted the Garibaldi Brigades, affiliated with the Italian Communist Party. They were often at odds with the Christian Democrats, of which Massimo was a member. Despite their differing political orientations, these and other partisan groups attempted to work together against their common enemies, the Fascists and the Nazis.

She was encouraged by Massimo's words. She had longed to prove herself a vital member of their squad, and his praise reassured her that the risks and sacrifices she endured could contribute to the long-hoped-for defeat of German occupation and Fascist rule.

"Will you share this information with the Garibaldis?" Isabella asked.

"Of course. I must warn them the Nazis are on to them. But perhaps I will contact the OSS agent myself. It may be advantageous to us in the long run." Massimo's loyalty to the Resistance was unquestionable, but he sought opportunities to advance in the Committee of National Liberation for Northern Italy, which coordinated the partisan efforts of various factions: right wing, left and moderate. "An alliance with the Americans will be of primary importance after the war. Of course the British will have a role, too, but the Americans are the key."

Massimo is very pleased—not only with me, but also with himself.

****

Isabella treasured the time with her family, and the relief it offered from the strain of life in Verona. In the sheltering circle of her mother and siblings, she found much needed comfort and support, and enjoyed the transitory illusion of normalcy.

Though her family didn't know of her espionage mission, her partisan comrades did. She noticed that some of the other women avoided her, especially Luisa, wife of their squadron commander, Filippo Oliveri. Isabella wondered how many details they had, but suspected from their apparent disdain that they knew about her involvement with Günter. Luisa had always been somewhat aloof toward Isabella, perhaps because Massimo challenged her husband's authority. She also suspected that Luisa, a devout Catholic, viewed Isabella as an immoral woman. *Not only am I living outside the sanctity of marriage with Massimo, but now I'm sleeping with another man, and the enemy, at that!*

Massimo drove Isabella back to Verona late Sunday night. When she got out of the truck, she noticed a light on upstairs and smiled, realizing that she would not be alone tonight.

"Did you forget to turn off the lights when you left, Isabella?"

"I don't think so. Perhaps Silvia came by today and left them on."

Massimo grasped Isabella by the shoulders and

looked at her with a heated gaze. "Why don't we go upstairs together? I'd like to see if the bed here is softer than ours."

Isabella felt a wave of panic. She feared a confrontation if her two lovers should meet. *Of course, Massimo knows about Günter, but he doesn't expect him to be waiting for me. With his temper, who knows what he might do?*

"I don't think that would be a good idea. Silvia might still be here." Isabella nervously glanced at the window, hoping that Günter would not pass by or look out.

"Very well, Isabella." His tight-lipped smile held no amusement. "I'll meet you as usual in the piazza Tuesday morning. You get to sleep late tomorrow." After a rough, bruising kiss, he departed.

Her anxiety ebbed as she climbed the steps to the apartment.

"Hello, Günter, have you missed me?" she asked as she entered.

He rushed to embrace her. "Tremendously, darling! Here, come sit down and tell me about your weekend. How is your mother?"

Isabella thought for a moment, being careful to remember which lie she had told him. "Oh, she's doing a little better. I think seeing me raised her spirits."

"I'm sure of that. It certainly raises mine!"

"And what did you do all weekend?"

"Nothing much. I accompanied some of my comrades out for an evening on Saturday. We went to a tavern, drank a few beers and regaled the other patrons with our horrendous singing! I enjoyed myself pretty well until..." He stopped.

"Until what?"

"Until some of my friends became too drunk to behave appropriately."

"But I'm sure *you* behaved like a gentleman.

What did they do?"

"I'm embarrassed to tell you this, but some of my fellow officers don't have proper respect for ladies," he said with a frown.

Suddenly Isabella tensed, as she remembered the intoxicated German officer whose offensive conduct led to her brother's unjust execution.

"What's wrong? You look upset."

"Nothing. I missed you, that's all." She nestled against his chest to conceal her sadness.

"I hope you don't think I did anything improper. I didn't even look at another woman."

Isabella composed herself and looked at Günter innocently. "I would never think that. I trust you. And you're allowed to look. Just don't touch!"

A curious smile flickered across Günter's face. "Oh, but I do like to touch. Come..." he said, gesturing for her to follow him into the bedroom. "Take off your clothes and lie down on the bed."

To Isabella, this was uncharacteristic of Günter. He was not usually so direct in his approach to lovemaking, but she did as he asked. He removed his clothes, too, and knelt next to her on the bed. His kisses were slow, delicate—barely touching her skin. He nuzzled her neck, just behind her right ear, then brushed his lips across her shoulder, along her arm to her fingertips. His mouth teasingly lingered there as he savored each one. Continuing his journey, he caressed her breasts with light strokes of his tongue, and gently tugged at her nipples until they became hard as stones. The silky hairs of her belly quivered as Günter's unrelenting lips moved downward to her navel.

She moaned, then reached above her head to clutch the rungs of the headboard. "I want you inside of me, Günter," she whispered.

"Shh..."

Isabella felt the warmth of his mouth against

her labia, which swelled to his touch like a rosebud maturing to full bloom. He responded to the rhythm of her body, as if he knew it better than she did herself. A rush of sensations swept over her. She lost all sense of time and place—the world seemed to fall away from her grasp. Searing waves of ecstasy surged through every inch of her, and she couldn't hold back her cries of delight. Günter slowly drew back, letting her pleasure resolve into a glow of contentment, then snuggled beside her and kissed her neck.

"Oh, Günter...that was so... I've never felt anything like that. But don't you want..."

"Not now, Isabella," he said as they both drifted off to sleep.

****

When Massimo approached Isabella a few days later in the piazza, she observed a swagger to his gait and the hint of a self-satisfied smile. He pulled her toward him and lifted her chin with one finger. His only greeting was a hasty kiss.

"I've met with Reynolds, the OSS agent," he whispered. "This is going to work out well."

"And it's lovely to see you, too, Massimo," she replied with a wry smirk.

A muscle twitched along his jaw and his lips tightened with impatience.

"So, what did he say?"

"He likes our plan. Of course, our squad will use your information for our own missions, but I can prove myself even more useful to the Allies than I'd hoped."

"Well, I'm glad to hear my work will be paying off." *Especially for you.* "What do you mean, 'more useful than you'd hoped'?"

"The larger brigades need the weapons the Allies provide. I'll make the connections. The Americans are more than happy to let us fight

130

behind the lines and keep the Germans and Fascists busy. The fewer Germans the Americans have to face at the front, the better. But Reynolds wants intelligence on supply shipments and troop movements at a steady rate, about twice a week."

"I'll have to think of something to tell Günter. I suppose I could explain that my mother's condition has gotten worse, that I'm needed at home a couple of nights a week to help with her care. But I'll say I've got to keep my job in Verona, too, since my family needs the extra money I provide. I just hope it doesn't make him suspicious."

"Why don't you break it off with him? You've already gained access to the offices. What do you need him for anymore? He doesn't share information with you."

Isabella tried to think up a convincing pretext. The truth was she didn't want to leave Günter just yet, but her reasons were not ones she could explain to Massimo. "Well...he might become angry and get me fired from Palazzo Maggiore. Then I'd have no access to German headquarters."

"I suppose that's true. Do you really think he would react that way?"

Deep down, Isabella knew it was unlikely Günter would. *Surely he'd be hurt, even angry, but he's not the vindictive sort.* "I don't know how he might react, but I don't think we can afford to risk it."

"All right, I guess you'll have to keep it up for now. I can't say I'm very happy about it, though."

"Remember, Massimo, this was your idea to begin with."

"Still, it isn't easy for me to picture you with that Nazi."

"It isn't easy for me, either." *Well, sometimes it's easy.*

****

The next day the rent was due for November, so Isabella stopped at her landlady's apartment to pay her portion before leaving for the palazzo. She and Silvia had agreed they would each pay half directly, on the first of the month.

"Come in, Signorina Ricci, what can I do for you?"

"Here is my half of the rent, signora."

"Oh, no, signorina, it has already been taken care of."

"But Silvia was only supposed to pay half. She must have forgotten about our arrangement."

"Signorina Matteo paid her share. The gentleman took care of the rest."

"What gentleman?"

"That German officer, the one who visits you so often." Despite her smile, there was a hint of censure in the signora's voice.

"There must be some mistake."

"Well, I suggest you take it up with him. It doesn't matter to me, as long as the bill is paid."

"All right, signora. Good day."

As Isabella walked to the palazzo, her bewilderment slowly changed to anger. *I won't be a "kept woman," especially of a Nazi. Who does he think he is?* A flush of shame heated her cheeks as she realized what she was becoming. *Not only am I a spy, now I'm a whore.* She thought of her one-time dream to study art history in Florence, perhaps to become a curator or lecturer some day. She would have been the first in her family to attend college, and as a woman that filled her with great pride. She had been disappointed when she had to return home to help on the farm, but at least it was honest labor and she was contributing to her family's welfare. Then when she'd joined the Resistance, she was gratified to be able to fight for her country instead of standing by mutely to witness the savagery and devastation.

But she was deeply conflicted about the mission for which she'd been chosen. She had told Massimo that she would do anything to help the cause, even to take up arms against the enemy. She knew of other female partisans who performed such tasks, especially among the Communist members. Some even commanded brigades. But in her squadron, it was nearly unheard of. When she'd accidentally reunited with her old school chum Silvia and learned of her Fascist associations, Massimo had conceived a way to exploit this connection. Isabella had thought he'd be appalled at Silvia's invitation to the party at Palazzo Fabriano. Instead, he'd shrewdly seen the opportunity in it.

When he'd first suggested that she surreptitiously attach herself to an important Fascist or German officer, she hadn't comprehended the extent of the assignment. But her devotion to Massimo compelled her to carry out whatever he asked, even if it meant compromising her integrity.

She now admitted to herself that she was hurt and angry that Massimo would willingly send her into the arms, let alone the bed, of another man. *If he truly loved me, why would he agree to this, even encourage it?* But she knew that Massimo was ambitious. He hoped the success of this operation would augment his chances of achieving prominence in the democratic post-war Italy they struggled to establish.

****

Günter and Isabella met later that day for their usual rendezvous behind the palazzo. His smile faded when she approached him, as he seemed to sense her anger.

"What's wrong, Liebchen?"

"I saw the landlady this morning to pay my rent. She told me you had already paid it. What were you thinking, Günter? How dare you! You make me feel like a whore!" Even she was surprised at the vehemence she unleashed.

Günter was stunned; it took him several seconds to respond. "Please, Isabella, I...I didn't mean it that way. I was just trying to help out. I would never think of you like that—*never!*" His eyes were filled with remorse. "I just thought that since we are practically living together... If anything, I see you as...as my wife. You're the most precious thing in this world to me! Please don't be angry."

She looked down at the ground, trying to take in all that he had said. "I don't know..."

"Forgive me, Isabella. I'm so sorry if I offended you. But I do feel responsible to help you with the expenses. I'm there almost every night. I want to take care of you, that's all. But it's nothing like what you said."

"I understand now." *He's too guileless to have conceived that I might interpret his intentions as anything but honorable.* She reached up and touched his face. "I forgive you."

He managed to smile despite their impassioned exchange. "Will you at least let me pay half of your half? It's hard for me to explain, but otherwise I'd feel that I'm taking advantage of you. You're my partner, my mate. I hope to marry you someday."

"Oh, Günter..." she murmured, and wrapped her arms around his neck. Deluged by a tumult of thoughts and emotions, she couldn't suppress the tears that streamed down her cheeks. "All right. You can help me out with the rent. But next month, it's my turn. After that we can split it."

He wiped the tears from her face and gently kissed her. "I love you very much, Isabella."

"I love you, too, Günter," she responded, wondering what those words actually meant to her.

Chapter 15

It had become Günter's routine to sleep at the barracks on nights when Isabella was not in the apartment. On one of these occasions, he retired to Albergo Venezia after a wearying day at headquarters, and found his roommate Kurt already there.

"I picked up our mail. There's something for you," Kurt said, pointing to Günter's cot.

"Thanks," Günter replied as he sat down on his bed and looked at the envelope, already opened by Army censors. "Damn," he muttered.

"Bad news?"

"It's from my sister Else. My father told me in his last letter that she'd decided to volunteer at a military hospital in Poland. She's only eighteen, for God's sake! You know how bad things are on the eastern front. She should have just stayed home and looked after our father."

"He isn't well?"

"No, he's all right but... Well, he's already lost one son and has another in the Army. Why should she put herself in danger like that?"

"She probably just wants to contribute to the war effort. I have a little sister in the Bund Deutscher Mädel. She's helping to serve food to bombed-out families in Hamburg."

Günter pulled out his wallet to show Else's picture to Kurt. "Look at her. She's barely more than a child."

"She's a pretty girl. Are you sure she's your sister?" Kurt teased as he looked at the picture. The white blouse of Else's school uniform set off two long blonde braids that hung down over her shoulders. "You'd better hide her away if I ever come to visit you."

"Oh, yes, I certainly will," Günter replied with a faint smile.

"Look, I think I'll go over to the mess. Do you want to come?"

"No, thanks. I'm not hungry right now."

After Kurt left, Günter lay on his bed and began to read his sister's letter:

Dear Günter,

I miss you very much and hope that you are safe and well. I'm sure Papa has already written to tell you that I've volunteered to work as a nurse's aide with the women's auxiliary. I'm getting used to my new surroundings, an evacuation hospital in Poland. At home I just felt so helpless, listening to the reports about our wounded soldiers, suffering and dying far from their loved ones. I didn't believe it was right for me to remain in comfort and security simply because I am a woman, while our men are risking their lives every day.

When my friend Gisela told me she was going to volunteer at a hospital near the eastern front, I knew I had to go. I thought that some young soldier might be lying in a hospital bed, scared and alone, and that I could offer him a bit of comfort. If, God forbid, you are ever wounded, then perhaps some kindhearted German girl will be there to help you, too.

Of course, I've no formal training as a nurse, but we did learn some first-aid skills in the Bund Deutscher Mädel and I try to make myself useful. In fact, they need every hand they can get since the casualties are coming in frightful numbers. I can dress wounds, administer medication (and change bedpans, of course!) and I've even learned how to give injections. No one here seems to care whether I have a nursing degree or not. If a doctor needs help, I step in and do what I can.

I see gruesome injuries that I can't even describe, and hear terrible things about combat from the soldiers who are sent here. They talk about the unbearable cold, the hunger, and the constant threat of death. I'm glad you're in Italy where the weather is not as severe as it is here, and at headquarters instead of in the field.

Sometimes I think that these soldiers are thankful to be wounded—to be away from the front. Here they have a warm bed, clean sheets, adequate food (if they are able to eat), and pretty nurses to tend to their needs. But what most of them appreciate more than anything is to have someone hold their hand, listen to their cares, and help them write letters home. Some flirt with me, even if they are seriously wounded. You needn't worry. I'm a lot stronger than most, and if they give me any trouble I just tell them that my older brother is a captain in the Wehrmacht! If that doesn't intimidate them, our doctors will protect me from any unwelcome advances.

Papa will miss me, of course, but I'm sure he'll be fine. With me away, he can offer another room to someone who's been left homeless by the Allied bombing raids. There's a program to move these people from Munich and other cities to villages like ours that haven't been heavily damaged. When I left, a soldier's widow and her two young children were living in what used to be Maria's and my room, and an elderly woman was in Otto's old room. I had moved into your room, but now Papa can give it to someone else.

As I work with the wounded, I think of the

dangers you are facing. I worry about you constantly, but am grateful that at least you are not so close to the front. I long for the day when we will all be together again.

Please take good care of yourself, Günter. I pray to God every day to keep you safe.

Your loving sister,
Else

Günter sat up, overwhelmed by feelings of frustration and anger that his sweet, innocent Else had to be exposed to such horrors. Though they were separated by nearly ten years, there had always been a remarkable bond between them. Günter adored his baby sister and paid more attention to Else than did either of their other siblings. Otto had no interest in playing with little girls; he was the eldest and focused his attention on more serious endeavors. Even Else's older sister Maria shunned looking after the child, perhaps jealous that she was no longer the darling of the family whom everyone fussed over and indulged. While most teenaged boys raced home after school to play soccer with their mates, Günter enjoyed spending time with Else—helping her with her lessons, reading stories to her, and teaching her to play the piano.

She was only thirteen when the war began. She'd lost her mother one year earlier, and was soon to lose her eldest brother. Günter recalled their parting at the railway station in Flüssbaden on the day he'd left for training camp so many years before. He remembered the pulpy softness of her cheeks as he'd wiped away her tears, and the fearful look in her eyes when she'd made him promise to return.

Though he'd been home on leave several times since then, he'd missed so many of the little things—piano recitals, graduation, first dance, first kiss. He didn't get to hear when she began to talk about boys in a different way, didn't get to guide her on which ones to stay away from. These were years lost and moments gone forever, moments of watching her blossom from child to young woman.

Reading her letter filled him with shame, too, as he realized that she would probably see more of the butchery of combat than he had in all his years in the Army. How lucky he'd been, skirting most of the fighting, experiencing little of the devastation of the battlefield. When he'd entered the war in France in the spring of 1940, the conflict there was nearly over. In the supply corps, he was able to view the war from an arm's distance. In the early years, he'd seen some of the dead and wounded, but that aspect of the war never became part of his daily existence as it did for the gunner or infantryman. Günter had been spared the worst of it, the eastern front, where both German and Russian troops suffered massive casualties and inhuman conditions. There, men lay in freezing, muddy trenches, stalked by the relentless specter of death, watching their comrades blown to pieces before their eyes.

From his desk at headquarters, he witnessed only a sanitized version of the war: statistics on casualties and on ammunition consumption, analyses of the deployment of equipment, rations and troops. It was not among his duties to see the faces, the bodies and the gore of the men behind those numbers. While both his own countrymen and the enemy struggled daily for survival, he enjoyed three hot meals and a leisurely fourteen-hour workday, with a whole day's leave nearly every week. All of that, and the extraordinary pleasure of a loving woman to share his bed. *Compared to the rigors of university life, war is bliss!* Günter thought with bitter irony.

Many times Günter had tried to reconcile his participation in the war with his personal ideals. To him, war was a futile, monstrous folly, the ultimate proof of man's failure to rise above base instincts and follow God's model of love and forgiveness. Günter was well educated; when he left university he had been working toward a degree in linguistics. He'd always been drawn to creative pursuits—language, music, literature and philosophy. But he knew that there were brutal forces at work and a scholarly life would not protect him or those he loved from destruction. Warfare was an inevitable component of human existence, he mournfully acknowledged.

But Günter was a man, not a martyr or an angel. He had his pride and recoiled at being thought a coward. Did he feel guilty that he'd chosen the safer route instead of volunteering for a frontline assignment? To some extent he did, but not enough to charge heedlessly toward death when he saw the opportunity to fulfill his patriotic duty while keeping his promise to Else, as well.

Chapter 16

Günter had accepted Isabella's explanation of her twice-weekly visits to her mother. As the weeks passed, the information she gathered proved valuable to the Allies and the Resistance. She had discovered the supply log, kept in a secure metal box in the bottom drawer of Major Gerhardt's desk. Fortunately, Günter's keys provided access to both the drawer and the box. There was little action now at the front, since harsh weather had stalled the Allied advance, but tracking the movements and types of supplies offered clues to German defensive strategies. The log provided specifics of where and when tanks, mortar and heavy artillery would be deployed. Though the Allies had chosen to delay their offensive until the spring, partisan brigades continued their assaults to the north, keeping the Germans engaged, and further exhausting the battle-weary Axis troops.

Massimo had asked Isabella to find out when the next trainload of ammunition was due to leave Bolzano for the front near Bologna, and which route would be used. She crept into the offices at the palazzo one night to search for the information. She had become accustomed to the pattern of noises she heard during her clandestine nights at German headquarters. She was no longer alarmed by the steady pacing of the guard on the floor above and could tell which soldier was on duty by the sound of his stride. The voices of the staff who worked

141

throughout the night on the upper floors did not distress her.

As she translated the log entries and copied them into her notebook, her concentration was broken by an unfamiliar sound. In seconds, she realized what was wrong. *Those footsteps—they're not from upstairs, but here on this floor!* Then she heard men's voices, German voices, not the muffled ones from the floors above but clear ones, right outside the office. For a half-second she froze, but her instinct for survival prevailed. She heard the jingling of a key in the door as she dove under Major Gerhardt's desk, grabbing the supply log, lock box, dictionary and notebook as quickly and silently as she could.

Before she could make sense of what was happening, the men were there inside the room. She wanted to scream, to flee, but she knew the slightest movement could be her undoing. She shook and her eyes filled with tears. But she discovered that if she concentrated on each breath, her lips tightly sealed, no sounds would escape. Crouched beneath the desk, she pressed her hands and feet against the floor to keep them from knocking against anything.

The two men spoke casually to each other, almost lightheartedly, in contrast to the deadly terror she felt. Though she struggled to comprehend what they were saying, she couldn't decipher all the words. She thought about reaching for the dictionary that lay by her side, but that was too risky. The Germans had turned on the lights and were walking from desk to desk, apparently looking for something. *Oh, God, what if they are looking for the supply log?* She considered putting it back in the drawer, but instantly realized how foolish that would be. *They'll find me anyway, if they approach this desk, and I can't make a move without giving myself away.*

Every second was agony, as if death might come

at any moment. But she admitted to herself that a swift demise would be easy compared to her fate if discovered. She would face humiliation, torture, and then finally, mercifully, death. The thought made her throat constrict painfully, as if a noose were being tightened around it. *Was this what Marco felt when he died?* Fear evolved into despondency. *Just breathe...slowly, deeply...focus only on that—don't think about anything else. Concentrate only on breathing.*

Her ordeal went on for what seemed like hours, although the time that elapsed was probably only about twenty minutes. When the men finally left, she waited another half hour to be certain they were gone. At last, she crawled out from under the desk. With trembling hands, she replaced the items she had used, painstakingly checking and rechecking that everything was exactly where it belonged.

She moved as silently and deliberately as she could to her basement hideout. When she reached it, she nearly collapsed from overwhelming terror and inexpressible relief. Burying her face in her blanket, she sobbed and convulsed until quieted by sheer exhaustion. Sleep never came that night, and she left the palazzo before four o'clock, though she didn't expect Massimo to arrive at the piazza until five. *I'd rather wait an hour in the cold than spend one more minute in the basement.*

As she walked to the piazza, she wondered if she would ever be able to return to German headquarters. *How will I explain this to Massimo?* But as she waited for him in the pre-dawn gloom, she realized that she must complete her assignment. *Massimo is counting on me. If I back out now, he will think me a coward and a failure.* She had assured him that she would not let him down, and her pride wouldn't allow her to admit defeat. Hadn't she promised herself to risk everything for the operation? Somehow, she would learn to suppress her dread, and continue her work for the Resistance.

She convinced herself that the frightening events of that night had proven her ability to persevere. She'd eluded capture, and despite excruciating inner turmoil, had been able to control her body's reaction to fear. Unbowed, she had accomplished her task, and survived to engage the enemy once more.

****

Physically and emotionally drained, Isabella decided to return to the apartment and not wait any longer for Massimo. He would probably be furious, but she knew that she hadn't the strength to discuss what she had just experienced. She needed solitude, and a warm, comfortable bed for her sleep-deprived body.

She didn't think Günter would be there, since he usually slept at his quarters on nights when she "visited her mother." But what if he were? How could she account for her appearance at four in the morning? Perhaps she'd had a fight with her brother and he threw her out of the house, forcing her to walk all the way back to Verona. *I must be mad if I expect him to believe that!* She fretted until she was able to concoct a fairly credible story just before reaching the apartment. Her mother had taken ill in the middle of the night and her brother drove into Verona to fetch the doctor. Since Isabella would have to return to the city later that morning, it seemed prudent to drive in with her brother now, rather than oblige him to make a second trip.

Still, it was a ludicrous tale, and she hoped she would not have to use it. When she arrived at the apartment Günter wasn't there after all, and she climbed into bed and nestled beneath the covers alone. Her tears began again, and she did not attempt to quell them; she needed to let loose the anguish of the last several hours. Though she had gotten some relief in the basement, she could find greater peace here in her bed, where she could unreservedly surrender to emotion.

After a long, but fitful sleep, Isabella awakened to a strange brightness in the bedroom. She jumped out of bed and rushed to look at the clock in the kitchen. It was nearly noon, already an hour past the start of her shift at the palazzo. She had never been late for work before and felt a wave of anxiety over the possible consequences. *I can't lose my job. I'd have no access to German intelligence, and then Massimo...* She refrained from pursuing that thought. Instead, she focused on getting ready as quickly as possible, and on how she would explain her tardiness to Signora Vettori.

She arrived at the palazzo an hour and a half late and immediately went to speak with the signora.

"I'm so sorry about this morning. My mother had a bad night, and then my brother's truck wouldn't start. If we had a telephone I would have called, of course."

"I'm very surprised, Isabella. You're always so reliable," the signora replied. "I was beginning to worry that something might be wrong. I'm sorry that your mother is ill, but I really can't keep you here if I can't depend on you."

"It won't happen again."

"How is your mother this morning?"

"Well, she was a bit better when I left. Her illness...it's very trying for all of us. My sisters are quite competent at taking care of her, but I feel that I must help out. I won't let it interfere with my job. Again, I'm very sorry about this morning."

"It must have been an awful night for you. You look as if you didn't get a wink of sleep. Why don't you just go home and rest? We can manage without you for one day."

"That's so kind of you. If you're really sure you don't need me today..."

"Go home, Isabella. But be on time tomorrow."

"Of course. Thank you, signora."

Before returning to the apartment, Isabella stopped at the bakery to leave a message for Massimo. In her note, she apologized for not showing up at the piazza, but told him everything was fine and that she would meet him as usual on Thursday. She left the information that Massimo had asked for in the care of Stefano, their operative at the bakery. She spent the day alone, getting some much-needed rest, and a respite from the strain of her covert mission.

****

At half past nine that night, Günter came to the apartment and let himself in with his key.

"Isabella, are you home?" he called out.

"I'm in the bedroom, Günter."

He came into the bedroom, turned on the light, and sat down beside her as she lay on the bed.

"Darling, is everything all right? Where were you today? I waited outside the palazzo at my break, and then when I left for the night. I was very worried."

"I did go to work, but Signora Vettori sent me home."

"Why? Are you ill?"

"I had a very bad night. My mother couldn't sleep at all; she was in a lot of pain. I didn't get any sleep myself." Isabella threw off the covers and sat up in bed. "The signora was very understanding. She could see that I was exhausted and told me to go home and get some rest."

"What does the doctor say about your mother? Is it possible that she could die?"

Isabella became very distressed at the thought,

146

and didn't know how to respond. "Yes, I'm afraid that she might," she replied hesitantly. She described the condition that killed her father, borrowing his symptoms to explain her mother's fabricated illness. "The doctor says this could go on for months, even years. But if it worsens, she might have very little time. Her heart is quite weak. Some days she can do a few things around the house. She can cook or go for a short walk. Other times she's almost a complete invalid and is bedridden for days."

Concern was etched on Günter's face. "It must be very difficult for you, for your whole family. I think I can understand what you are going through. My mother was sick for a long time too, before she died."

"What did she die of?" She noticed that his eyes were tinged with red.

"Cancer. She lingered for months, and at the end she suffered a great deal. Then a year later the war started. My brother signed up right away; he was sent to Poland and was killed. He must have been among the first casualties of the war. I didn't think my father would be able to go on...but somehow he did."

It was all too much to bear: her terrifying night at the palazzo, recalling her father's death, and now hearing about Günter's personal losses. Isabella began to weep, and as Günter took her in his arms her sobbing increased. She clung to him desperately, and her heart overflowed with tenderness. She remembered that morning—how she'd avoided Massimo at a time when she most needed consolation. Now, in Günter's embrace, she found a depth of affection and solace she knew Massimo could never provide. *Günter loves me so much. Could it be possible that I love him, too?*

Chapter 17

One morning as Isabella waited in the piazza she was surprised to see Luigi, Massimo's subordinate, drive up in the truck.

"Where is Massimo?" she asked as he approached.

"He went to Milan to attend a meeting of the Committee. He asked me to meet you to collect whatever information you have."

"What kind of meeting?"

"There are representatives of all the partisan factions. They're organizing strikes and possibly civil insurrection throughout northern Italy. He hopes to learn more about the operations of the Committee and their connections with the Allies."

"Why didn't Filippo go? He's our commander."

"He's been occupied with leading sabotage missions. We succeeded in derailing a German supply train. Imagine, Isabella, our small group accomplished that, thanks in part to the intelligence you uncovered! He and Massimo have enlisted more men for our squadron. We're gaining recognition among the Allied commanders."

"Did anyone die in the train wreck?" She worried about Nazi retaliation against civilians if any of their soldiers were killed.

"A few Germans died and a number were injured."

"What kind of reprisals did they order?"

"The usual."

"How many, Luigi?"

He sighed as he reported the gruesome toll. "Fifty men from a nearby village were taken as hostages and shot."

"So, my information caused the deaths of fifty innocent civilians. Their blood is on my hands, too! If our men had given themselves up..."

"You mustn't look at it that way. If we yield to their brutality we might as well surrender all of Italy to the Nazis! We can't let them deter us. We're at war. Regrettably many innocents will die, but we must keep fighting. If we gave ourselves up we'd be letting the Germans win. Remember, we are working to defeat the enemy and free our people. Future generations of Italians will thank us."

"I suppose you're right...but it's hard."

"Do you have anything for me?"

She handed him several pages of handwritten notes. "When will Massimo be home?"

"He'll return in a few days. We're planning another operation. It should be over by the time he gets back."

"So, I'll meet you here on Thursday, then?"

"Yes. And keep up the good work!"

****

Isabella met Luigi a few days later in the piazza. When he neared, a sense of foreboding enveloped her and she felt her stomach clench.

"Ciao, Isabella," he said flatly. His usual vigorous manner was subdued by a darker mood. Looking off in the distance, he avoided her eyes.

"What is it, Luigi? What's wrong?"

He exhaled a grim sigh, then met her anxious gaze. "It's a disaster. Well, not the mission. We did manage to blow up the bridge, but..." He paused and seemed at a loss for words.

"Yes?"

"We lost three men in the explosion—Filippo,

Cesare and Donato."

"Oh, Dio!" Trembling, her eyes stung with tears. "But Cesare's wife just had a baby! And Filippo? Luisa must be beside herself. How could this have happened?"

"The timer on the explosives malfunctioned. The rest of us were far enough away, but those three... We were lucky to be able to retrieve the bodies, or at least what was left of them." Luigi straightened and cleared his throat. "But we accomplished our task; now the Germans will have to reroute their supplies. We'll continue to frustrate them at every turn."

She looked at him strangely, amazed at how quickly he cast off his sorrow, focusing on military success instead of the loss of their comrades.

"I've got to see if I can help out somehow, and if nothing else, pay my respects. Can you meet me here later this morning, say nine o'clock? I'll tell Signora Vettori that I've had a death in the family and must return home right away."

"All right."

By the time Isabella returned to the apartment, Günter had left for work. She went to the palazzo and discussed the situation with the signora. She was generous to Isabella, telling her to take the next few days off to be with her family. *I'll need to tell Günter, too.* She warily entered the administrative offices, so familiar to her in the voiceless seclusion of night, but a strange, bustling hive of activity in the daytime. She approached his desk, aware that some of the other officers glanced at her curiously.

"Günter..."

"Isabella, I'm surprised to see you here. I thought you weren't on duty until eleven."

"Can you come and speak with me?"

"Of course." He followed her out into the hallway.

"I wanted to let you know that I need to return

to my family for a few days. I've already cleared it with Signora Vettori."

"Is it your mother?"

"No," she responded, her eyes cast down. "There's been a death in my family. My uncle...he died in an automobile accident yesterday."

"How terrible! Oh, I'm so sorry." He touched her cheek. "Is there anything I can do? Can I drive you home?"

"My brother is meeting me in the piazza at nine. I don't know exactly when I'll return. I'm not certain what the arrangements are."

"Are you sure I can't go with you?"

"Yes, I'm sure."

"When do you think you'll be back?"

"I don't know. Maybe Monday or Tuesday."

"Shall I wait for you at the apartment?"

"All right."

He held her close, and then kissed her on the forehead. "I'm very sorry, Liebchen."

"Thank you, Günter."

****

Gloom hung over the farmhouse filled with somber mourners when Isabella arrived. She found Luisa sitting in the main room, surrounded by family members and the women from their group. Isabella approached to offer her condolences.

"Luisa, I'm so sorry." Isabella embraced her and held her hands as she knelt before her. "Filippo was a great man, a true hero to our cause. We'll never forget him."

Luisa was so distraught she was barely able to respond. "Thank you, Isabella," she said through sobs.

Massimo didn't return until the next day, just in time to attend the funerals. He was devastated to learn of the tragedy, but in spite of his grief, Isabella could tell that he was pleased with the outcome of his trip to Milan. He suggested they go to their cabin to speak privately.

"I didn't want to discuss this in front of the others, but this turn of events gives us a chance to move in another direction. Filippo and I had our differences, as you know. Of course, I'm sorry for his death, but now I can expand our dealings with the Allies. Filippo was an excellent strategist, but I don't believe he had the foresight to concern himself with Italy's future after the war."

"So your goals are more political than military? Do you plan to curtail our sabotage operations?"

"No, we'll keep them up. I'd like to recruit more men to our squad. I do plan to escalate our offensive, but also to further develop our relations with the Allies, especially the Americans. The OSS man I've been meeting with—I think he can contribute to my future plans."

"*Your* plans?"

"I won't lie to you, Isabella. You know I have aspirations beyond this minuscule operation of ours. As commander of our squadron..."

"Are you certain you hold that position now?" she cut in.

"Who else do you think? I was second to Filippo, and probably a stronger leader than he," he answered with a touch of indignation.

"I guess you're right. But at least wait until he's cold in his grave before installing yourself in his place."

Isabella asked Massimo to drive her back to Verona Tuesday morning, in time for her eleven o'clock shift. She'd thought about returning Monday night but didn't want a recurrence of Massimo's suspicions about seeing the lights in the apartment. *Günter will be waiting for me, and I can hardly ask him to sit in the dark so my other lover won't be jealous!*

****

As time slipped by and the close of 1944 approached, Isabella continued her efforts in gathering intelligence and felt Günter's affection grow with each passing day. The dread of capture never left her, despite her skill at escaping detection. The nights she spent in the basement afforded little rest: she never allowed herself peaceful sleep, for fear of discovery if she did not wake in time to avoid her fellow workers. The stress of her work for the Resistance was taking its toll—on her spirit as well as her body.

One evening upon meeting Isabella behind the palazzo, Günter suggested they dine at their usual restaurant, the trattoria close to the apartment. When they arrived, the proprietor greeted them warmly.

"Ah, Captain Schumann, Signorina Ricci, how are you this evening? It's getting cold out there, don't you think? Here, let me seat you near the fire."

"Thank you, Rodolfo."

"The chef is trying out a new dish; I'd like you to taste it. What can I bring you from the wine cellar?"

"Why don't you surprise us?" Günter replied.

"Very good, Captain." Rodolfo bowed slightly and withdrew.

"Isabella, you look so tired tonight. Is everything all right?"

"Yes, I'm fine."

"That doesn't sound convincing," he said, taking her hand in his. "I think these frequent trips to your mother are wearing on your nerves. Why don't you take a week off and go home? You'll be able to spend more time with her, and maybe get a little rest yourself."

"Won't you miss me?"

"Of course, darling. I'd come visit you every day if I could. But I know you don't want me to meet your family."

She detected a note of melancholy in his voice. "You'll meet them someday, Günter. It's just not the right time." Isabella regretted the lie. She knew they would never meet.

"I understand. But still, you should take the time off."

"I can't right now. I've already imposed on Signora Vettori's kindness too often."

"Well, I hope I can cheer you up a bit." A smile lit his eyes. "I have something for you."

"Really? What is it?"

"Let's wait until we get back to the apartment," he said with a wink.

When they arrived at the apartment, Isabella felt exhaustion engulf her, in spite of her curiosity to discover Günter's surprise.

"Why don't you go and get comfortable?" he suggested as he removed his tunic and relaxed on the sofa.

"All right, I'll be right back."

Isabella walked to the bedroom, sat down on the bed, and slipped off her skirt and blouse. Too tired to rise, she tossed them onto a chair. *I'll lie down for just a minute*, she told herself as she stretched out.

She hadn't realized how long she'd been sleeping when she felt Günter sit down beside her.

"Isabella, are you asleep?" he whispered.

She turned toward him, barely opening her eyes. "What..." she murmured.

"I was beginning to wonder what had happened to you. It's been half an hour."

"I'm sorry." She yawned. "I don't know why I'm so sleepy."

"Don't worry. You just rest now." She felt him tuck the covers around her, then gently kiss her cheek.

"Good night, Liebchen," was the last thing she

heard.

****

Isabella opened her eyes, squinting at the brightness of the room. *How long have I slept?* She reached over for Günter, but his side of the bed was empty. Looking across the room, she saw him standing before the mirror combing his hair, then donning his field-gray peaked officer's cap. In silence she watched him, stealing a glimpse of his reflection. *How handsome he looks, even in the uniform of the enemy.*

"You're up early, Günter."

"Good morning, sweetheart," he said as he walked over and kissed her. "I tried not to disturb you when I got up. You were sleeping so peacefully. But it's not early anymore."

Tossing off the covers, she sat up in bed. "What time is it?"

"Almost seven o'clock. I'm afraid I must leave very soon. But first, I have something for you. I wanted to give this to you last night, but you fell asleep as soon as we returned from dinner." He drew a small package from his pocket and placed it in her hand. "Go ahead and see what it is." She looked up at him, puzzled, then untied the string and carefully unfolded the paper.

"Oh, Günter! You shouldn't have—you *really* shouldn't have!"

She turned his gift over in her hand, awed by the luminous strand of pearls fastened with a delicate gold clasp. But her surprise turned to hesitation, then uneasiness.

"What's wrong? You don't like them?"

"No, it's not that. They're lovely, really they are...but..."

"What is it then?"

"It's just that..." Isabella fought back a tear before continuing. "Günter, don't you know what kind of a girl accepts presents like this from a man?" She thought of Silvia and her collection of trophies—jewelry, clothes, furs, expensive perfumes—and of all the men they memorialized. "You're already helping to pay my rent. Don't you know what this makes me?"

"It makes you someone who is loved very dearly. The ones you borrowed from Silvia that night—you liked them so much. I thought you should have some of your own."

She was astonished that he remembered that detail, so many months ago. "I don't think I should..."

"Here, at least try them on." He took them from her hand, opened the clasp and placed them around her neck. "Go, look for yourself," he said with a nod toward the dresser.

She stood and stepped before the mirror. "They're so beautiful!" She pivoted slightly from side to side, admiring the way they glowed against her skin in the soft light of the morning. "I...I don't know what to say."

"How about 'thank you'?" he said with a smile.

"I don't know. They're just perfect and you're so sweet, but...I really can't...I mean, I shouldn't...I mean..."

"Look at it this way," he offered. "You can think of them as 'borrowed' if you like. If we ever part, you can return them to me. Of course, I hope that never happens."

"I'm not sure...perhaps...well, all right. I don't think I've ever had anything so fine. I really do love them," she said with the smallest trace of guilty delight.

"Good. But I really have to leave now. The colonel will be very cross with me if I'm late. I'll see you later, then."

"Yes, of course. And thank you, Günter."

He kissed her, then hurried to the door. "You make me very happy, Isabella."

She stood in front of the mirror for another few moments, entranced by the opulent gems, how the light played off mercurial tones of silvery white, golden ivory, and the palest hint of pink. She looked up and gazed into her own eyes as if they belonged to someone else. She thought of Günter, the man who shared her bed almost every night, and of Massimo, whom she seldom met now, and then only for brief encounters. Her world was becoming unfathomable. All of her touchstones had turned to sand.

She tried to turn to memories of a simpler time: the family farm where, as a girl, she helped to milk the cows and tend the chickens, gathering eggs for sale at market. She recalled the innocent pleasure of sitting in the kitchen with her brothers and sisters, enjoying Mamma's fresh-baked bread and the quenching tartness of Papa's homemade wine. She thought of convent school, of how she laughed and played with Silvia and the other girls, of the fragrant herb garden in the cloister, and the nuns—severe but kind—in their pristine black and white habits.

She looked up again into the mirror, searching for some clue to identify the woman she saw before her, one who seemed almost a stranger. *Who am I now? A naïve girl, a freedom fighter, a whore?* She lay back on the bed, trying to free her mind of troubling questions. She imagined that she floated in air, warmed by the sun and caressed by billowy clouds, unfettered from the earth. There was no war, no conflict, no deceit; all thoughts save tranquil ones were banished from her brain. But in her mind's eye one unrelenting image refused to depart. It was a face, with a warm smile and eyes as deep and blue as the ocean. It was Günter's face.

Chapter 18

After his midday cigarette break with Isabella, Günter arrived back at his desk to find a handwritten document, in Italian, left for him to translate into German. He sat at his typewriter to begin work on the translation. From the heading, it appeared to be a witness's statement of an incident that had occurred in the village of San Vincenzo about a month earlier. Günter had heard about the reprisals that the Army exacted there. A sniper attack on an Axis supply shipment resulted in the killing of two German soldiers and the wounding of several others. The actual perpetrators, partisans who were believed to have come from that village, were never apprehended. In retribution and as a deterrent to further acts of rebellion, twenty men from the village were shot. This type of brutal retaliation was expressly delineated and authorized by Field Marshal Kesselring's orders, issued months before. Severe measures were to be used against partisans, including the arrest and killing of hostages, in an effort to deter saboteurs. But the field marshal had also declared that unjustified attacks on innocent civilians by German military personnel would not be tolerated, and that any violators would be prosecuted.

But as Günter perused the affidavit, he was horrified to discover that the reprisals at San Vincenzo had far exceeded the field marshal's orders. According to the witness, a Catholic priest from the local parish, German soldiers indiscriminately gunned down scores of civilians. He claimed that some villagers had fled the onslaught and sought refuge in the church, which was then set on fire by the Germans. The priest described in shocking detail how the soldiers rounded up the congregants, mostly women and children, as they escaped the flames and mowed them down with machine-gun blasts. The entire village was then burned to the ground. The numbers of victims from each local family, close to one hundred in total, were listed in the document.

Before he could even begin his task, Günter stood and headed for the washroom. His hands shook and his throat was tight with agitation. To quiet his nerves, he splashed his face with cool water and took a few deep breaths. He didn't want to believe it, but the priest's statement conveyed an air of truth. Disturbed though he was, it was Günter's duty to translate the document and bring the contents to the attention of his supervisor.

****

"Max, you've got to see this," Günter said urgently to his immediate superior, Major Gerhardt. "I've translated an affidavit from a witness to the San Vincenzo incident. You won't believe what he says happened there!"

"Let me see your translation." Günter handed the document to the major and waited while he read it. "I see," Max said without expression.

"There will have to be an investigation. The field marshal should see this right away."

"Don't clamor about this, Günter. The field marshal has more important things to worry about right now."

"Perhaps I should tell the colonel..."

"I wouldn't do that if I were you. The colonel is already aware of what went on at San Vincenzo. Is

159

this your only copy of the translation?"

"No, I have another. I always keep a copy for my file."

"That won't be necessary. Where is the original affidavit?"

"It's on my desk."

"Give me the original and any copies you have."

"But..." Günter hesitated.

"Just get them."

Günter retrieved the documents and handed them to the major.

"I wouldn't discuss this with anyone else. Just let the senior staff handle it, all right?" Gerhardt told Günter in a dismissive tone.

"Max, I don't understand how you can be so detached. Some of our soldiers could be guilty of the mass murder of innocent civilians. You don't seem to be bothered in the least!"

"Between you and me, I'm quite sure nothing will come of this. Take my advice. Just forget you ever saw this document."

"But what about the field marshal's order? Men who commit such butchery should be treated as criminals!"

"I'll tell you this once, as a friend, and then we won't speak about it again. If you don't learn to keep your mouth shut, you'll find yourself in serious difficulties around here. And if you go to the colonel or the field marshal about this, you'll probably find yourself at the front, or worse."

"So, this will all be swept under the carpet, then? We're to just make believe it never happened?"

"You know, Günter, you're really not cut out to be a soldier, let alone an officer. If you want to survive the rest of this war, you'd better toughen up and stop being so damned sentimental about everything. Now I don't want to hear another word about this. You understand? That's an order,

Captain."

"Yes, sir. I understand," Günter responded, scarcely able to suppress his contempt. "May I have a few hours' leave, Major? I have some personal affairs to attend to."

"Yes, go ahead. Just remember what I told you, Günter."

****

Günter walked the narrow streets of Verona. At first he had no particular destination in mind, but soon he found himself headed toward the riverfront. There he could escape the midday drone of the city and watch the ceaseless, silent flow of the Adige. A gray, overcast sky darkened the waters while the blustery chill of late December pierced his wool tunic, sending shivers through his body. He realized he'd forgotten his greatcoat in his haste to flee headquarters and needed to find shelter from the cold. He rejected the idea of returning to quarters, where he wouldn't be able to avoid his comrades. He needed a refuge of solitude, someplace for quiet reflection to seek solace for his grief-laden heart. He walked back in the direction of the palazzo but continued past, turning down Via Portici to the Church of Santa Maria degli Angeli. He had stopped in for Mass several times before and felt welcome, despite never seeing another German uniform there.

Romanesque arches and stout marble columns gave an austerity to the dimly lit medieval church. All around, dozens of votive flames glowed, each embodying a fervent plea for heavenly intervention, or a prayer of thanksgiving. Günter entered and headed for the small chapel with the beautiful statue of the Virgin. After lighting a candle, he knelt down to pray. He wasn't devoutly religious and had little tolerance for arbitrary dogma and castigation. Discounting doctrines of sin and damnation, he focused instead on teachings about love and forgiveness. Günter was drawn to the sanctity and transcendence of the Church and experienced a serenity there that defied description. To him it was not the infallible, solitary source of all truth but a nurturing well of virtue and grace, a link to divine benevolence.

Mass was about to start in the main sanctuary, so Günter went there and found an empty pew toward the back of the church. Despite his efforts to remain attentive to the liturgy, his thoughts kept drifting back to the horrifying descriptions of the massacre and to the callous reaction on the part of his superior officer. But he concluded that the major was probably correct; nothing would come of this incident, and if Günter protested it would likely result in an assignment at the front. Gerhardt's advice, though repugnant to Günter, was in his best interests.

At the end of the Mass, Günter remained in the pew, enjoying the quiet of the near-empty church. He didn't realize that hours had passed when he was roused from his contemplation by the soft voice of an elderly man. Günter looked up and recognized the white-haired priest who had quietly taken a seat in the pew in front of him. He had celebrated many of the services Günter attended, and he sensed his kindness and sincerity, not only from his homilies, but also from his warm, compassionate nature.

"Good afternoon, Captain. It's so nice to see you today. We don't have many Germans attending services here. I've seen you on several occasions and thought I should introduce myself. I'm Father Michele and I'm the pastor here. Do you speak Italian?"

"Yes, Father. My name is Günter Schumann. I'm stationed a few blocks from here at Palazzo Maggiore."

"You've been sitting here quite a long while

today. My parishioners don't usually spend the entire afternoon in church, but you're certainly welcome to stay. Is there anything I can do for you, Günter?"

"Well no, not really...but..." Günter hesitated. He looked into the gentle eyes of the old priest. *Do I dare unburden my soul?*

"What is it, my son? Is there something you wish to tell me?"

Günter stared out toward the altar and the crucifix that hung high above it. He closed his eyes and rubbed his brow. Perhaps it was the stark contrast of the priest's comforting voice with the impassive one of the major that caused a heavy sigh to break from Günter's lips.

"I really don't know where to begin. I guess I'm just feeling a little lost."

"It's all right. Take your time. I've no place to go for a while. Tell me your troubles; perhaps I can help to relieve them."

Over the next hour, Günter related his worries and cares, all the conflicts of trying to be a good soldier and a good Christian, of loving his country but hating its regime. He spoke of the shame he felt wearing the same uniform as the men who committed atrocities he'd long suspected took place but never wanted to believe. Today, he saw them confirmed in the affidavit he'd been ordered to forget.

Emotionally spent, Günter listened to the soothing words of Father Michele. "You have done nothing to feel ashamed of, my son. I can see that you're a decent man burdened with an agonizing dilemma. God knows this and He knows your heart. Believe in Him and you will find your way."

"I'm sure you understand that I could never go to the Army chaplain with this. I could be court-martialed just for saying some of the things I've told you."

"You needn't worry about that, Günter. I know how to keep secrets. I've protected many even weightier than yours."

"I know, Father. I trust you. And I'm grateful for your time and your counsel. Thank you so much."

"I hope I've been able to give you some consolation. Now just remember to keep praying."

"I will."

Chapter 19

Silvia approached Isabella one day to invite her and Günter to a retreat at Federico's villa. Isabella had been curious to see the place, and relayed the invitation.

"Federico and Silvia have asked us to join them at his villa for the weekend. I think I can arrange to get Saturday and Sunday off at the palazzo."

"I won't be able to get away for more than a few hours on Sunday," Günter replied. "You can go without me, if you like."

"We can go together on Sunday, can't we?"

"You should take the whole weekend. You've been working very hard and deserve some time off. What if I come for a little while on Sunday and then bring you home? That way you can spend some time with your friend Silvia."

"All right. I'll tell Silvia." *It will be pleasant to get away from Verona for a short holiday. I wouldn't mind some female companionship, and a little gossip, too!*

****

On Saturday morning, Federico sent a car to bring Isabella to the villa, about an hour's drive from Verona, on the shore of Lake Garda. Along the journey, she was delighted by the picturesque scenery and glorious views of snow-covered mountains beyond the crystalline lake.

The villa was smaller than Villa Bagliotti but equally imposing and elegant. It had been in

Federico's family for generations, a symbol of the prosperity of their ancient vineyard. As the car pulled up to the front of the mansion, Silvia ran out to greet her.

"Cara mia! I'm so happy you're here. We are going to have such a wonderful time together!" Silvia said as she took Isabella by the arm and led her into the villa.

"This place is absolutely magnificent!" Awestruck, Isabella followed her friend through hallways lined with exquisite paintings and beautiful tapestries. Regal furnishings, embellished with intricate inlay and silk brocade filled the salons; elaborate carvings enhanced majestic pilasters and lofty ceilings. "Are these paintings originals? Some of them look like old masters!"

"Yes, I believe they are. Some have been in Federico's family for centuries, or so he says," Silvia replied with a laugh. "Come, let me show you to your room."

They headed upstairs to a bright, airy guest suite with a separate drawing room and bedroom. A small terrace looked out onto the lake. In the bedroom was a tremendous four-poster bed appointed with a canopy and a downy coverlet in a pattern of pink and yellow rosebuds, echoing touches of pink and yellow throughout the suite. There was even an adjoining bathroom of sparkling white tile and brass with a spacious dressing area.

"Oh, Silvia, it's lovely. And it's as big as our apartment! I do wish Günter were here."

"I'm sure you do!" Silvia said, glancing at the sumptuous bed.

"I mean, he'd love the view from here," Isabella remarked, indicating the terrace. "You don't really think I meant that he would share this bed with me. We're not married, so he'd need his own accommodations, of course. What kind of a girl do you think I am?" Then they burst into laughter and giggled like schoolgirls.

Federico joined them for a splendid luncheon, where he was able to flaunt the finest selections from his family's winery. In the afternoon, Federico attended to business affairs, leaving the two friends to enjoy each other's company. Isabella and Silvia took a brisk hike down to the lake and caught each other up on their romantic adventures.

"I've never seen you so happy. You must be in love," Isabella said to her companion.

"Yes, I don't quite believe it myself, but I can't remember ever feeling like this. Federico has me completely enraptured! And what about you, Isabella? Is it true love for you and Günter?"

"I don't know. Günter's very sweet, but..." She hesitated.

"Then what is it?"

How can I explain it to Silvia? I hate to lie, but I can't tell her the truth. "I don't think I want to be in love right now."

"Why not?"

"I prefer to be free, I guess." She had struggled for months to maintain an emotional distance from Günter. Though she couldn't deny his wonderful qualities, or the tenderness of his affection, she had suppressed any feelings of love. "Besides, how can I imagine a future with him? He's German and I'm Italian. After the war he'll return to Bavaria and forget about me. Why should I risk a broken heart when I know this affair will not last?"

"I don't think Günter will forget you so easily. I've seen the way you look at each other. You're both very much in love, even if you don't want to admit it."

Isabella shook her head, endeavoring to dismiss Silvia's comment. *You may be able to love a Fascist, but how can I love a Nazi?*

****

That night after dinner Isabella retired to her bed, hoping to fall asleep quickly. But the conversation with Silvia earlier that day weighed on her mind. She realized how weary she was, after months of internal battles and outward pretense. *In a different world I could give myself completely to a man like Günter, but life is more complicated than that.* As she drifted off to sleep, she prayed that her labors and sacrifices would not be in vain, that she would not lose her heart or her spirit before concluding her mission.

Günter arrived early Sunday afternoon, just after lunch. After giving him a tour of the villa, Silvia invited him to join the others in an elegant salon and introduced him to Federico.

"I'm so sorry you missed luncheon. Can I get you anything to eat?" she asked.

"No, thank you, Silvia. I'm fine for now." He moved over to Isabella and put his arm around her. "I've missed you, sweetheart," he whispered.

Silvia glanced at Isabella with a knowing smile. Isabella shook her head slightly, trying to convey to Silvia that she was reading too much into everything.

"Here, Günter, you must try some of this," Federico said as he produced a crystal decanter. "Have you ever tasted a forty-year-old cognac? It's the absolute nectar of the gods!"

"No, I can't say that I have. My drinking experiences are limited, I confess. But I certainly enjoy a fine bottle of wine, or a good draft of beer— Bavarian, of course," Günter said cheerfully. "I'll give it a try." He took a sip of the amber liquor proffered by Federico, coughing slightly at its potency. "It's quite strong."

"One has to build up a tolerance, my friend. But if you prefer wine, I must give you a few bottles of our finest vintage. I'd like to know what you think of it."

"Thank you, Federico. I understand that your family has owned the winery for generations."

"Yes, that's true. But I've got my hand in several enterprises. How is your business going these days?"

"My business?"

"The war business, of course," Federico said with a laugh.

Günter sighed. "Well, it's not pleasant, I can tell you that. My field of study was linguistics, before the war. I hope to return to it as soon as possible."

"Not too soon, I pray. I, for one, like having you Germans around. I've made a fair profit off the Wehrmacht so far," Federico said with a trace of condescension. A look of annoyance shadowed Günter's face and he didn't reply.

"You know, I admire the Nazis very much," Federico continued. "Your Führer is a remarkable leader. He is able to command allegiance to an extent that our Duce, unfortunately, has not been able to achieve. I've said this to Il Duce myself, mind you. He's been too lenient, too merciful at times. If he'd been as single-minded as Hitler, Italy would be unified today. Hitler wouldn't have tolerated the kind of dissension we've experienced here. Take the Jewish question, for instance..."

"Yes, the Jewish question...one of many," Günter interrupted. "Please excuse me; I need to stretch my legs." Then he stood and headed out of the room. Isabella hurried after him.

"Are you all right?" she asked.

"I don't care to discuss such things, that's all. Politics is not my favorite subject." His lips thinned into a frown. "I suppose I should go back in, but I almost feel as if Federico is baiting me."

"I'll try to turn the discussion to another topic, all right?"

Günter stroked her cheek. "You're a true peacemaker, my dear."

When they returned to the salon, Isabella succeeded in guiding the conversation in a different direction, and Günter was able to tolerate his host for a few more hours. By late afternoon, he hinted to Isabella that he wanted to leave. She consented and told Silvia that Günter had to return earlier than planned due to an important meeting with his commander.

Silvia linked her arm in Günter's as she accompanied him to the door. "I'm sorry you have to leave so soon."

"Duty calls, Silvia. But thank you for a lovely afternoon," Günter said, and kissed her on both cheeks.

"We'll see you at Mussolini's party, won't we?" Silvia asked.

"Mussolini's party?" He glanced at Isabella, his brows drawn into a question.

"Yes, I told Isabella I could get invitations for both of you. It will be the social event of the season! I just couldn't bear it if you don't come, Günter."

"I'll let you know if we can make it, Silvia," Isabella assured.

Günter held his hand out to Federico. "It was nice to meet you, Federico. Thank you for your hospitality."

"You must come again soon, my friend!" Federico replied.

****

During the ride back to Verona, Günter was unusually quiet. Isabella tried to soothe him with an affectionate word, but he barely responded and seemed lost in his own thoughts. When they arrived back at the apartment, she keenly sensed his disquiet.

"You seem upset. What is troubling you?"

"Nothing." He sighed, then headed to the bedroom. Isabella followed and found him standing by the window, looking out pensively at the red tile rooftops of Verona.

"I can see you didn't enjoy today's visit with Silvia and Federico. I don't think you liked Federico very much. He seemed to irritate you."

"Oh, he's all right, I guess. That is if you like pompous stupidity!"

"Günter!" Isabella was shocked at his antipathy.

"I'm sorry. I probably shouldn't say such things. I hope my displeasure was not apparent at the villa. I'd hate to be discourteous to our hosts, and I certainly wouldn't want to embarrass you. I suppose Federico is entitled to his opinions."

"What was it about his views that bothered you so much?"

"I'd rather not talk about this now, all right?"

How strange. He's always been so open. But the finality in his tone convinced her it would be best to just leave him alone. "I'll go and make us something to eat, then. It's too bad you didn't want to stay for dinner at the villa. Federico's chef is fabulous."

"Fine," he replied, then turned back toward the darkened panorama of the city.

****

Dawn had just broken when Massimo drove Isabella to the remote meadow on the outskirts of Verona later that week. She shifted uneasily in the front seat of his unheated truck. The frosty air made her shiver, so Massimo rubbed her hands in his to keep them warm.

"So, you really want me to attend this party for Mussolini?" Isabella asked. "You don't want me to start spying on *him* now, do you?"

When she'd told him about Silvia's invitation to the gala in Il Duce's honor, Isabella recalled the misgivings she'd had months earlier about the party at Palazzo Fabriano. Her instinctive response to the offer was one of distaste. Despite genuine affection for Silvia, and the opportunity to enjoy wonderful music, good food and lavish surroundings, she did not relish the idea of socializing with her enemies. Yet Massimo always found ways to further his status through Isabella's connections, and he'd urged her to accept.

"We can't pass up a chance like this," Massimo replied.

"A chance for what?"

Isabella wasn't sure whether Massimo's hesitation denoted thoughtfulness or apprehension on his part. After a few moments of silence he looked at her with cool resolve.

"To kill him."

"What?"

"Silvia's lover is close to Mussolini, isn't he?"

"Yes," she responded warily.

"He can introduce you. Let me see... Poison. Yes, that's the only way, I think. You can put some into his drink, or... You'll have to make the most of whatever chance you get."

"What are you talking about? You actually want me to poison Mussolini? Are you insane?"

"Imagine, Isabella. We'll be renowned." Gazing off dreamily he mused, "It was Massimo Baricelli who brought about the end of the detestable tyrant, ushering in an era of democracy for all Italians..."

"Massimo, would you please be serious."

"I *am* being serious."

"You're going to 'usher in an era of democracy' by committing murder?" she mocked.

"It wouldn't be murder but retribution!"

"If you want to effect justice in this way, you can do it without me."

"I would, but you're the one who's invited to this party."

She stared at him in wonder. "You *are* serious. But how?"

"I know where I can get these things. It will be slow acting. I'll make sure of that. Slow and agonizing! You'll have plenty of time to get away before anyone realizes that something is wrong. No one will ever suspect you."

"I don't know, Massimo. I don't think I can."

"You didn't think you could spy, but look at how much you've accomplished! I'm very proud of you, carina. Have I ever told you that?"

"But to kill someone..."

"Don't you believe he deserves to die?"

"Well, maybe. But why me? I don't want to be a murderer."

"You won't be a murderer. You're a soldier. I've killed, too, Isabella. This is war. When you joined the squadron you told me you'd do anything for the cause. Then when I put you in the kitchen with the other women it wasn't enough for you. You wanted an active role. I admire you for that. I know you can do this."

She looked into his jet-black eyes and saw the potency and fortitude she'd always esteemed. For the year they'd been together he was her source of strength, the bulwark she leaned on when doubt or fear held her back.

"I just... Can I at least think about it?"

"Of course. I want you to be sure. The party's in a week, you said?"

"Yes."

"It will take me a few days to obtain what we need. Why don't you go ahead and accept the invitation? Then you can let me know what you decide." He moved closer to her and pressed his warm cheek against her chilly face. "You're my brave little warrior. I'll be so proud of you," he whispered. He slid his arm around her waist and took her lips with his ravishing mouth. For a second she pulled away.

"I'm...I'm so cold," she murmured.

"Don't worry, my love. I'll keep you warm."

Chapter 20

Silvia had arranged invitations for Isabella and Günter to the gala in Mussolini's honor. The party was to be held at a grand villa in Verona, the home of one of Il Duce's oldest friends and supporters. Though the guest list was scrutinized for security reasons, Isabella's association with Federico and Günter's status as a German Army officer readily cleared their admittance.

When Isabella told Signora Vettori of her invitation to the exclusive event, the housekeeper gladly allowed Isabella to leave earlier than usual to get ready. Günter would not get off duty until much later, but he promised to meet her at the villa.

Isabella reached home a little before eight o'clock, with just enough time to dress and arrive fashionably late for the party. She'd decided to wear the same black taffeta gown she'd worn at Palazzo Fabriano on the night she'd begun her covert mission. The strand of pearls Günter had given her hung down the low-cut neckline of the dress. As she stroked the gems with her finger, she remembered how happy Günter had been that morning when she'd accepted them. Standing before the mirror, she applied a touch more makeup and wondered if anyone would be able to peer through the alluring façade to her treacherous design.

The festive sounds of the gala emanated onto the street in front of the villa when Isabella arrived. German soldiers and members of Mussolini's

175

personal guard monitored entry to the building, but she presented her invitation and was admitted without question.

Though a grueling war and the bleakness of winter forced most Italians to survive on scant provisions, there was no trace of privation here. Gourmet delights of every kind—succulent roast meats, fresh fish, mountains of pastries, and luscious cakes—were displayed in abundance. But her aversion for such gluttony, combined with the terrible prospect of her homicidal scheme, quashed any appetite Isabella might have had.

She was relieved to spot Silvia, surrounded as usual by a flock of male admirers. When Silvia saw Isabella, she dashed over to greet her.

"Cara mia, you look absolutely stunning! But where's Günter? Isn't he coming?"

"He's still working at headquarters, but he should be here later. What about Federico? I was hoping he might be able to introduce me to Il Duce." Mentioning her target made Isabella's stomach flutter with panic, but she fought to conceal her anxiety.

"Oh, I'm sure he'd be happy to. I'll tell him as soon as I see him."

For the next hour or so, Isabella wandered around the villa, trying to formulate her approach and escape route. There was no sign of either Federico or Il Duce, though Silvia had assured her that both were on the premises. Isabella assumed that Mussolini and his ministers were spending the party in private meetings and had little interest in entertaining other guests.

Finally, Federico came up to her. "Silvia says you'd like to meet Il Duce. He's very busy right now with pressing matters of state, but I think I can get you in to see him a little later."

"Oh, good. It would be such a thrill for me."

"I'll look for you when he has a free moment. But you must excuse me now, as I'm expected in another salon. It's so tiresome to be on duty even during a lovely party like this," he added with a smile.

"Of course. Thank you so much, Federico."

After waiting another half hour for Federico's return, Isabella determined to pursue her objective on her own. She had noticed the large man who was standing to the side of the main salon. His humorless expression and daunting presence told Isabella that he was not among the revelers but part of the security detail. Yet his frequent glances, and even an occasional smile in her direction, indicated an opening. Fortified with a couple of glasses of champagne, Isabella decided to attempt an encounter without Federico's help. She walked over to the man.

****

Günter arrived at the party just past ten o'clock, after an unscheduled meeting with Colonel von Haeften. He wandered around the villa looking for Isabella for a short while before he saw her conversing with one of Mussolini's bodyguards. She didn't see him, so Günter stood a ways off and watched. He observed how the man leered at her, and reached to fondle a tendril of hair that had escaped the grasp of its pin and dangled along her neck.

"Don't be jealous, Günter," Silvia whispered as she came up behind him and placed her hand affectionately on his arm. "Believe me, you're the only man in the world for her."

Günter turned to Silvia and smiled. "How can you be so sure? Did she tell you that?"

"She didn't have to. Come on, dance with me."

"I'm not a very good dancer. And I'm sure you'd rather dance with Federico anyway. Is he here?"

"He's here somewhere. I've hardly seen him at all tonight; he's too busy chatting with his cronies. As you can see, both of our lovers have deserted us. Let's console each other."

Silvia coaxed Günter onto the dance floor. She gently squeezed his hand as he put his arm around her waist.

"That's right, Günter, just a little faster now," she encouraged as he struggled to keep in step with the music.

"What kind of dance is this?" he asked in exasperation as he watched the other dancers and tried to copy their movements.

"It's a foxtrot."

"A waltz I might be able to manage, but this is beyond my capabilities."

"But Isabella told me that you're a musical genius! She said you have a wonderful voice and that you play the piano, too."

"Then my talent must be limited to my vocal cords and fingers. It doesn't seem to extend to my feet."

"Don't you have to use your feet to play piano?"

"Well, yes, but they don't have to propel me across the floor. I'm afraid I'm not very good at this. Though I'm not much of a soldier, I think I'm better suited to a foxhole than a foxtrot!"

Silvia burst into laughter. "You're so funny, Günter! And you're doing fine, really." Günter kept glancing toward Isabella, so with a slight shift of her body, Silvia tried to turn him away from the distraction. "Oh!" she exclaimed as Günter trod on her foot.

"Oh, dear, I'm terribly sorry! Why don't we take a little rest now before I seriously injure you?"

"Only if you promise me the next waltz," Silvia replied with a wink.

"It's a deal. But I warn you, you'll be dancing at

your own risk."

Günter led Silvia to a nearby settee. After procuring two glasses of champagne, he sat down beside her.

"You know, Günter, I've learned something in the last few months. I used to think I knew a lot about men. They were my avocation, you might say." She laughed. "I thought I had them all figured out. But then I realized something."

"What was that?"

"That I didn't know what love was. Well, I mean I didn't know what *being* in love was. I never imagined I could feel the way I feel about Federico. He actually cares about me—about *me*. Oh, I know he can be a bore sometimes, but deep down he's really sweet. And he doesn't just want sex."

"You know, we *do* think about other things," Günter protested.

"Oh, yes. Business, money, politics..."

"So what do women think about?"

"Why, men, of course!" Then she leaned in closely and uttered in a soft, earnest tone, "Isabella is a very lucky woman. Don't ever let her go, Günter."

"I won't."

****

"I would like so much to meet Il Duce," Isabella said, trying to ignore the wolfish gaze of the brute who stood before her. *I've never seen a man so large.* She couldn't even see past the expanse of his shoulders. Then she felt a hand on her buttocks and pushed it away. "Il Duce?" she repeated.

"And why, mia piccina, do you think Il Duce would be interested in meeting you?" The rejected hand attempted another maneuver at her waist.

"Do you know Federico di Balduccio? He's my friend, and he promised to introduce me to Il Duce, but I just don't know where he's gone off to. I only want to tell him how much I admire him and how grateful I am for everything he's done for Italy." *I can't believe I said that without choking on the words.*

"Wait here," the bodyguard told her with a smirk before walking away.

****

"There's Clara Petacci, Günter. Doesn't she look gorgeous? I wonder where she got that dress," Silvia remarked, in awe of the sequined white gown flaunted by Mussolini's mistress.

"Um...yes, it's a lovely dress." Günter saw that Isabella was finally alone and wondered how he could politely excuse himself from Silvia's company.

"I should go say hello. Would you like to meet her? I can introduce you."

"Not right now. But you go ahead," Günter replied.

"All right. But I'll be back for our waltz."

****

Günter approached Isabella, who was still waiting for Mussolini's bodyguard to return.

"Hello, darling. Are you enjoying yourself? I'm happy to see you wearing these," he said as he touched her pearls, then slid his finger along her throat, and down the décolletage of her gown. "You look beautiful tonight."

Though usually calmed by his presence, Isabella felt an unexpected discomfort at Günter's appearance. It was almost as if she feared that he could read her mind and knew of her fatal plan.

Günter clasped her trembling hand. "What's wrong?" he asked.

"Nothing. I...I'm waiting to meet Il Duce. I was just talking to his bodyguard. He's going to introduce me."

"I didn't realize that you were such a great admirer of Mussolini."

180

"Well...oh, there he is now," she said as the guard drew near. "Günter, would you mind terribly..."

"What, you want me to disappear so you can have Il Duce all to yourself?"

"Please don't be annoyed. But if you'll excuse me for just a minute..."

"Of course," he said flatly. "Anything you wish, my dear." He shook his head and walked off.

Isabella felt her insides twist as she turned from Günter to Il Duce's brawny protector.

"Come with me, signorina," he offered. His hand wandered from her waist to her hip as he led her to another salon.

How am I possibly going to do this? she asked herself as she surveyed the room. *You can't just go up to someone and poison him!*

Mussolini was sitting on a sofa surrounded by other men, smoking cigars and drinking. She recognized the brutal profile of the tyrant—a harsh but weary face—evincing command, yet suggesting the ignominy of failure. He'd been reduced to a figurehead under Hitler's domination, without whose protection he would have been vanquished. Like the Nazis, Mussolini was now reviled by most Italians, save for a few steadfast supporters. But an air of authority remained.

She fumbled with the clasp of her black satin purse, then withdrew the silver lipstick case that Massimo had prepared. The bodyguard walked over and whispered to his leader while pointing in Isabella's direction. With a nod, Mussolini indicated his consent, and signaled for her to join him.

She clutched the small silver tube as she approached. The other men moved away to allow their Duce some privacy with his attractive visitor. The bodyguard remained close by, but turned away from them, unaware that he was turning his back on a deadly threat.

Mussolini stood to greet Isabella and extended his hand. She nodded demurely, and then sat down beside him. She recalled the protests she'd attended years earlier, the pamphlets she'd distributed denouncing the Fascist regime and demanding the overthrow of its ruthless dictator. She wondered how her compatriots would view her now, as she smiled at the object of their hatred. She wondered how her mother would view her now, as she contemplated assassination.

Isabella glimpsed the drink that Mussolini had set down on the table before him, but she endeavored to focus her eyes on the man instead.

"So, what can I do for you, signorina?"

"I...I just wanted to tell you how much I appreciate what you have done to make our country strong." Of all the lies she had told these past months, all the pretense and treachery she'd committed in the name of liberty, this disgusted her the most.

"Thank you." He looked off, as if bored with the conversation. "If you'll excuse me..." Abruptly, he stood to join a group of men across the room. He left his drink behind on the table. The bodyguard moved toward his charge, ignoring Isabella for the moment.

With astounding fortune she'd been left alone and unguarded, with Mussolini's life literally in her hands. She knew this was her best and probably only opportunity. She could slip the powder into his glass and disappear without any disturbance. Of course, there was no guarantee he would return to finish his drink, but she was unlikely to get another chance. She agitatedly fingered the lethal silver case. *What if someone else drinks from the glass? What if an innocent person mistakes it for his own? I should stay to ensure that doesn't happen. And do what then? Casually knock it out of his hand before he takes a sip?* With that thought she flinched and the cylinder tumbled from her hand.

"Oh, Dio..." she gasped. The lipstick case rolled away, arriving at the feet of the bodyguard. If not for her cry of alarm, he would probably not even have noticed.

"Is this yours?" he asked as he walked over and handed it to her.

"Uh...yes. Thank you," she sputtered and hastily claimed it.

Mussolini was still engrossed in conversation across the room; the bodyguard had again turned his back to Isabella. She sat transfixed, breaking her gaze on Mussolini's glass only by nervous glances toward Il Duce, to his warder, and to the silver tube in her hand.

She remembered Massimo's words when they'd first conceived the plan: "Don't you believe he deserves to die?" he'd asked her. She'd evaded a response then, and had since pushed the thought from her mind.

Men like Massimo had the cool assurance to condemn others without reservation. When the enemy stood before them they never faltered; they knew it was time to act and not to question. *Yes, Mussolini probably deserves to die, if anyone does.* He'd eliminated political opponents and exacted summary justice in a merciless quest for ascendancy. Certainly he'd brought about the deaths of innocents, and no righteous court would acquit him.

She knew she was already accountable for loss of life. The intelligence she'd uncovered at German headquarters had been used against the enemy. She'd had a hand in killing, if indirectly. And like any soldier, she justified this as defending her country from a cruel invader.

But to kill in cold blood? Isabella quivered. No, it would stop here. Someone else could be the hero and bring down the oppressor. She wouldn't become judge and executioner, wouldn't stain her hands even with the blood of the guilty.

In a whirl of emotions, Isabella fled the salon and hurried to the restroom. She barred the door, sat down, and tried to subdue the tremors that racked her body. Eventually, she calmed down enough to notice that she was still clutching the silver lipstick case. Her grip was so fierce that the muscles in her hand ached when she finally released it.

She'd failed in her mission, yet it was not disappointment at a lost opportunity that lingered. The overriding emotion was relief. Not only had the hated Duce received his reprieve, but she had, too. She would not have to live with murder on her conscience.

She opened the tube and dumped the poison into the toilet, wondering how to dispose of the lipstick case. She removed the slim glass vial that had contained the powder and tossed the outer silver case into the waste can. Then she wrapped the vial in a hand towel, crushed it beneath her heel and shook the contaminated shards from the towel into the toilet. She had to be sure that no one would accidentally come into contact with any trace of the poison.

Still shaken, Isabella returned to the main salon. She thought of the party at Palazzo Fabriano and the unease she'd experienced there, the same nauseating feeling in the pit of her stomach. But in the months since then she'd progressed from naïve girl to cunning spy, and now...almost to assassin.

She saw Günter standing by himself across the room, drinking a glass of champagne, looking somewhat withdrawn and dejected. When she approached, he barely turned his head to look at her.

"Are you finished?" he asked.

"I... Would you mind taking me home now, Günter?"

"I really can't leave yet. I've promised Silvia a dance."

"But I...I don't feel well."

"What's the matter?"

"I...um...I think I've had a little too much to drink."

"Yes, maybe you have." His voice was laced with reproach.

"Or perhaps it's something I've eaten. I feel a bit queasy."

"Fine, let's go. But first let me say 'Good night' to Silvia. She's been very gracious to me this evening."

He left Isabella standing there and went off to find Silvia.

****

When they returned to the apartment, Isabella observed an unusual coolness in Günter's demeanor. After escorting her inside, he turned to leave.

"Good night, Isabella," he said as he reached for the doorknob.

"Where are you going?"

"I think I'll sleep at the barracks tonight. I have to be up very early in the morning."

"You get up early *every* morning."

He sighed. "The truth is, I don't feel much like sleeping with you tonight."

"What do you mean? Why not?"

"What do you need *me* for? You have your precious Duce to take care of you!"

"Is that what's bothering you? That I wanted to meet Il Duce tonight? Surely you're not jealous of *him*?"

"Are you sure that it was Mussolini who interested you and not his thug? You should have seen yourself tonight! My God, you just let that man

185

put his hands all over you! And then you disappeared. What was I to think?"

"I don't know, Günter. What *do* you think? Don't you trust me?"

"I really don't want to talk about this anymore." As he opened the door Isabella grabbed his arm to stop him.

She realized now that she'd been so absorbed by her own tribulations that she hadn't considered Günter the entire night. "Please don't leave like this. Believe me, nothing happened. Please, come and sit down." She tugged on his arm until he relented and sat beside her on the sofa. "You're right. I pretty much ignored you the whole evening. I am sorry about that. But I wanted to meet Il Duce. You can understand, can't you? I was excited, that's all. Wouldn't you feel that way if you got a chance to meet your Führer?"

"What I saw tonight... It was a side of you that didn't appeal to me." He hesitated before continuing. "I never really thought about what your political views might be, but I didn't imagine you a devoted Fascist."

Me, a Fascist... The thought almost made Isabella laugh. "And would that be a bad thing? If I were a Fascist? The Nazis and Fascists are allies, after all."

"I'm not a Nazi."

She looked at him strangely. "But you're an officer in Hitler's Army."

"There are many officers who are not Party members."

"But surely you must agree with Hitler's ideology? How else could you serve him so conscientiously?"

"I really have to go." He got up and headed toward the door.

"Günter, wait..."

186

"So you think I'm a Nazi?" His tone grew severe. "Perhaps you worship your beloved Duce, but don't assume for one minute that I feel the same way about Hitler!"

"You joined the Army."

"I was drafted, Isabella. Didn't I tell you that? But if I hadn't been... Well, I'm not going to lie. I probably wouldn't have signed up, anyway. I suppose that makes me a coward, doesn't it? You don't know what it's like for me sometimes. I mean... I love my comrades. I'd give my life for them. But when I have to listen to the way some of them extol our valiant Führer... I can't possibly tell them what I really think. But I don't expect you to understand."

"I want to understand." She reached for his hand.

"I just can't talk to you about these things. Especially now that I know what your feelings are."

"You *don't* know what my feelings are." All these months she'd guarded her political stance, assuming Günter would distrust her, even cast her aside, if he knew what she really believed in. She couldn't bear the thought that he disdained her now, thinking that she supported Mussolini. "Please, Günter, talk to me."

Günter sat on the sofa and rested his elbows on his knees. He closed his eyes and held his head in his hands. A palpable silence hung in the air for a minute or more. Finally, he looked at her with tremendous sadness in his eyes. "If I tell you something, you must not repeat it. I've never told this to anyone."

"Of course. You can trust me."

"For twelve years, now, unspeakable brutality has reigned in Germany, yet I've remained silent. There are some who resisted...but I was always too afraid. Few who question the government survive. I just tried to stay alive and prayed the regime would

187

be defeated someday. But defeated by whom? Surely not by cowards like me! And then when I was drafted—what could I do? The truth is that I despise Hitler and everything he stands for. When I think of what he has done to my country... He's a monster! Have you ever heard the things he says? I want to vomit every time I have to say 'Heil Hitler'! But I do love my country, and I won't be a traitor. I would be shot if my superiors ever heard me talk like this. Do you want to know what kind of man I am, Isabella? I'll tell you. I'm a hypocrite and a coward!" His body shook with rage, and despair veiled the luster of his eyes.

"No, Günter," she murmured. "You mustn't think of yourself that way. I know you're loyal to Germany and to your comrades, but to be forced to serve a government you hate... It must be unbearable. But it doesn't make you a coward. You have a conscience. And I...I can't explain why I wanted to meet Mussolini tonight. But I'm *not* a Fascist. I hate Mussolini as much as you hate Hitler!"

My God, what have I just admitted? Yet any distress she might have felt before, any fear of revealing too much suddenly vanished.

When she looked at him now she didn't see a German officer; she saw only the man she loved. The last barrier to her heart shattered and her feelings poured forth unrestrained. Drawing close, she wrapped her arms around him.

"I love you so much, Günter!" She had said those words before, but never allowed herself to believe them. She realized now that she had deceived herself for months—she knew she was deeply in love with him.

They held each other and didn't speak. Isabella caressed the tense muscles of his shoulders, trying to ease his pain with her loving touch. She ran her

188

fingers up the back of his neck and stroked his soft, thick hair. Her pulse quickened, and she pressed her lips against his with a fervor she hadn't felt before. As their ardor rose, they hastily stripped off their clothes. Günter laid her down on the floor and drenched her body with kisses. With mounting urgency, he grasped her buttocks with one hand while the other traced a burning path from the curve of her throat to her taut, quivering belly. She clung to him, burying her face against the damp skin of his chest, and impetuously raked his back with her fingernails. For an instant they paused, pledging their love in a silent, ardent gaze, and then arousal flared again—he parted her lips with his insistent mouth and they locked in an embrace. Her body arched toward his and she welcomed him into her. In that moment she became his completely. Seized by an irrepressible passion, they surrendered to desire until Isabella cried out and Günter shuddered intensely, reaching a tumultuous climax.

They lay beside each other breathing heavily as their hearts slowly recovered their normal pace. Isabella nestled close to Günter and rested her head on his shoulder. Then he turned and kissed her tenderly on the forehead.

"Forgive me," he entreated.

"Forgive you for what?"

"For the way I acted, like a jealous fool. I should have trusted you."

"It's all right, Günter."

"I should have trusted my own heart. You're everything to me, Isabella. Don't you know that? You're my whole world. How could I ever have doubted you? When this war is over, I only pray there will be someplace for us to spend our lives together."

Isabella's eyes welled up with tears as she tried to imagine if such a thing could possibly come true.

It will never be for us. She could no longer deny that her love for Günter was real and profound, yet she saw that a future with him was hopeless. She knew then that she had no choice but to leave him. She knew that her mission was over.

Chapter 21

The first rays of morning light barely illuminated the cobblestones of Piazza delle Erbe as the frigid January winds slashed through Isabella's frayed wool coat. Wrapping her arms around herself, she shivered from cold and trepidation. It would be difficult enough to explain to Massimo that she'd failed to kill Mussolini. How was she now to tell him that she'd resolved to abandon the operation entirely?

Isabella had given so much for Massimo. She'd risked her honor, her self-respect—even her life—for their scheme to succeed. She had been afraid to break free of his influence, to allow her own feelings to rule her. How would he respond to her decision to end the ploy?

While Günter had remained merely an enjoyable distraction she could abide the deceit, telling herself that victory for the partisan cause would erase the scars on her conscience. She would disappear back into her former life and Günter would be none the wiser. He would return to his homeland, eventually forget her, and pick up his life where he'd left it. Neither of them would remain devastated forever. In the end, righteousness would prevail and all her indiscretions would be forgiven.

But now she had made her last sacrifice—her heart. She had fooled herself for months, thinking she could walk away unscathed. *I should have backed out long ago.* She couldn't imagine a life with

191

Günter; neither of them would ever betray comrades or country. Now that she realized how deeply she loved him she had to get out, before irreversible damage was done. But what else had she lost in all of this? Likely, her relationship with Massimo would never be the same. Günter was the man she loved. She could no longer deceive him, nor could she stay with him, knowing how she'd used him.

Finally, Massimo drove up in his truck. Her stomach clenched as she reached for the door handle. Climbing in, she was struck by his icy glare.

"I listened to the radio this morning, gathered intelligence from every source I could find. It appears that our Duce still lives! In fact, from what I hear, he's never been more fit in his life. The poison I gave you is slow-acting, but not *that* slow!"

"Massimo, please..."

"I want to know exactly what happened last night."

"I just couldn't get close enough. There were too many people around."

"So you never even got near him?" Isabella shook her head. "What an incredible waste. This was our chance, Isabella! I could have made a name for myself."

"Yes, at *my* expense. If I'd been caught I would have been killed! You had nothing to lose here— nothing. All the glory for you and any unpleasant consequences for me. Why didn't you risk your *own* life and do it yourself?"

"I wasn't invited to the party. I don't have Fascist friends like you do."

"Stop it, Massimo, just stop it! I've had it with all of this. I'm through. Do you understand?"

"Fine, Isabella. No more assassination plots. You can go to all of the Fascist parties you want to and just enjoy yourself. No killing required."

"Don't patronize me."

"Well, I suppose it wasn't your fault. If you couldn't get close enough... Maybe it just wasn't meant to happen last night."

"It's not only about last night. I'm through with it, *all* of it."

"What are you talking about?"

"This spying has gone on for too long. I'm not going back to Palazzo Maggiore. I want to come home." Her voice wavered. "Have you...have you any idea what I've been through, what I've risked? I can't do it anymore!"

"Is it Schumann? Is he treating you harshly?"

"No, it's not that. It's just that I can't stand to lie anymore. Haven't I done enough? Can't I just stop now?"

His tone softened. "I know it's been hard for you. You've contributed so much to our cause. You're a brave and dedicated soldier. But soldiers don't quit."

"You can't make me go back there!"

"No, of course I can't. It's your decision, Isabella. But I need you to return to German headquarters one more time."

"Why?"

"I think you made some error in those last dispatches you copied. The intelligence didn't make any sense. In fact, it led us in the opposite direction from where we needed to be."

"I don't understand. I was scrupulous with my translation."

"I need you to return and check the supply log again."

"I don't know..."

"One more mission. You can't just leave us hanging now. You must confirm the information you gathered. If you get it right this time, we can intercept the next leg of the shipment. I know I can count on you."

She felt torn in her loyalties. She had vowed not

to deceive Günter again, but how could she let down her comrades? She'd gone this far; surely she could endure one last night of espionage.

"All right, Massimo. But this will be the last time—I swear it! I'll do it tonight. Günter will be leaving for headquarters in another hour. I'll pack up my things when he leaves. Can you come over to the apartment at ten o'clock and take my belongings with you?"

"Yes."

"Then meet me here tomorrow morning at five. Today will be my last day at the palazzo. Of course, I won't be giving Signora Vettori any notice. They'll never know what happened to me when I don't show up tomorrow. I'll sacrifice my final wages to get out of that place!"

"And what about Schumann? Will you give him any notice?" Massimo asked with a touch of sarcasm.

Isabella felt an ache in her throat at the thought of leaving Günter without even saying farewell. *How can I face him now and tell him it's over, especially after he shared his most private thoughts with me just yesterday? I can't possibly tell him I'm leaving him. But I must see him again.*

"No, I won't tell him I'm leaving. I'll just say good-bye to him this morning as usual." *But I cannot reveal that this will be the last time.*

****

Isabella returned to the apartment as Günter was dressing. She'd planned what she would tell him and how to disguise her distress.

"I've just seen my brother in the piazza. Mamma is very sick. I must go to see her tonight. He'll pick me up after my shift. I don't know how long I'll be gone. You might as well sleep at the barracks until I return."

"Oh, Isabella, I'm so sorry about your mother. Is there anything the doctors can do for her?"

194

"I...I don't know." She looked down, trying to hold back her tears.

He lifted her head gently with his hand and caressed her face. This only increased her despair as she looked into his adoring eyes, and her anguish broke through in sobs.

"My poor darling!" He enfolded her in his arms. "I wish I could go with you. I'll pray for her."

"Thank you, Günter. You'd better hurry or you'll be late."

She broke away from his embrace, ran to the bathroom, and tried to compose herself. *Why did I come back here to say good-bye? I can barely face him.*

A little while later Günter knocked on the bathroom door. "Isabella, I must leave now. Come out so I know you're all right."

She opened the door and threw her arms around his neck. "I love you so much, Günter!"

"I love you, too, Liebchen. Will you call me at the palazzo from your mother's house and let me know how she is doing?"

"We don't have a telephone. But I'll have my brother bring you a message if anything changes. Hopefully, I'll be back in a few days." This last falsehood nearly brought on another barrage of weeping, but she called upon all of her strength to suppress it.

With a last tender kiss he departed. She sank down onto their bed, and gave way to grief. She then began wandering through the apartment, gathering her possessions as she glanced at reminders of her time with Günter—small gifts they'd given each other, one of his shirts lazily flung over a chair in the bedroom, the dried flowers she'd kept from the first bouquet he'd given her. *Will I ever be able to forget him?* She imagined what he might think when she didn't contact him. *How long will he wait before he begins to worry? Would he try to find me somehow? Can I just disappear without a word?*

She decided that she would leave him a note—a final farewell, an attempt at closure. It was the least she could do, considering the heartache she knew he would suffer. It took her a long time to compose. There were so many things she wanted to say, so many things she couldn't tell him. In the end, it was a simple good-bye, no explanations or excuses. She told him she loved him but that they must never see each other again.

****

Later that morning, after Massimo had picked up her things, she walked to the palazzo for her last day of work. She tried to comfort herself with the thought that her life of deception would soon be over and she could return to her home and family. But all day she fixated on the image of Günter's face when they parted. She fretted about her final mission, anxious for it all to be over. She was careful to avoid him, even skipping their cigarette break together. She prayed that he would not come looking for her. As the hours crawled by, she tried to busy herself with work; she offered to polish all of the silver to avert even a moment of idle reflection.

When nine o'clock finally came, she feigned her departure as usual and crept down to the basement. After nearly an hour, she felt it was safe and made her way up to the second floor. The palazzo was quiet; not a step was heard from the floor above as she let herself into the administrative offices and closed the door behind her. In the dim illumination of her flashlight, she found her way to Gerhardt's desk. She unlocked the bottom drawer and removed the metal box that contained the supply logs. Grabbing the Italian/German dictionary from the top of Günter's desk, she sat on the floor, unlocked the box, and pored over the contents. She compared the entries in the log with those in her notebook. The information matched what she had copied the last time she was there. She checked again, referring to the dictionary to make certain her translation was correct. She verified that a large supply of ammunition had left Bolzano, via the eastern route near Rovigo, to the final destination of Ferrara, just as she had previously noted. Assured that she had not made any errors, she wondered if perhaps Massimo had made the mistake. *He must have misinterpreted my notes.* After about an hour of work, she was finished. She replaced the documents exactly as she had found them and put the box back into the drawer. She sighed with relief as she opened the door, glad that this miserable task was behind her.

Stepping into the hallway, she found herself confronted with an unimaginable obstacle—a barrier of gray-green uniforms obstructed her passage. With a gasp, she glanced up at their faces. The two SS men glared down at her, grabbing her before she could even consider trying to flee. It would have been fruitless. She had no chance of escape.

Chapter 22

After spending the night in his barracks, Günter arrived at the palazzo and was surprised to learn that the daily staff meeting had been cancelled. Neither Colonel von Haeften nor Günter's immediate superior, Major Gerhardt, were anywhere in the office. He supposed they were called away to a meeting that did not involve him. But there was plenty of work waiting for Günter at his desk, and he didn't need supervision to tackle it. By mid-afternoon, he had gotten through most of it when a private came into the office and approached him.

"Captain, the colonel would like to speak with you."

"The colonel? I haven't seen him all day. Where is he?"

"He's downstairs in the small conference room, sir."

"All right. Thank you, Private."

Günter was puzzled to hear that the colonel was on the premises. Not having seen him, he'd assumed that he was away from the palazzo. *Well, perhaps he just returned,* he thought with little concern as he made his way down to the conference room. When he entered the room, a strange sense of uneasiness swept over him.

"You sent for me, Colonel von Haeften?"

"Yes, come in, Captain Schumann. This is Major Dietrich of the Waffen-SS. You know Major Gerhardt and Sergeant Müller, of course. Please sit down."

Günter took the seat indicated by the colonel and immediately felt the tension among them. They were all watching him, following every movement he made.

"Is something wrong, Colonel?"

The colonel looked troubled but managed to keep his tone even. "You might say that, Captain. Or perhaps I should say 'Lieutenant.' You'll be lucky if you get out of this with just a demotion."

"Sir?" Günter struggled to remain calm as his heart beat so fiercely that he imagined everyone in the room could see it throbbing right through his chest.

"Captain Schumann, may I see your keys, if you please?"

Still mystified and fearing imminent doom, Günter felt inside his front trouser pocket and handed over a large ring of keys in various shapes and sizes. The colonel set out several crudely made keys on the table and began to seek matches between the two sets. All remained silent for several minutes as the colonel found a mate for each of the loose keys with those on Günter's ring.

"Tell me, Captain," the colonel said as he looked up, "do you know a woman by the name of Isabella Ricci?"

Günter's jaw dropped and his hands began to shake. His mind reeled, trying to reconcile the disparate notions...keys...demotion...Isabella? But nothing made sense. "Yes," he replied cautiously.

"And what exactly is the nature of your relationship to her?"

His eyes darted among the other four pairs, searching for a clue as to how he should respond.

"I suggest you just tell us the truth."

Günter stared down at his hands and took a deep breath before looking up and meeting the colonel's gaze. "We are lovers." No one spoke for several agonizing seconds. "Please, Colonel, tell me what this is all about."

The colonel's tone shifted to one of almost fatherly concern. "Did you know that your girlfriend is a spy, working for the partisans?"

"What..." Günter was on his feet in a second. "What do you mean?" He stared at the others, as if somehow they could help him to understand. Then he turned to his commander. "I don't believe you!"

"Please sit down, Captain Schumann! I see you are as shocked as we were by this revelation. That will mitigate matters for you, but I must say that you are at the very least incredibly stupid! How you could let yourself be deceived by a woman, I cannot understand. The only explanation is that you are one of those young men who allow another organ besides the brain to do their thinking!"

The colonel went on. "This woman somehow made duplicates of your keys and used them to break into the command office. She was able to access lockboxes that contained secure information about supply routes and shipments. We began to suspect a security breach somewhere, so we planted false information in various places to uncover the source. Once we narrowed it down to those boxes, we set the trap and caught her right in the act, with the duplicate keys in her possession. We questioned her for hours, but she would tell us nothing of consequence. Major Gerhardt recognized her as someone he had seen with you on several occasions, and that is how we put the rest of it together, except for one thing. How do you suppose she got to your keys?"

Günter lifted his head to reveal the face of a stricken man. "I don't know, sir. Maybe she did it while I slept. Where is she?"

"We have her here in custody. You know, of

course, what we do with spies?" Günter nodded. "Since she will not reveal the names of her associates or their location, she is really of no use to us. Perhaps you could try talking to her, Captain. She may be more compliant if you speak to her alone. Tell her we will spare her life if she tells us what we want to know."

"Is that true?"

"No, but you'll convince her it is. Either way, she'll be shot in the morning. Sergeant, please show Captain Schumann to the interrogation room." The colonel stood and put his hand on Günter's shoulder. "I know this is not easy for you, Günter. Come see me again when you are finished with her. I have a few more questions for you."

Günter followed the sergeant downstairs to the basement and through a long hallway. Müller knocked on a door, which was then unlocked and opened by a guard inside the room. Günter entered and Sergeant Müller returned upstairs.

"Corporal, would you please wait outside?" Günter asked the guard.

"Yes, sir. Call me if you need me," he offered as he exited the room, closing the door behind him.

Isabella was seated in a wooden chair on the far side of the windowless room, her bound hands resting on her lap. She looked up at Günter with bleary eyes but said nothing. Her face was red and swollen and there was dried blood in the corner of her mouth. A large purple bruise extended from her right ear down to her jaw line. Her clothes were torn, her hair in disarray.

Günter glared at her for at least a minute, his hands clenched at his sides, before he could begin to speak. "How...how could you do this? You traitorous bitch!" he erupted. "I've no idea who you are! How could you do this to me?" He raised his fist and saw her flinch, then turned and picked up a chair and heaved it across the room where it struck the wall and landed in pieces.

"Everything all right, Captain?" he heard from outside the door.

"Just fine, Corporal." He stepped toward her again and lifted her with a firm grip on both upper arms. "Tell me who your comrades are and it will go easier for you."

She cried out in pain, tears overflowing her eyelids. "Please let go of me." He released his grasp and she slid back into the chair. He pulled up her sleeve to reveal an ugly distention of her left arm. "I think it's broken."

He turned from her in disgust—both for her crime and for the treatment she'd received. He fought to hold back his tears before he looked at her again. "If you don't tell them what they want to know you will be shot."

"I have nothing to tell them, and even if I did, I know they would shoot me anyway. You are not a very good liar, Günter."

"Yes, and you'd be a good judge of that!" He leaned against the wall and for the first time allowed the tears to run freely down his cheeks. "You're right; I won't lie to you. You're to be executed in the morning."

Neither said a word for several minutes, Günter resting his head against the wall and Isabella sitting with her head bowed.

Suddenly she looked up at him again. "I must ask you something." Her voice quivered.

"What is it?"

"Do you...do you think...you can ever forgive me?"

He stared at her in astonishment. "Forgive you? You've ruined my life and now you want me to forgive you? I'll probably be court-martialed because of you! You'd have better luck asking God for forgiveness. In fact, I think you would be wise to start asking Him now. You haven't much time. I've nothing else to say to you, Isabella."

"Günter..." She wept, but he turned toward the door.

In that instant a deafening explosion knocked them both to the ground. Another blast followed, seconds later. They heard screams and chaos erupting on the floor above them. Günter was covered with dust but otherwise unhurt. He looked over at Isabella, who had managed to push her body up, with her hands still bound, to a sitting position. As Günter got to his feet, the door opened.

"Are you all right, Captain?" the guard asked.

"Yes, I think so. What in God's name was that?" They stepped into the hallway but could see little through a thickening haze of dust and debris.

Günter stood there for a moment or two, dazed, trying to decide what to do. "Corporal, go and find out what's happened. I'll stay here with the prisoner. Report back to me right away."

"Yes, sir," replied the guard as he raced off down the hall.

Several minutes later, Major Gerhardt appeared at the door. "Günter, we've been bombed! The whole building is on fire—we've got to get out of here! You'll have to shoot her. We can't take any prisoners with us now."

Günter stared at the major, and then looked at Isabella. Then he turned back to the major and asked in disbelief, "You mean now?"

"Yes, now! If you can't do it, I will."

Günter slowly drew his sidearm, cocked it and pointed it at Isabella's chest. His right hand trembled, so he tried to steady it with the other.

After several seconds, Major Gerhardt drew his own pistol. "I understand. You're man enough to fuck her, but not man enough to do your duty! What a pathetic excuse for a soldier you are. Step aside. I'll take care of this."

As Gerhardt raised his arm to fire, a shot rang out from Günter's gun. The major's body crumpled to the ground with a bullet through his face. His lifeless eyes stared blankly as blood gushed from the back of his head.

Günter lowered his arms and stood there, paralyzed by revulsion and self-loathing. *"Mein Gott...what have I done?"*

"You saved my life!" gasped Isabella.

Günter felt a sudden, violent wave of nausea overwhelm him. He knelt down and vomited.

"Come on, let's get out of here!" Isabella struggled to her feet and tugged at Günter's sleeve until he rose. "Please untie me," she pleaded as she held her hands out to him.

In a stupor, he holstered his sidearm, drew his dagger and cut through the cords that bound her wrists. Pulling him by the arm, she all but dragged him to the open door.

"We should head toward the back of the building," she insisted. "If we go that way, there's a chance they won't see us. I know the basement well."

They groped along a darkened passageway and reached a staircase. Dodging crumbling plaster as the disintegrating palazzo creaked and groaned above them, they ascended and found an undamaged exit.

Günter turned and looked at Isabella, then at his own uniform. They were both filthy and spattered with blood—Major Gerhardt's blood. The perilous gravity of the situation into which his instinctive act to protect Isabella had propelled him began to penetrate his consciousness. Circumspection and subterfuge were now critical. Günter opened the door and looked out. There was little activity in the alleyway, but he could see crowds gathering on side streets to watch the conflagration. Rescue efforts would be focused at the front of the building as it quickly became a blazing ruin. He took her hand and led her down the alleyway, keeping close to the wall for cover.

"You should try to make a run for it, before anyone starts looking for you. Go to the Church of Santa Maria degli Angeli on Via Portici. Tell Father Michele I sent you. He's a good man—he'll help you."

"Come with me, Günter!"

He looked at her with scorn. "I've already committed murder and treason for you. I won't become a deserter, too."

"If they find out what you've done, they'll shoot you!"

"Then let's hope they don't find out. I'll take my chances. Now get out of here before I change my mind about letting you escape." His hand went to his sidearm, as if to warn her. "Go!"

With one last glance at Günter, Isabella ran down another alleyway and disappeared.

By the time Günter got to the front of the palazzo, it had been nearly consumed by fire. The fire brigade succeeded only in keeping the flames from spreading to nearby buildings. Several floors had already collapsed and Günter prayed that his crime would remain mutely entombed beneath tons of rubble. As he searched around for his colleagues, he spotted Colonel von Haeften sitting on a low wall, attended by a medic.

"Are you all right, sir?" Günter asked as he approached.

"Yes, I'm fine," the colonel responded after a fit of coughing. "Major Gerhardt went to find you. Have you seen him?"

"No, sir. Did everyone get out?"

"The field marshal and his staff are safe, thank God. We're missing a few men from our unit:

Gerhardt, Ehrler, Steinhoff, and Graf. Would you leave me be, please?" he said with annoyance to the medic. "How did you manage to get out, Captain? Oh, and where's the girl, our prisoner?"

Günter had prepared for this query. "She's dead, sir. I felt it best to shoot her, under the circumstances." He looked down at the ground and tried to relax his breathing. He knew that his voice trembled when he spoke, but hoped his commander would take it as grief instead of deceit. It was, in fact, a mixture of both.

"I see," the colonel said as he glimpsed the specks of blood on Günter's tunic. "Well, that's an end to it then. We will punish the bastards who did this. You'll need to tell me everything you know about the girl, where you met her, who her friends are, and so forth. Now go see what you can find out about our missing men. We'll convene at SS headquarters. Report to me there this evening."

"Yes, sir," said Günter as he moved on to search for his missing comrades.

Chapter 23

Ducking into doorways and stealing along narrow streets, Isabella reached the Church of Santa Maria degli Angeli several blocks from the palazzo. She opened the door and stopped briefly to bless herself with holy water. *I should probably bathe in it,* she thought sacrilegiously, as she glanced down at her dirty and disheveled appearance. It occurred to her that perhaps her guilt-ridden soul needed cleansing, too. Late afternoon Mass was in progress, and a small number of worshippers were scattered throughout the church. She skirted the perimeter of the sanctuary and found a tiny chapel where she could rest unobserved. She sat in a pew in the back corner, and as exhaustion, pain and remorse overtook her, she began to weep profusely. Looking up at the merciful face of the Virgin, she felt compelled to pray. Her injured arm braced gingerly with the other, Isabella rose to kneel beneath the statue.

"Blessed Mother, protect him!" she whispered. "He is so good, so innocent. He only killed to save me. Please don't let him die!"

She sobbed despondently but struggled for restraint, lest she draw attention to herself. Mass had ended and the church was now very quiet. She heard someone approach, then realized that the young celebrant was standing over her, his face evincing benevolence.

"Excuse me, signorina. Are you all right?"

"Are you Father Michele?"

"No, I'm Father Sebastiano. Can I help you in some way?"

"Is Father Michele here? A friend told me I should speak to him."

"He's resting in the rectory. Here, why don't we get you something to eat, and you can wait for him in the back."

Isabella looked at her torn and filthy clothes. *He probably thinks I'm a beggar.* He offered his hand, but she clutched her injured arm against her body. Awkwardly, she stood and turned to him. His concerned expression heightened to alarm as he observed her battered face.

"Are you hurt? Perhaps we should call a doctor."

"No, not yet. Please let me wait for Father Michele first."

"Well, at least come with me so we can get you cleaned up. Don't worry, my child, no one will hurt you here."

"All right. Thank you, Father," she replied and followed him through a door at the back of the church to the rectory. He led her into the kitchen.

"Ah, Santa Madonna!" exclaimed the middle-aged woman who stood before the stove. "Look at this poor child! Father, where did you find her?"

"She was praying in the little chapel of the Virgin. Signora Leone, this is... Oh, I'm sorry. What is your name, my child?"

"Isabella."

"Isabella, Signora Leone is our housekeeper. She will take good care of you while I check on Father Michele. Why don't you give her something to eat, signora?"

"Of course, Father."

The older woman looked at Isabella and shook her head. She got a bowl from the cupboard and filled it from the simmering pot of soup on the stove.

"This is for the Fathers' supper tonight, but it's nearly done, so you can be the first to taste it. Here, sit down and eat, my dear." She held out a chair.

Isabella's hand trembled as she tried to lift the spoon. She set it down and returned to cradling her left arm with her right. The pain was nearly unbearable.

"What's wrong with your arm, Isabella? Let me look." The housekeeper examined her, taking in the bruises and the spattering of blood on her dress. Her nose wrinkled, as she seemed to detect the strange, burning odor emanating from Isabella's clothing and hair. "You were in that fire on Via Scaligeri, weren't you?"

"Please, signora, don't say anything. I really must speak to Father Michele."

At that moment, a frail, white-haired priest entered the kitchen. "Is this the young lady who is looking for me? Father Sebastiano tells me your name is Isabella and that you wish to speak with me. What can I do for you, my child?"

"Father Michele?" He nodded. "Please, could we speak alone?"

Signora Leone raised her eyebrows slightly and sighed, then followed the younger priest out of the kitchen. Father Michele sat next to Isabella at the table.

"Father, do you know Günter Schumann? He told me you could help me."

"Yes, I know Günter. Is he a friend of yours?"

"Yes." She swallowed hard. *I've got to trust him. I've nowhere else to turn.* "Father, I'm hiding from the Nazis. If they find me they'll kill me."

"Did they do this to you?" he asked, his voice filled with compassion. Isabella nodded. "Why?"

"I'm a partisan. I was searching for documents at German headquarters in Palazzo Maggiore when they caught me. They were going to shoot me, but..."

She stopped. Would the priest protect Günter's secret, too? *He sent me here,* she reminded herself. "Günter helped me escape. He told me to come here and see you."

"The fire at the palazzo today, I heard it was a bombing. Do you know anything about that?"

"No, Father, I swear I don't. If it was partisans I don't think it was my group. But it was pure luck that it happened when it did. Otherwise I wouldn't have had the chance to escape."

"I don't believe in luck, my child. It is all part of His plan. Where is Günter? Is he all right?"

"I...I don't know." She began to weep again. "I begged him to come with me. If the Germans find out that he helped me..." She couldn't finish the thought. The toll of the day's events bore down on her, and she laid her head on the table as she broke down in sobs.

"Come, my child, everything will be all right. Let us pray together." He gently placed his hand on her head and began: "Ave Maria, gratia plena, Dominus tecum. Benedicta tu in mulieribus, et benedictus fructus ventris tui, Iesus..." When he finished, he left to find Father Sebastiano. Isabella had nearly passed out from grief and exhaustion.

Father Michele instructed the young priest to go and get Dr. Giambalvo. "Tell him she may have a broken arm but we cannot bring her to the hospital. He must treat her here, if at all possible. Do not discuss this with anyone else. No one must know she is here. You understand?"

"Yes, Father. I will return as quickly as I can."

Signora Leone and Father Michele managed to get Isabella to take in a little food and water. Then the signora showed Isabella to a guest room and helped her undress. When she saw the bruises and welts covering Isabella's body she gasped.

"Oh, Dio mio! Who did this to you?"

"You've been so kind to me, signora. But can we please talk about this tomorrow?" Isabella looked down and blinked away a tear.

The housekeeper nodded sympathetically. She washed Isabella as best she could, gave her clean clothes from the collection they kept for the poor, and then helped her into bed.

When the doctor arrived and examined her, he diagnosed a slight fracture of the humerus. He prepared a cast and sling, gave her a dose of morphine and advised several days of bed rest.

Father Michele saw Dr. Giambalvo to the door. "Thank you so much, Doctor. I know you will be discreet about this. Her life may be in great danger."

"I haven't lost a patient from a broken arm yet," the doctor assured. "Don't worry, Father, no one will know about her, not from me, anyway."

****

Isabella awoke, sluggish and disoriented, in the clean white guest room of the rectory. When she attempted to rise, a jolt of pain shot through her body and her left arm throbbed in agony. The cast on her arm was obvious, but she couldn't remember the injury. She laid her head back on the pillow, trying to recall where she was and what had occurred. Images randomly bombarded her brain: the terror of her arrest, her brutal beating at the hands of her captors, a panicked escape from a burning building... She couldn't quite put the pieces together. Somehow she knew that her life was in danger, though she couldn't remember why. She sank down into the bed and pulled the covers over her eyes. *If I stay here I will be safe.* Suddenly, there was a knock at the door.

"Who's there?" Isabella called out.

"It's Signora Leone, Isabella. May I come in?"

Isabella didn't recall the name. *I might as well let her in. I can't hide here forever, especially if I don't know where I am.* "Yes, all right."

A plump, mature woman entered the room, bearing a tray. When she set it down next to the bed, Isabella saw the bread, cheese, and steaming pot of coffee and realized she was famished.

"Is that for me?" Isabella asked.

"Yes, of course, my dear. How are you feeling?"

"I...I have some pain...my arm...and my side."

The signora helped Isabella as she struggled to sit up. "Here, you must be very hungry," Signora Leone said as she set the tray on Isabella's lap and poured a cup of coffee for her.

"Thank you." Isabella hesitated. "I'm sorry, but I just can't remember what happened. Where am I?"

The signora smiled and patted Isabella's hand. "It must be the morphine. You're in the rectory of Santa Maria degli Angeli. You came here yesterday to see Father Michele. He sent for the doctor to look after you. Don't you remember the fire at Palazzo Maggiore?"

Palazzo Maggiore... Isabella was silent for several moments as the pieces began to fall into place. "Oh, God! He was going to shoot me...then Günter..." She stopped abruptly and started to tremble. *What has happened to Günter?*

The signora's eyes widened. "Someone was going to shoot you?"

"I need to speak to Father Michele," Isabella said, ignoring the question.

"Why don't you finish your breakfast first? I will come back in a little while to help you dress. I'll let the Father know that you wish to see him."

"Thank you, signora."

Isabella had finished everything on the tray when Signora Leone returned and helped her into the clean clothes they had provided. They improvised with a large, pullover sweater to avoid repositioning her injured arm. The signora led her down the hallway to Father Michele's study.

"Come in, my child. How are you feeling today?"

"My arm hurts, and my side. I think I might have a broken rib. I'm a little dazed, too. At first I couldn't remember what happened to me, but it's starting to make sense now. Thank you for taking care of me, Father."

"Not at all, my dear. I'll make sure Dr. Giambalvo comes to see you today. Now, is there someone from your family we can contact? They must be very worried about you."

Suddenly, Isabella remembered that she was supposed to meet Massimo at the piazza. *When was that? God, that must have been early yesterday morning! He must be terrified for me.*

"I must get a message to Massimo, my...fiancé." She tried to think of a way to reach him, and then remembered the bakery. "Can someone bring a note for him to the San Lorenzo Bakery on Via Mazzini?"

"Of course," Father Michele said as he handed her a piece of paper and a pen. She composed a brief note, telling him she was safe but in hiding, and that he should come as soon as he could to Santa Maria's to get her.

"This must go directly to Stefano at the bakery and no one else," she insisted as she handed the note to the priest.

"I'll make sure that he gets it, Isabella."

Chapter 24

The German staff worked late into the night, assessing the casualties and damage from the fire and setting up temporary facilities at SS headquarters, a block away from the palazzo. They deduced that the tremendous damage which left the building in ruins was the result of two strategically placed incendiary bombs. The field marshal and General Staff had been in the basement war room at the time of the bombing and escaped without injury. Of the two hundred or so in the building, thirty-four perished, many of the bodies never to be recovered. Additionally, the loss of important documents, maps and intelligence reports was enormous; it would take weeks to reconstruct the information. The SS personnel accommodated their colleagues as best they could, but space was at a premium and there was talk of moving some of the operations to Palazzo Fabriano, outside the city. Security procedures were scrutinized to prevent another such calamity.

Günter reported to Colonel von Haeften, who had set up a temporary office in a small conference room. Major Dietrich, the SS officer whom Günter had already met, was there also.

"Come in, Captain Schumann. Please sit down."

"Thank you, sir. I have figures on the casualties. It appears we've lost thirty-two men, as well as two women from the domestic staff, not counting Signorina Ricci, of course," Günter reported, remembering that Isabella was supposed to be dead.

"Forty-seven were injured, nineteen seriously."

"These criminals will pay. Major Dietrich and his men are already working on leads. But if we don't find the culprits, we've enough detainees at Scalci prison to carry out a reprisal in accordance with the Führer's edict." Günter knew that meant ten Italians would die for every German killed in the attack. "But I've a few questions for you, Captain. Tell me everything you know about Isabella Ricci. Where did you meet her and with whom did she associate?"

Günter hesitated. *Must I inform on Silvia and Federico? What other friends of Isabella's do I know?* It suddenly struck him how little he knew about her. "Sir, I met her at a party in Palazzo Fabriano in September. She came there with her friend, Silvia Matteo. But I've no reason to believe that Silvia was involved in any of this."

"That will be for us to determine. Who were her other friends?"

"I really don't know, sir. Silvia Matteo is close to Federico di Balduccio, whom I believe is a member of the Fascist Party and associated with Il Duce. Isabella told me little of her family or other friends. I can't even tell you where they live."

"Didn't that seem a little odd to you? You were lovers for several months and you didn't even know where she lived?"

"Honestly, I never really thought about it before. I did meet her brother Leonardo, but no one else from her family. She told me she grew up on a farm outside of Verona but I've no idea where it is." *She kept so much from me, but I was too bewitched to see it.* In a sense he was relieved she hadn't told him the name of her village. He would be pressured to advise the colonel, and that would put her family in danger. And what if she were hiding there? If she were ever found alive he would surely be executed for treason.

His survival was now irrevocably linked to hers.

"You don't know where her family lived, and I know she didn't visit you at your quarters. So where did you go to carry on your liaison?"

"We always met at Silvia's apartment. Silvia had moved into Federico's villa, so Isabella and I really had the place to ourselves." The colonel asked for the addresses of the apartment and the villa, and Günter could do nothing but comply. *Hopefully, she has the sense not to go there. If she does, both of our lives are over.*

"That will be all for now, Captain Schumann. I'll let you know if we need anything else from you."

"Sir..." Günter faltered.

"Yes, Captain?"

"Sir, I wonder if...I mean...am I to face any charges?"

"I don't know yet. Unfortunately, we are quite short of personnel at the moment. If I have you arrested I will be at a loss to replace your services. And now with Major Gerhardt gone, I need to depend on you even more. Besides, I'm inclined to believe you are innocent of any complicity in this espionage plot. If you were involved, you'd have merely given her the information she wanted. She wouldn't have risked capture by breaking into the offices at night. Major Gerhardt assured me of your loyalty to the Fatherland. He told me that you're rather naïve but was certain you could never commit treason. Nonetheless, I'll ask that you keep your movements confined to here and your barracks for the time being. Is that understood?"

"Yes, sir. Thank you."

****

Early the next morning, Major Dietrich and some of his men converged on the apartment, scrutinizing every inch of the place, opening every drawer, cabinet and closet, dumping the contents on

216

the floor and sifting through them for anything suspicious. A few letters were discovered and turned over to Dietrich, who knew Italian. On top of the dresser in the bedroom was a note, found beneath a small packet, and both were handed to Dietrich. The packet consisted of a string of pearls in a neatly folded handkerchief. The note appeared to be of a personal nature:

> *Günter,*
> *You told me I could return these to you if we ever parted. Sadly, I must leave you. Please do not try to find me. I cannot explain why I am compelled to do this—you would never understand and, believe me, it is better that you don't know. It was nothing that you did. All I can tell you is that there is a part of my life you know nothing about. Just know that I will always keep you in my heart. I love you very much, but we must never see each other again. God keep you safe, Günter.*
> *Isabella*

The colonel did not need to seek out Federico and Silvia; instead, they came to him. They had learned of the fire the previous night and were terribly concerned about Isabella. When they went to the apartment to see if she was there, they found it in shambles, as if robbers had raided it. The landlady told them that German soldiers had been there, turned the place upside down, and interrogated her about whom she had seen coming and going. Silvia was bewildered and frightened, but Federico insisted that the only place to find answers would be German headquarters. When they arrived at the interim command center, they were shown to the room Colonel von Haeften now occupied. Major Dietrich was there and interpreted for the colonel.

Federico introduced Silvia and himself. He

spoke before the colonel had a chance to ask them anything. "We just came from Signorina Matteo's apartment. It was completely ransacked, and we were told that German soldiers had been there. We were looking for her close friend, Isabella Ricci, who is staying there. Do you know anything about this, Colonel?"

"So, you're a close friend of Signorina Ricci? Tell me, how well do you know her?"

"We went to school together and we've been sharing that apartment for several months. She worked at Palazzo Maggiore, as you may know. Can you please tell me if she is all right?" Silvia responded anxiously.

"It's so strange that you should come here today. We were going to invite the two of you here for an interview. Thank you for saving us the trouble of finding you." Silvia and Federico exchanged nervous glances. "Sergeant," the colonel called out.

"Yes, Colonel?" he said as he entered.

"Please go and find Captain Schumann. He's probably in the staff room we've set up on the third floor. Tell him I need to see him right away."

"Yes, sir."

Silvia and Federico waited uneasily for several minutes until Günter entered the room. He looked at them, and then looked down in embarrassment. He wondered whether they would be suspected of any involvement with Isabella's espionage, and how the colonel would explain her supposed death to them.

"Günter! Where is Isabella? Is she all right?" Silvia asked, her tone urgent.

Günter didn't know how to respond, but the colonel jumped in immediately. "I'll ask the questions here, all right? Signorina, what can you tell me about Signorina Ricci's political inclinations and activities?"

"I don't know a thing about them! We've never

discussed politics. Now would you please tell us what is going on?"

"All right, Signorina Matteo. Your friend Isabella was a spy for the partisans. We discovered her with classified documents at Palazzo Maggiore. We also suspect her involvement in yesterday's bombing. She's dead. She was to face a firing squad this morning, but amid the confusion of yesterday's disaster Captain Schumann took matters into his hands and dispatched her himself."

After a moment of stunned silence, Silvia turned to Günter and cried, "Tell me this isn't true, Günter! You...you killed her? She loved you so! Please tell me it isn't true..." Silvia dissolved into tears.

Günter struggled to maintain his composure. "She was a spy, Silvia. I was only doing my duty."

Federico attempted to comfort Silvia, then stated with disdain, "Sir, do you have any idea who I am? I assure you, Il Duce will not be pleased when he finds out how we've been treated here."

"We are simply trying to gather information. Do you realize that thirty-four people died in the attack on the palazzo? I am certain Il Duce, as well as our Führer, will be grateful for your full cooperation," the colonel replied. "Major Dietrich, why don't you take these people to another room to continue your interrogation—I mean...conversation? I'd like to speak to Captain Schumann alone for a moment."

"Of course, Colonel," Dietrich said as he escorted Silvia and Federico out of the room. Silvia glanced contemptuously at Günter as she left.

"Captain, Major Dietrich found this at Signorina Matteo's apartment this morning. I believe it belongs to you." The colonel handed the small packet and its accompanying note to Günter, who opened it to reveal Isabella's pearls. After quickly reading the note he handed both back to the colonel.

"I don't want these, sir. I don't want any

reminders of her."

"I asked Dietrich to translate the contents of the note. It was enough to convince me of your innocence. I believe you were completely duped by this woman. But I think you should take these back. Those pearls must have cost a small fortune, especially on captain's wages. I'd hate to think that a subordinate of mine would be foolish enough to dispose of valuables so heedlessly. You can always sell them."

The colonel held out the pearls and the note until Günter took them back. He deposited both in his breast pocket.

"If there's nothing else, sir..."

"Well, there is one other thing. I would be negligent in my duties if I did not discipline you in some way for your inadvertent participation in this regrettable affair. I've decided that a letter of reprimand in your personnel file for 'fraternization' will suffice. There is no need for formal charges, provided your record remains without further blemish. It should be of little consequence to your military career, unless you had hopes of making colonel before the end of the war."

"No, sir. And thank you."

"That's all for now, Captain. You may return to your work."

After he left the room, Günter wondered why his commander had chosen to be so lenient. Perhaps the colonel felt that having to execute his own mistress was punishment enough.

****

The next day, Colonel von Haeften received a report from Major Dietrich on the progress of his investigation. He found no reason to hold Federico or Silvia, especially after confirming Federico's credentials with Fascist Party officials. They were released, with a personal apology from the field marshal himself. Information gained from informants pointed to several suspects in the bombing of the palazzo. Those captured and interrogated knew nothing of Isabella Ricci, leading Dietrich to conclude that she probably was not involved in the bombing, and that a separate partisan group was responsible.

Günter was relieved to hear this news. As much as he despised Isabella's treachery, he couldn't bear to imagine that she had participated in the murder of thirty-four people, among them close friends and comrades, including his roommate Kurt Graf. But Günter's pain was somewhat assuaged by the knowledge that apprehension of the actual perpetrators reprieved over three hundred political prisoners who would have been executed in their stead.

Chapter 25

Massimo received Isabella's message the day it was delivered and drove immediately to Santa Maria's to get her. When he saw her, he touched her face, tracing the darkened bruise that ran along her cheek. Anguish was etched in his gaze. He drew her into his arms with tender restraint, as if she were a porcelain doll that would shatter in his embrace.

Father Michele did not want her to leave yet, concerned that she was not well enough to travel, but Massimo insisted he would look after her vigilantly and would summon a doctor as soon as he got her home. When he expressed his gratitude to the priests for their care and shelter, Isabella thought she discerned the glimmer of moisture in his eyes. Not since the aftermath of Marco's death had he shown her such softhearted affection.

"I owe my life to all of you," she told the two priests and Signora Leone as Massimo helped her into his truck.

During the ride back to the farm, Massimo asked Isabella several times how she was feeling.

"Are you in much pain?"

"Yes, but I'll feel better when we're home."

"I was worried when you didn't show up at the piazza. And then when I heard about the fire... I didn't know what to think. You said in your note that you were hiding at Santa Maria's. Were you hiding from the Nazis? Will you tell me what happened?"

"Please, can we talk about this later? I'm so tired."

"Of course." He reached over and squeezed her hand. "I just want you to know how happy I am that you're safe."

"I know, Massimo."

At the farmhouse, their partisan companions greeted her warmly. Everyone had been anxious, fearing that she had died in the fire at Palazzo Maggiore. None knew of her arrest and escape from the Nazis.

Later, in the privacy of their cabin, Massimo was almost in tears, trembling as he spoke. "I was so worried about you, carina. I thought I had lost you forever."

"I nearly died, Massimo! You've no idea what I've been through," she said as she began to weep softly.

"Tell me...please."

"The Nazis caught me just as I was leaving the administrative offices. They tortured me for hours, but I told them nothing!"

"Oh, God, Isabella! I should have realized. I thought you were injured in the explosion."

"They locked me in a room in the basement and beat me. But they didn't break me—I swear it!" she sobbed. "They were going to shoot me."

"You must have been terrified." He stroked her face and kissed her on the forehead. "Did you escape during the fire?" A tear trickled down his cheek. Isabella had never seen him weep.

"Yes, but only because of Günter. He saved my life! After the explosion his superior officer, Major Gerhardt, came down to the interrogation room and ordered Günter to shoot me, right then and there. When Günter couldn't do it, Gerhardt pulled out his pistol and would have killed me himself...but Günter shot *him* instead! Oh, Massimo, if it weren't for

Günter, I'd be dead now!"

He held her gently in his arms, careful not to hurt her. They didn't speak for several moments.

Suddenly he gasped. "This is all my fault! You didn't want to return to the palazzo. If I hadn't made you go..."

"Don't blame yourself. You couldn't have known what would happen."

"I'm so sorry. I should have protected you."

"It's all right. It's over now. Please, can you make a fire for me? It's so cold in here."

"Of course, carina. Come, you should rest." He led her to their bed and helped her as she lay down and pulled the covers up to her chin. "Don't worry, Isabella, you're safe now. I'll never let anything happen to you again."

****

After a few days, Isabella asked if there was room for her in the main house. She told Massimo that it was too cold for her in the cabin, that she couldn't handle the spartan conditions in her weakened state. The only room available was tiny, barely larger than a closet, but she gladly accepted it. She dared not return to her family's home. She feared that if she were ever captured by the Germans, her family would suffer for it. It would be better to be found with other partisans who had already pledged to risk their lives for the cause.

As the weeks passed, her body grew stronger but her mind remained troubled. She had given up subversive work for the Resistance, helping only with household and farm chores. Massimo suggested she come back to their cabin, but she put him off with a variety of excuses: the cold, the inconvenience, that her body was not strong enough to bear physical intimacy. She was afraid to tell him the truth—that she had fallen in love with another man.

He found her alone in the kitchen one day and approached her again about their sleeping arrangements.

"I miss you so much, carina. Why won't you come home to me?"

"I can't live in that cabin anymore. I suppose I got used to the warmth and comfort of the apartment in Verona. I just can't abide the rustic life now."

"But you don't even want to come for a visit? You know, during the day? You don't have to spend the night. Don't you want to be with me?"

Isabella could see the apprehension and loneliness in his eyes. She felt dreadfully guilty at the thought that she was about to break his heart, but knew it was time to be honest with him.

"I can't go back to the way things used to be. I'm sorry. But I just can't live with you."

"You mean you don't love me anymore? It's that Nazi, isn't it?" The line of Massimo's mouth grew taut. "Are you in love with him?"

She looked at him for a moment, then her lashes dipped down. "Yes. I didn't mean for it to happen this way. I never wanted to hurt you. I only tried to do what you asked of me."

"How could you, Isabella? Falling in love with the enemy?"

"I didn't want to fall in love with him. I tried to resist. I'm sure you don't want to hear this, but he's really a wonderful man. Anyway, it doesn't matter now; I know I'll never see him again."

"I think you should return to your family," he said, his voice brittle.

"You know I can't go back there yet. Please don't hate me. I do care for you. I love you like a brother."

"I don't hate you. But what use is it to long for someone you'll never have?"

"There is no use to it, I know. But I can't help

225

how I feel. Perhaps I'll forget him in time, but it's too soon now. I need to be by myself for a while. I'm sorry, Massimo. You're very dear to me, you know."

"Yes, I know...like a brother," he replied, then walked away.

****

In the weeks following the bombing of Palazzo Maggiore, Günter occupied himself with the exhaustive work necessary to resume operations. The General Staff was moved to Palazzo Fabriano, with heightened security measures in place. Günter's administrative unit remained in the building shared with SS headquarters. He volunteered for extra duty whenever possible, attempting to take his mind off his disastrous relationship with Isabella. He asked Klaus to try to sell the pearls and to keep a generous commission for himself. Klaus accepted the assignment, happy for a chance to earn a little extra money.

For reasons he couldn't quite grasp, Günter kept Isabella's note. He read it repeatedly, as if to punish himself for his gullibility. Despite his efforts to forget her, he often lay awake at night, reflecting on her declarations of love and their tender moments of passion, wondering if it had all been an illusion. Recollections of blissful encounters tormented him, as the image of her lovely figure and face, her silken hair and expressive brown eyes invaded his unguarded moments and haunted his dreams.

But another specter disturbed Günter's consciousness: he agonized over his culpability in the death of Max Gerhardt. At first, he blamed Isabella for driving him to murder, but candid reflection convinced him that this was not her transgression but his own. Though she was accountable for deceit and betrayal, it was his choice to kill. She did not ask him to do it. Yet if he hadn't pulled the trigger and ended Max's life, Günter knew that the sight of his beloved dying before his eyes would have tortured him the rest of his life.

There was one place where Günter could try to relieve his anguish. Though he had not attended church since the disaster, he decided to seek its shelter and attempt to find solace for his wounded soul. He visited Santa Maria's one afternoon but was too overwrought and ashamed to enter the confessional. He knelt before the statue of the Virgin in the tiny chapel and prayed for strength. His heart was still heavy as he rose to leave, and then he saw Father Michele approach him.

"Günter? It's been quite a while since I've seen you. It must be weeks, since before the fire at Palazzo Maggiore. How are you, my son?"

"Well, Father...I'm all right. Physically, anyway."

"Your friend was very worried about you. She feared for your life," the priest whispered.

"How is she?"

"When I last saw her she was still recovering from her injuries, but I'm sure she's healing well now."

Günter didn't know how to respond. As her erstwhile lover, the man who had saved her life, he should be relieved to hear this, but as a loyal German officer... He didn't know what he should think or feel.

Father Michele scrutinized Günter's face. "I can see that something is troubling you. Would you like to tell me about it?"

"I...I don't know if I can, Father."

"Come. Let's have a talk."

He motioned to Günter to join him in a pew near the back of the empty church. After a lengthy silence, Günter began to confide in the priest as he poured out his heart, his deepest regrets and heaviest sins. Father Michele held Günter's hand, trying to ease his sorrow. Then Günter recited the Act of Contrition as Father Michele gave absolution.

"I will continue to pray for you, my son. You must not surrender to despair but must try to accept God's grace. God has forgiven you. You must try to forgive yourself."

"I will try, Father."

Chapter 26

Günter awoke and sat up in his cot with a sigh. He looked over at the empty bed across the room and the lump in his throat rose again, as it always did when he remembered that Kurt was gone. The awareness that his own bed had lacked the warm, soft body of a woman these last three months did nothing to ease his sullen mood.

He'd been fortunate to get three hours of sleep, considering the depressing progress of the war. It was common now at headquarters to work through the night. But at least there was adequate food there and a barracks to return to for occasional respite. Men at the front were lucky to get four ounces of stale bread and half a sausage a day.

The news from home wasn't any less dismal. His father's last letter noted the inexorable Allied advance on the eastern and western fronts and decried the relentless aerial bombings. Even their village had been hit. *It's a wonder his letter got through at all*. He supposed the censors didn't bother to black out defeatist language anymore, though he still feared reprisals against his family. Germans were hanged for less than that.

Talk at headquarters was getting bleaker, and even senior officers advised capitulation to minimize further casualties. Unlike Hitler, who would have sacrificed the last German soldier in his insane scheme to preserve the Reich, most generals knew better. But the Führer would not hear of surrender, and Günter and his comrades were cautious of what they discussed in front of the committed Nazis in their ranks.

****

Headquarters was more chaotic that morning than when Günter had left a few hours earlier.

"Sir, the colonel wants to see you," his aide informed him as Günter tossed his cap onto his desk.

"Thank you, Sergeant," he replied, even as he headed to Colonel von Haeften's office. Günter paused a moment to straighten his tunic and brace himself for what was likely very bad news. It was foolish to expect anything else at this point in the war.

"Please, Captain Schumann, sit down," offered the colonel with a wave toward the chair facing his desk. "Orders have come from High Command to accelerate our withdrawal. Of course, we expect this will be a temporary measure until supply lines free up again. As you know, most of the division has already been transferred to the Austrian border. We're to vacate headquarters in two days and regroup in Bolzano. However, we won't abandon this post entirely. We'll need to maintain a small staff here to hold our position in Verona. The tide may still turn." He hesitated for several moments, then lowered his voice and leaned in toward Günter. "May I be frank, Captain?"

"Of course, sir."

"If we can't return, if the situation deteriorates further, many on the General Staff will have a lot to answer for."

"To the Führer?"

"To the Allies. It pains me to admit this, but our conduct of this war..." The colonel stood and gazed out the window. "It's not something I'm proud of. If we lose, we'll be held accountable. The punishment will not be lenient." He turned to face Günter.

"There are files that must not get into Allied hands. We may still need them, so they can't be destroyed. Not yet. Someone must remain here to supervise. Someone I trust."

"I understand, sir."

"I've already written up the orders. I'm leaving Lieutenant Bauer and eight enlisted men in your command. We'll maintain radio contact from Bolzano and keep you apprised of the Allied position and any tactical changes. But if communication is severed... Well, then you'll have to determine the timing of your retreat. You're to remain here as long as possible in the event of a reversal." The colonel handed Günter his orders. "I know I can count on your discretion."

"You can, sir."

Günter returned to his desk and sat down, a gnawing tightness in his chest. He knew that the war was lost; the colonel had all but acknowledged it. To remain behind with such a small unit would be dangerous for the men under his charge. Their welfare was now his responsibility.

He did not relish the task of destroying evidence of official misdeeds to save top generals from prosecution. This was not the way Günter would have chosen to serve his country, but he resolved to fulfill his duty, nonetheless.

****

The next day, Klaus approached Günter in the courtyard at headquarters amidst the frenzy of the withdrawing Army. They quickly stepped aside as soldiers rushed by to load equipment and supplies into trucks.

"Captain Schumann, may I speak with you?"

"Of course, Klaus. It's good you found me. I've been wanting to say good-bye, and I'm glad I didn't miss you. I suppose you'll be driving the colonel to Bolzano?"

"No, sir."

"Another assignment, then?"

"Well, I asked the colonel if I could stay behind with you."

"What?" Günter was stunned that a private would dare ask the colonel for reassignment.

"He said I could. He'll find another driver."

"But why, Klaus? Why did you request this?"

"You've been so good to me, sir. When I got the news about my family... You're the only one I could talk to about it. You listened, you..." Klaus's lip trembled, as he seemed to fight for composure.

"It's all right," Günter said as he laid a hand on the young man's shoulder. "I know how hard it was for you. And you and I have been though a lot together, haven't we? But you should go with the colonel. It'll be riskier to remain behind."

"That's why I want to stay."

Günter didn't know what touched him more—Klaus's grief at losing his family in the firebombing of Dresden two months earlier, or this remarkable gesture of loyalty.

"Well, I will need a driver. Thank you, Klaus."

****

It had been two days since Günter's last radio contact from High Command, when he'd been told that the Americans had just taken Bologna and were on the verge of breaching the Po. He knew that the Allies would be upon them in days. To wait and surrender was perhaps the safest option, but to the men it would be an act of cowardice. Günter decided on retreat, hoping to reach Bolzano before being ambushed by the partisans or overtaken by the American advance.

After being informed of their captain's plan, the men completed their task, burning the last of the sensitive documents. They worked through the night and departed at daybreak. A troop truck was employed for the journey, with Klaus at the wheel and Günter beside him. The rest of the men rode in the back.

They had reached the countryside, about fifteen miles north of Verona, when Klaus was momentarily distracted by commotion in the rear of the truck.

"Captain," Klaus asked as he turned toward the din, "what do you think is going on back there?"

"Never mind about that," Günter replied. "Just keep your eyes on the road."

A split second later, Günter was stunned to see an elderly peasant inching his way across the road only a few yards ahead.

"Klaus, Achtung!"

Alerted by Günter's cry, Klaus swerved to avoid the old man, and the truck careened off the road, sideswiping a tree, and overturned. Klaus's full weight slammed into Günter as the truck landed on its side.

"Ach, du lieber Gott..." groaned Günter, his head pressed against the dashboard, one arm twisted awkwardly behind him and Klaus's knee jammed into his gut.

Klaus reached to pull himself through the driver's side window above him. Kneeling on the side of the truck, he wrenched the door open and leaned in, extending a hand to his superior.

"Are you all right, sir?"

Günter shifted his weight and waved away Klaus's hand. "I'm fine. Go check on the others."

Günter hurried to pull himself out and rushed to the back to see to his men. They were heaped on top of each other, moaning and struggling to move. Slowly, a few disentangled themselves and scrambled out, then returned to assist their comrades. A corporal, holding his left arm against his side and grimacing in pain, tugged on another injured man with his right, urging him to stand.

Günter and Klaus guided a barely conscious soldier out of the truck and helped him to sit on the ground a short distance away.

Once everyone had managed to get out, Günter began to assess the injuries. The most serious wound was a severely broken leg sustained by a private who had to be carried from the wreckage. There were two men with broken ribs, another who suffered a fractured arm and one a broken wrist, as well as two with possible concussions. Only Günter, Klaus, and two others were relatively unharmed, bearing only bruises and lacerations.

Further inspection confirmed that the truck was now useless. Fluid and steam spurted from the engine and the wheels on one side were bent at irregular angles. Without heavy equipment, there was no way of righting the vehicle. The mechanics in the troop concluded that even if they could get it back on its wheels, it would not run.

Amid the chaos of the accident, Günter had forgotten about the old man whom Klaus had barely avoided flattening beneath the wheels of their truck. *Perhaps he's gone off for reinforcements*, Günter mused, aware of the contempt with which most Italians viewed the Germans. Günter preferred to believe that the peasant would be too frightened to pursue the matter, happy enough just to escape with life and limb.

There was little to do besides wait. They attended to the injured with the scant medical supplies they had brought along and tried to make them as comfortable as possible. Günter considered sending a small party to walk several miles to the nearest village for help, but feared a hostile or even deadly reception for his men. He preferred to risk capture by the encroaching Americans, from whom he expected humane treatment, rather than confront civilians or insurgents. The Allies were sure to pass by eventually, so his little unit might as well conserve their energy.

About an hour had passed when Günter was informed that three small military vehicles approached them from the south. As they drew close, Günter identified German-made motorcars, VW kübelwagens with their Nazi insignia painted over. His worst fears were realized: it was a band of partisan guerrillas. *They seldom take prisoners.* He considered the condition of his men and concluded that an engagement would be suicidal. He ordered them to surrender and approached the vehicles to attempt negotiations with the squadron leader.

The partisans jumped from their vehicles and readied their machine guns. One of them disarmed Günter as others surrounded and disarmed his men. His hands raised, Günter asked to speak to their commander. To his great surprise, Günter recognized the man who approached him, the apparent leader of this group.

"What are you going to do with us?" Günter inquired.

"What do you think, Captain? We have no facilities for taking prisoners."

Günter knew he had nothing more to lose and would attempt to use whatever influence he could to save his men. "I know you. You're Leonardo—Isabella's brother," he whispered to the man who stood before him. "Don't you remember me?"

"My name is not Leonardo, and Isabella is not my sister," the man uttered scornfully. Then a glimmer of recognition flashed across his face. "Of all the Nazis to happen upon," Massimo said with a laugh. "This must be my lucky day!"

Günter prayed that Isabella had told her brother, or whoever this man was, how he had helped her escape, at the risk of his own life.

"How is Isabella?" he whispered.

"She's fine, except for all the pining for her long-lost German lover. I know she'll be heartbroken when I have to inform her of his execution."

Massimo signaled to Luigi, waiting nearby for orders. "Get them ready to fire," he said in a hushed tone when his lieutenant approached. "I don't want survivors."

A frantic pounding in Günter's chest rose as he watched Luigi dash over to the partisans. Each man primed his weapon as Luigi moved from one to another with whispered instructions and a glance toward the Germans.

"Please, Leonardo, or whatever your name is, have mercy on these men. Do with me what you wish, but spare them, for God's sake!"

"Have you Nazis ever shown us any mercy?" Massimo asked.

Günter looked down in desolation. "No, probably not. And I'm sorry for that, if you can believe me." He now looked Massimo directly in the eyes. "These men are not combat soldiers. They are clerks and mechanics. They've never killed anyone. I give you my word on it."

"And you, Captain, have you ever killed anyone?"

"Yes, to defend my life or someone else's. Isabella can tell you."

"She already did," Massimo acknowledged, then gestured to Luigi to hold fire. "Tell your men that they will be marched back toward Verona and turned over to the Allied authorities. Anyone who does not cooperate will be shot."

"Thank you, Leonardo. May God bless you for this."

The back of one kübelwagen was loaded with the confiscated weapons and another carried the private with the shattered leg. Günter and his men were marched to the partisan base, five miles south

236

toward Verona, then another fifteen due east. The three vehicles followed them close behind. A few miles from the farm, Massimo ordered the convoy to halt.

"Take these men to the base and wait for the Americans. Shoot anyone who tries to get away," Massimo instructed Luigi. "I'll take care of this one," he added, indicating Günter. "I've a few questions to ask him."

Massimo remained with one of the cars and had Günter placed, his hands bound behind him, in the front passenger's seat. Once the prisoners were marched out of sight, Massimo climbed behind the wheel and drove off the road to a desolate spot. He ordered Günter out of the vehicle, led him several yards away, and then pushed him down on his knees.

When Günter felt the cold steel at the base of his skull, he tried to prepare himself for a brief interrogation, followed by a bullet to the back of his head. *So this is the end.* He suppressed a tear as he thought of his family back home in Bavaria, and of his one true love who had so cruelly betrayed him. He now prayed only for the fortitude to die with a modicum of dignity.

"Do you want to know why I'm going to kill you? It's retribution for the atrocities you Nazis inflicted on the Italian people. But I have another reason for wanting you dead."

Günter reflected on the irony that he, of all German soldiers, who loathed everything that the Nazis epitomized, would now pay for their crimes.

"Can you guess what it is, Schumann? Do you know why I despise you so much?"

Günter was not anxious to surrender his life but had tired of Massimo's pointless derision. "I really don't need to know the reason. If you're going to shoot me, just do it and get it over with!"

"First, I want to even the score for your violation of my woman. A quick, painless death will not compensate me for the injury you have caused."

"So, you're Isabella's lover, then? Compensate *you*? What is she, your property? I swear to you that I believed she was unattached. She had me completely fooled, you know. But I always treated her with the utmost respect and affection. I never wronged her, even after I learned of her deceit. I truly loved her...and I thought she loved me, too."

Agonizing seconds passed as Günter waited for the click of the trigger. His heart leapt to his throat when a shot thundered past his ear. A spray of dirt stung his face, and he realized the gun had discharged into the ground just a few feet away.

The man behind him exhaled a dispirited sigh. "Damn you," Massimo muttered, his tone thick with resentment. "You're the one she loves, not me."

Günter turned and watched in bewilderment as his captor walked back to the kübelwagen and drove away.

Chapter 27

The Germans were brought to the farm where Massimo's group was based. Never having dealt with prisoners before, the partisans didn't know quite how to handle them. Blindfolded, their hands tied behind them, the men were made to sit silently by the side of the barn and warned they would all be executed at the first sign of resistance. The most badly injured were allowed to lie down on the ground but were given no medical attention. Several armed men guarded them closely.

The rest of the partisan band, scattered about the farm and in the house, began to approach the curious assemblage. Isabella and the other women, who had been working in the kitchen, drew near to observe the spectacle.

"Where is Massimo?" Isabella asked Luigi.

"He took one of the prisoners with him to question. He should have returned by now."

"What are you going to do with these men?"

"For some reason Massimo wanted to spare them. I don't understand it myself. We've never taken prisoners. But the German captain, the one he took with him, he somehow convinced Massimo not to kill them. We'll turn them over to the Allies as soon as they've liberated Verona. We don't want to keep them here any longer than we have to."

A chill ran down Isabella's spine as she listened to Luigi's words. *The German captain... Could it possibly be Günter?*

"Luigi, where did Massimo take this captain? What is he going to do with him?"

"I don't know. Personally, I hope he shoots him and leaves his body to rot. It would be a pity to have expended all of this effort without spilling a drop of Nazi blood."

"What a despicable thought!"

"I'm surprised you would say that after what they did to your brother. Excuse me, Isabella. I have things to do." He walked away.

She surveyed the group of prisoners. Most of the men looked exhausted and terrified. A few of the injured quietly moaned; others sweated profusely and breathed heavily. She felt compassion for them and resolved to offer what little comfort she could. Surely her compatriots wouldn't deny these men the small decency of a drink of water.

She went back into the house, returning with a pail of water and a cup. Kneeling beside each man, she offered a drink as she spoke in German.

"Wasser?"

Most accepted. As one of the men expressed his thanks, she thought she recognized him. Pushing the blindfold off of his eyes, she gasped.

"Klaus, where is Günter? Was he...was he with you?" she asked urgently in broken German.

His jaw dropped in astonishment. "Fräulein Ricci? I thought you were dead! Yes, Captain Schumann was with us, but one of them took him away. I fear the worst for him."

"What's all this about, Isabella? Why are you speaking to that man?" demanded one of the partisan guards.

Isabella was now on the verge of tears. "I know him from Palazzo Maggiore. He means no harm; please don't hurt him."

Luigi had returned and observed this exchange. "Isabella, why don't you go back to the house and wait for Massimo? The rest of you can go about your business, too," he said, and he watched the others disperse.

Isabella hurried back to the farmhouse and ran up to her room before anyone could approach her. She curled up on her bed, tightly hugging her pillow as her body convulsed in sobs. All the months she had wondered about Günter, not knowing whether he was alive or dead, all culminated in one appalling image she could not expel from her mind: Massimo holding his revolver to Günter's head and pulling the trigger.

****

A short time later, Isabella heard Massimo's voice and ran down the stairs to confront him.

"He's dead, isn't he?" Isabella's words were more an accusation than a question. Her cheeks burned with fury while her heart rent in despair.

"I don't know what you're talking about."

"Günter! You've killed him, haven't you?"

"Leave me be," Massimo replied with annoyance, then turned and tried to walk away.

She grabbed him by the arm and began beating him with her fists. "You bastard! You're a murderer, Massimo!" she wailed.

"Get hold of yourself, Isabella," he snapped as he held her wrists in restraint. "He was alive the last time I saw him. I'll have Luigi drive you back there so you can see for yourself!"

Massimo yanked her by the wrist, bringing her outside the farmhouse to where the prisoners were being guarded.

"Luigi, I need you for something. Drive back to the spot where I left you—you know, about three miles west on the main road. Off the road there, about a half mile north, look for that Nazi captain I took with me. He couldn't have gotten far."

"He's alive, Massimo?" Luigi asked.

"He was when I left him. Bring him back here. He can join the rest of them. Oh, and take Isabella with you," Massimo said as he pushed her toward Luigi, then walked back to the house.

****

As Isabella rode beside Luigi in the kübelwagen, she prayed that Massimo had told her the truth, that she would find Günter alive. When they reached the point where Luigi thought Massimo had separated from the others, he turned off the road and headed north. They hadn't driven far when they spotted a man sitting on the ground, his hands pinioned behind him, his head bowed. Luigi had barely stopped the car when Isabella jumped out.

"Günter!" she cried as she ran to him. He looked at her without uttering a word. "Are you all right?"

"Yes, I suppose."

She helped him to his feet and tried to loosen his bonds. Luigi stopped her, seized Günter and led him to the vehicle. After tightening the cords around Günter's wrists, Luigi put him in the back of the car and drove off toward the farm. Isabella tried to catch Günter's gaze, but he wouldn't look at her, instead staring straight ahead with an air of enmity and resignation.

At the farm, Günter was removed from the kübelwagen and brought to where his men sat by the barn. One of the guards began to blindfold Günter, but Isabella stopped him.

"Please, I just need to speak to him first," she entreated. The guard looked quizzically at Massimo, who was standing nearby. Massimo shrugged and nodded his consent, allowing Isabella to lead Günter a short distance away.

"I've been so worried about you, Günter. I feared you were dead!"

"Well, as you can see I'm still among the living." His chilly tone betrayed no emotion.

242

"I...I don't know where to begin... I don't know how I can express to you how sorry I am..."

"Don't bother, Isabella. It doesn't matter anymore."

"It matters to me."

"It's over. Just let things be, now."

"Won't you at least look at me?" she pleaded.

"I'd rather not," he replied as he stared down at the ground. Then he raised his head and looked at her, his expression bleak. "Why don't you just go back to Leonardo and leave me alone?"

"Leonardo?"

"You know, the man you introduced to me as your brother Leonardo. Don't you remember, back at Silvia's apartment? He's your lover, isn't he? I know he was eager to blow my brains out, but he spared me because you told him how I saved your life. I guess I should thank you for that. Now that makes us all even, doesn't it?"

"He's not my lover anymore. You're the only man I love," she whispered.

"Please, Isabella, don't insult me with your lies. Can't you just leave me be?" There was anguish in his voice, and Isabella knew it would be cruel to press him any further. She touched his arm tenderly, but he merely looked away. With a forlorn sigh, she turned back toward the house.

She glanced at Massimo as she passed, her eyes dimmed by regret. "I'm finished. You can put him with the other prisoners."

****

That evening, Massimo drove to Verona to find out whether the Allies had reached the city. He left Luigi behind to look after the prisoners. As night fell and the temperature dropped, Isabella approached Luigi to discuss the treatment of the Germans.

"You can't leave these men out here all night; it's starting to rain heavily and it will be quite cold.

243

Some of them are badly injured. They could die out here," she protested.

"I'll be weeping over that," he spat. "And what do you propose we do with them?"

"Why don't you put them inside the barn? At least it's a little warmer in there. And take off those blindfolds and untie them. What do you think they are going to do? Report back to German High Command with our location? They're not going to try to escape with four armed guards surrounding them."

"Are you in charge? Massimo must have forgotten to tell me I'd been relieved of my post. You know, I can almost understand your misplaced affection for that captain, considering all of the humping you did, but you're really starting to sound like a traitor to me."

Isabella looked at him with contempt but strove to control her anger. "Listen, Luigi, I don't love the Germans any more than you do. But even our animals are given shelter from the cold. Whatever his reasons, Massimo decided to spare these men. I don't think he'd be pleased to find some of them dead when he returns."

Luigi glowered. "Fine, Isabella. We'll treat them as our honored guests."

He walked into the barn to inspect its suitability and security as a temporary prison. After discussing the plan with the other partisans, Luigi instructed the guards to remove the blindfolds and bring the Germans into the barn. Their hands were untied but they were not allowed to walk about freely or converse together. The seriously injured private was carried into the barn by two of his comrades. The man was in obvious pain and distress; he was sweating despite the cold and shivering uncontrollably.

Günter appealed to Luigi for a minimal gesture

of humanity. "This man is gravely ill. Can't you at least send for a doctor?"

"No, but if you want us to put him out of his misery we can accommodate you," Luigi responded icily with a glance toward one of the armed guards.

Günter's eyes narrowed, and he took a step closer to Luigi. The guard leveled his rifle at Günter.

Isabella was standing nearby when she saw the confrontation and raced over to intervene. "Please," she whispered, "don't challenge him, Günter. He'll kill you all!"

"Schweinehund," Günter muttered under his breath. With a slight nod to Isabella he retreated. Then he sat down on the ground next to the private and grasped his hand. "It'll be all right, lad," he said softly.

Isabella returned to the farmhouse, where she recruited Carla and Vittoria to help her. They rounded up as many blankets as they could find around the house and brought them out to the barn. Then while the two others searched the kitchen for scraps of food and bread for the prisoners, Isabella approached the ailing private and knelt beside him. He was burning with fever, so she wiped his forehead with a dampened cloth.

"Danke schön! Das ist sehr nett von Ihnen. Sie sind ein Engel!" he uttered, his voice frail.

"What did he say, Günter?"

"He thanked you and said that you're very kind—like an angel."

****

Massimo didn't return until late the next morning. Accompanying him were several American soldiers with a troop transport. As the German prisoners were loaded into the truck, Isabella ran out of the house to see what was happening.

"Massimo, where have you been all night?"

"We've retaken Verona! I think I've made some

245

valuable connections with the American commanders. We spent half the night discussing strategies and the Allied advance. The war could be over in days, Isabella! They were even impressed by the compassion I showed to these Nazis. Most partisans they've met haven't been as merciful."

Isabella couldn't remember when she had seen Massimo this jubilant. "I'm happy for you."

As she turned to go back to the house, her glance caught on Günter. He was making sure that his injured men were properly looked after before joining them in the truck. *Yes, of course, and I am now nothing to him.* Eyes downcast, she had just started away when she heard someone call her name. It was Günter. She approached him reservedly.

"I just wanted to thank you for the kindness you showed my men last night," he said.

"It was the least I could do. How is the man with the broken leg?"

"He didn't make it. It was an open wound; the infection spread too quickly. He probably died from shock."

"I'm so sorry." She looked into his mournful blue eyes and wondered if she would ever see him again. "Good luck, Günter. May God be with you," she added, her voice choked with emotion. She barely heard his words as she rushed toward the house, tears streaming down her face.

"Good-bye, Isabella."

Chapter 28

Silvia pressed her body against the wall just outside Federico's study. The urgency in his voice troubled her. She inched closer to the door, listening intently to his side of the conversation.

"Of course I heard. Both dead, shot first and then strung up like dogs. Disgusting. So, you'll meet me at Gianni's place in Lugano? Tomorrow, for sure. I've got a passport and the other papers, not that it means anything to those bastards. How much? Yes, I have the money. Swiss francs, of course. I guess we'll have to pay them all off. Look, I've got to go. What? No, I'm coming alone. I'm sending Silvia to her parents. No, it's for the best, really. I can't thank you enough. Of course I would, you know that. Grazie, Alessandro, mille grazie. Ciao. No, I won't forget. Ciao."

When she heard the click of the receiver, Silvia stormed into the room.

"Sending me to my parents, Federico?"

"You were listening? For how long?"

"Long enough. And why is it any of Alessandro's business what I do?"

"Silvia, I don't have time for this."

"Don't have time to talk to me?"

"Listen, do you have any idea what's going on? The partisans are rounding everyone up. They'll probably kill us all!" He drew a long breath and raked his fingers through his hair. "You don't understand what's happening now."

247

"I understand that we need to get out of Italy. I understand that the war is over, that Mussolini is dead, and that the partisans will take their revenge on anyone else they can find. And I understand that we need to get to your friends in Switzerland as fast as we can. How many paintings can we fit in the car? And your grandmother's crystal vase—I'll wrap it in the Persian rug. I'd rather not leave that behind, either. Oh, and the tapestries. We'd better take the Mercedes; it'll hold more."

"We're not taking the Mercedes, I am. You'll take the Fiat and drive to your parents. You'll be less conspicuous that way." He glanced at her elegantly tailored suit and fox stole. "And change into something simpler. You don't want to draw attention to yourself."

"Why should I go to my parents? They don't even speak to me anymore. I can write to them from Switzerland."

"You're not going to Switzerland. Not now, anyway. You'll be safer here in Italy. Once things settle down I can send for you."

"I'm going with you."

"No, Silvia. It's too dangerous. Look what happened to Il Duce!"

Though he fought to remain calm, she could see the panic in his eyes. His thin black mustache quivered for a second before he turned away.

"I'm going with you," she asserted, "and that's all there is to it. I'll pack the furs and the jewelry you gave me. We can use them for bribes if we have to."

He walked over and held her gently by the shoulders. "It's too dangerous, amore. If anything happened to you, I'd never forgive myself. Please go to your family. It will only be for a little while, I promise."

"I'm not going to leave you. Whatever happens, I

248

want to be with you."

"You could be killed, like Il Duce's mistress Clara Petacci! They shot her, too, you know."

"I won't leave you. You're the only thing that matters to me anymore." He shook his head and let out a weary sigh. "I love you, Federico," she murmured, and slid her arms around his neck.

He held her for a brief moment. "All right, but don't bring too much. Now, hurry up; they could be here anytime. And don't forget to change your clothes."

****

When they'd crammed as many treasures as they could into the Mercedes, Federico helped Silvia into the car, then drove down the half mile of private drive from the villa toward the main road. They were within one hundred yards of the road when a convoy of military vehicles—two American jeeps, a German kübelwagen, a couple of motorcycles and a pickup truck—approached and blocked their path.

"God damn it, Silvia! Why didn't you listen to me when I told you to leave?" Federico reached beneath the seat for his pistol, but then froze; the horde of men barring their way with machine guns and rifles ensured that resistance would be futile. "Stay here and let me handle this," he told her sternly.

Federico was about to open the car door when a burly man armed with a revolver drew near. Behind him were two men with rifles aimed at the Mercedes. As those three detained Federico and Silvia, a few others entered the villa. All were dressed in civilian clothes, but the tattered red bandanas tied loosely around their necks identified them as members of the Garibaldi Brigades.

"Put your hands up, both of you," ordered the man with the revolver. Federico and Silvia complied. The man opened the driver's door with his left hand while he held his gun in his right. "Get out." One of the others opened the passenger's door. When Silvia hesitated, the third man roughly pulled her out and pushed her up against the car.

"Leave her alone!" Federico yelled.

"Balduccio?" the partisan asked. Federico nodded. There was no point in denying who he was. He had enough enemies who could easily identify him. "Who's she?"

"She's nobody. She's not even a Party member. You've no reason to hold her." Federico glanced over and saw several men sitting in the back of the pickup truck. Some looked as though they'd been beaten, and all had their hands bound behind them. Two were fellow members of Mussolini's inner circle, but he looked away without acknowledging them.

The partisan leader told his men to search Federico for weapons and then bind his hands and put him into the truck. As Federico was led away, Silvia broke free from her captors and tried to run toward him.

"You're not taking him!" she cried.

One of the partisans seized her from behind before she could reach Federico. She tried to pull away but he held both of her arms in a firm grip. She strained to thrust her elbow into his ribs and brought the heel of her shoe down sharply on his instep. He hollered in pain, then slapped her hard across the face, knocking her to the ground. Federico shouted and struggled with his guards but was forced into the truck and held at gunpoint.

"Marta, Angelina, come here now!" the Garibaldi leader called out as he yanked Silvia up from the ground. Blood trickled down from her split lip and mingled with the mud that spattered her face and clothes. Two young women got out of the kübelwagen and ran toward them. Each grabbed one of Silvia's arms and held her securely.

The men who had gone into the villa came out to report that the house was deserted.

"Good. Let's go," the partisan commander said. He directed his comrades to prepare to pull out.

"What about her?" asked one of the women holding Silvia.

"Leave her here. We don't need her."

"No, I'm going with him!" Silvia protested.

"As you wish," the partisan said with a shrug. "Tie her hands and put her with the others."

Silvia was bound and led to the truck.

"Let her go. She hasn't done anything!" Federico pleaded as she was shoved into the back of the truck.

"She wants to come along for the ride," the Garibaldi sneered as one of his men slammed the tailgate shut.

Silvia scrambled toward Federico, who was sitting against one side of the truck. A fellow captive moved out of the way so she could sit next to him. She leaned against Federico's arm as the truck began to move.

"Why?" he asked her, his voice husky with grief.

"Because no one else ever really loved me. And because I don't want to live without you."

"They're going to kill us."

"I know," she replied.

The truck picked up speed and its involuntary passengers were harshly jostled about. Silvia slid down, laid her head on Federico's lap and closed her eyes. He struggled against his bonds, frustrated that he couldn't hold her in his arms. With difficulty, he leaned forward and pressed his cheek against her blonde curls.

"I love you," he whispered.

She began to weep softly. "I love you, too."

****

In the wake of the German surrender, Massimo spent much of his time establishing bonds with his new American comrades and with ascendant Italian politicians. One day when he returned to the farmhouse, he approached Isabella and beckoned her to sit beside him on the sofa in the main room of the house. His expression unsettled her.

"I'm afraid I have some sad news for you."

"What is it?"

"It's your friend Silvia. She's dead."

Isabella began to weep. "Oh, no...what happened to her?"

"The partisans are rounding up Fascists all over northern Italy. Her lover, Federico di Balduccio, was an important man in the Fascist regime. When he was arrested, she refused to leave his side. Both of them were executed."

"But how do you know this?"

"I was at a meeting with other partisan commanders. There was a list of the Fascists who were apprehended, and I recognized her name. One of the Garibaldis told me what happened."

"Oh, Massimo...how could they do it? I'm sure she was innocent; she knew nothing of politics. She had such a kind heart. It just isn't right!" she cried as she shook her head and sobbed.

Massimo put his arm around Isabella and tried to soothe her, stroking her hair and holding her head lightly against his shoulder. After several minutes her tears began to subside. "War is an ugly business, Isabella. We've all lost many friends and loved ones. Maybe it's time you returned to your family. I'm sure they'll be safe now; you needn't hide from the Nazis anymore."

"Are you asking me to leave?"

"You don't belong here anymore. I hope we can still be friends, but I know I've no claim to you. You're such a gentle soul, carina. I will always love you, you know."

"I want to remain friends, too, but you need to

find someone who will love you."

He replied with a smile that didn't reach his eyes. "Perhaps."

"I'll go and get my things together. Will you take me home, Massimo?"

"Of course."

****

When they heard Massimo's truck drive up to the farmhouse, Isabella's brothers and sisters came out to see who had come. They ran to embrace her, tears of happiness flowing from all eyes. Over the last few months, while Isabella remained in hiding with the partisans, she'd forbidden her family to visit. She feared they might be implicated if the Germans ever captured her again. Though Massimo had exchanged messages between them, nothing could equal the joy of holding them in her arms.

Together they entered the house, where Isabella enjoyed a touching reunion with her mother. Her family had been aware of her risky life as a partisan but knew nothing of the espionage operation or how close she had come to death. *May they never find out,* she prayed daily.

"Please, Massimo, won't you stay for a while?" Leonardo entreated. "You've brought our precious sister safely home. At least join us for a meal." The others pleaded along with Leonardo, and Massimo could not resist their offer.

After supper, Leonardo pulled his friend aside for a private discussion. "Thankfully the war is over now. Don't you think it's time you propose to my sister? I can assure you that married life is a blissful condition, as my wife Anna will confirm! Believe me, nothing would make us happier than to welcome you into our family. In fact, we consider you part of the family already."

Massimo was surprised at the topic of conversation, but touched by the generous

253

expression of friendship. "You know that I love her very much, but I don't think Isabella wants to marry me."

"Has she rejected your offer? Perhaps I should speak to her."

"No, Leonardo, I don't think that's a good idea. It would be best to just let her be for a while. She's been through a lot; we should give her some time." Massimo didn't think it necessary to mention that no offer had been made.

Leonardo puzzled over his friend's words. "What exactly has she been through? I hope you didn't put her in danger."

"Surely you know that a partisan's life is always in jeopardy. If Isabella wants to talk about her experiences, she will. It's not my place to do so." Massimo hoped this would end the discussion. He did not relish the thought of Leonardo learning about his sister's involvement with Günter, or of her near fatal encounter with the Nazis. He certainly did not want to be the one to enlighten him.

****

During the months that followed, Isabella endeavored to resume a normal life with her family, occupying herself with farm chores, housework and cooking—anything to cast Günter from her mind. But as hard as she fought his memory, a day did not pass that she didn't think of him or worry about his welfare. She painfully recalled his steadfast devotion, as well as his rage when he learned of her deceit. She missed Silvia too, and mourned her loss. Though they hadn't spoken since schooldays until the chance meeting that day in Verona, Silvia had become her closest friend and confidante. *If it hadn't been for Silvia, I would never have met Günter.*

Of her two sisters, Isabella was closer to Laura, her junior by three years. With Marco gone, she was now the youngest member of the family. Francesca, two years older than Isabella, was prudish and docile; her only ambition was finding a husband and pursuing a career of domesticity and childbearing. Laura, rebellious by nature, was in awe of Isabella's thrilling exploits. Isabella recalled her relief when she'd convinced her sister not to join the Resistance, but shuddered, imagining Laura battered as she'd been at the hands of the Nazis.

Laura approached Isabella one early morning as she gathered eggs in the henhouse.

"Isabella, you've been very distracted lately. Something is upsetting you."

"What makes you think that?"

"You've been brooding for weeks. Is it about Massimo?"

Isabella longed to confide in someone. Even Silvia had not known all of her secrets, especially the most devious. *Can I take the chance and tell Laura my troubles?*

"No, it's not Massimo," she replied with a wistful expression. She sighed before admitting the truth. "There's someone else, Laura, someone I can never have."

Laura's eyes widened. "Who is he?"

"His name is Günter. He's a German officer, now a prisoner of war in American custody."

"A Nazi?" Laura was stunned. "How did you meet him and what is he like?"

"He's not a Nazi, just a captain in the German Army." Isabella was at a loss to know where to begin and how much to tell. "He's the sweetest, kindest man I've ever known. I met him through Silvia, an old friend of mine from convent school."

"I remember her name. I thought you'd lost touch with her years ago."

"I happened to run into her in Verona one day." Isabella didn't want to discuss Silvia now; it was difficult enough to talk about Günter.

"Tell me more about Günter. What does he look like? Is he like Massimo?" Laura inquired with fascination.

"Well, he's tall, with dark brown hair and the most beautiful blue eyes." Isabella couldn't help but smile as she pictured him in her mind. "He's very handsome. And not at all like Massimo, not in the least! Günter is easygoing and gentle. He's polite, intelligent and refined. He treated me like a queen." A dull ache began to rise in her throat.

"He sounds almost too perfect! But you look so sad, Isabella. Won't you be able to see him again?" Laura placed a soothing hand on her sister's shoulder.

"We...we had a falling out. I don't think he wants to see me."

"Why not?"

"It's a very long story. I did something he may never forgive me for."

"I know what it is. He found out about Massimo!" Laura declared with a slight grin, seemingly pleased at her deduction. "You were seeing them both at the same time, weren't you?"

"Well, yes...but it's very complicated."

"And what about Massimo? Does he know about Günter?"

Isabella now questioned the advisability of confiding in her sister. There were too many things that were impossible to explain. "Yes, and he knows that it's Günter whom I truly love." She began to weep. "I just don't think he will ever take me back!"

"If you love him that much, why don't you go to see him? What do you have to lose?"

"He's probably in a prison camp, but I've no idea where. Even if I find him, I doubt they'll let me see him. And then they'll send him back to Germany and I'll never see him again! For all I know he may already be there. I know I must try to forget him, but...but he never leaves my thoughts!" She put her face in her hands and sobbed.

Laura put her arm around Isabella. "I've never seen you like this. I think you should try to find him. I can see that you love him very much. If he sees that too, I'm sure he will take you back. I can't believe what you did could be so unforgivable."

Isabella was quiet for several moments before she raised her head and wiped away her tears. "Maybe you're right. I could try to see him again. But I wouldn't know where to start looking."

"Don't some of your partisan friends have connections with the Allies? Perhaps they can help you."

"I just don't know if that's best for me. But thank you for understanding, Laura."

"Of course. Isn't that what sisters are for?"

"Oh, yes, cara mia, it is!"

****

Four months had passed since Isabella had last seen Günter. Perhaps he no longer remained in Italy; some prisoners of war had already been repatriated. She considered Laura's advice—what had she to lose by attempting to see him? But even if she found him and he forgave her, did they have any chance of a future together? She decided to risk devastating disappointment and employ any means she could to find him.

Chapter 29

Massimo had moved to Rome to work with the Allied Military Government and the American commanders as they sought to return control of the country to Italian governance. He solidified alliances and insinuated himself amongst the most influential and ambitious politicians. Having proven his valor and leadership as a partisan commander, he stood poised to rise into prominence. He continued to write to Isabella, and she kept up the correspondence, wanting to preserve their friendship.

Isabella asked her brother Leonardo to drive her to the train station in Verona. She was to board a train for Bologna, and then change for another to Rome. The trip would take nearly eight hours; she wanted to catch the nine o'clock train to arrive in Rome before evening.

"So, you are going to Rome to see Massimo?" Leonardo asked as he drove her to the station.

"Yes. He works at the Palazzo Governativo. I hope to find him there, if not today then tomorrow."

"Have you decided to accept his offer of marriage?"

Isabella knew this would fulfill her family's dream. *They've always loved Massimo, and now he seems destined for success.* Although this would send her far away to Rome, it promised a comfortable life for Isabella. As head of the family, it was Leonardo's duty to make certain that his sister was well provided for. *Apparently Leonardo doesn't realize that Massimo has never actually proposed.*

"I don't know." She wasn't ready to disclose the real purpose of her trip.

"Then why are you going all the way to Rome?"

"I must speak to Massimo. I will explain when I return."

"And when will that be?"

"I don't know yet. It shouldn't be more than a few days. I'm hoping Massimo will help me find a hotel room."

"You won't be staying with him?"

"No, Leonardo." She wanted to tell him it was none of his concern, but thought it was wiser to let the matter drop.

****

From the train station in Rome, Isabella caught a taxi to the Palazzo Governativo. It was just after five o'clock, and she hoped to find Massimo before he left for the day. As she rode through the city, she marveled at its enormity. She had never been to Rome before; what a naïve country girl she felt! They drove along broad avenues, passing glorious monuments to centuries of diverse eras: ancient and medieval, Renaissance and Baroque. Despite the devastation of war, the grandeur of the Eternal City was unmistakable.

As they pulled up in front of the immense palazzo, she questioned the wisdom of her mission. But she focused her resolve and proceeded to the reception desk just inside the entrance.

"How may I help you, signorina?" the clerk asked.

"I'm here to see Massimo Baricelli. He works in the office of Military Administration. I believe he is expecting me."

The clerk rang through to Massimo's office. "There's a young lady here to see Signor Baricelli. Her name is..." He waited for Isabella to identify herself.

"Isabella Ricci."

"Isabella Ricci. Yes. Thank you, signore."

He hung up the telephone and turned to Isabella. "You can go up. It's on the second floor, down the hall to the right." He pointed toward the grand marble staircase ahead.

"Isabella! It's so wonderful to see you!" Massimo was waiting for her at the entrance to the office. After a moment of hesitation, he kissed her on both cheeks. "How was your trip? Please come inside. You must be exhausted." He led her into the office, then down a long hallway to a small conference room. "I'd bring you into my office, but I share it with several others, and you might prefer to speak in private. I was so happy when you wrote to tell me you were coming. I can't wait to show you Rome! How are you? Is your family well?"

"I'm fine, Massimo, and so is my family. And you?"

"I'm very well. Your letter was vague. Can you tell me why you've come all the way to Rome? I'd like to think it was just to see me, but I sense you have another purpose."

"Well, I hope that you can help me." She was weary from her trip but anxious to tell him why she was there, lest he make incorrect assumptions. She took a deep breath and then looked into his eyes. "I'm sure you remember Günter Schumann. I know he is in American custody, but... Well, I want to find him. I thought that since you have connections with the American military officials you could at least point me in the right direction." She observed his reaction closely, hoping that their long friendship would be sufficient to persuade him to help her reunite with his rival.

He paused for a few moments and frowned. "I see. I should have realized that you did not come here to see me. So you're still in love with him, then?"

"Yes. I've tried to forget him, but I can't. Maybe he still hates me, but..."

"You think that he hates you? Why?"

"The way I used him... I don't know if he'll ever forgive me for that," she responded, her voice almost breaking.

"But what do you hope to accomplish by finding him?"

"I need to see him again. I couldn't live with myself if I didn't at least try to reconcile with him."

"And you think I can help you with that?"

She noted the edge of resentment in his tone. "I don't know, but I didn't know where else to turn. I believe you still care about me. Perhaps I've no right to ask you this, but... I'm sorry. I shouldn't have come."

"It's all right, Isabella. I'm glad you're here. But I really don't think I can help you." Isabella bit her lip and looked away, trying to hide her disappointment. "Do you have a place to stay in Rome?"

"No. I was hoping to find a hotel room."

"Well, I will be leaving soon for the evening. Let me help you find one. Can you wait here a little while so I can finish up?"

"Of course, Massimo."

Isabella was impressed by the limousine and driver Massimo had at his disposal. They drove to a small but elegant hotel not far from the palazzo. She waited in the car while Massimo inquired within. He came out to tell her they had a room available and then helped her with her suitcase as she settled in.

"Can I pick you up here for dinner? I'll meet you in the lobby in an hour. That will give you a little time to rest."

"All right."

****

As they dined at an excellent restaurant on Piazza Navona, Massimo spoke animatedly about his ambitions for a role in the nascent Italian Republic.

"I hope to realize my dreams in Rome. The next several years promise to be very exciting. I know I can contribute to Italy's future. I used to think that you wanted to share this with me."

"I long for a free Italy, too, but my dreams are very different from yours. If Günter will not take me back, I will try to get on with my life. I may move to Florence to pursue my studies. I've put them off for so long now." Isabella paused, then looked into his eyes. "I'm very sorry if I've hurt you, Massimo."

There was an uneasy silence before Massimo responded. "Do you know why I spared him that day? As much as I hated him and everything he stood for, I couldn't bring myself to kill him. I thought about what he meant to you and I just couldn't go through with it. But I still can't understand how you could fall in love with a Nazi."

"You don't know him. He isn't a Nazi. I won't violate his confidence, but believe me, he's a good man. Not everyone in a German uniform is evil. I couldn't love him if he were."

After an awkward moment, they continued their conversation, mostly on inconsequential matters, and then Massimo escorted Isabella back to her hotel. When they entered the lobby, she went toward the front desk.

"I want to ask the clerk if he has a copy of the train schedule."

"Why? You're not leaving so soon, are you? You just got here today."

"I'm not here on holiday, Massimo. You know why I'm here. Please don't be offended. It is good to see you again, and I'm glad we got to spend a little time together. But if you can't help me, there really isn't any reason for me to stay in Rome."

"Isabella, wait..." Massimo reached for her arm as she began to turn away. "You said you don't know if you have the right to ask me for help. Well, maybe I had no right to ask you to spy, to put your life in danger. Hell, I almost got you killed!"

"That wasn't your fault. You didn't force me to do anything."

"No, but I do owe you at least a little consideration. Let me see what I can find out about Schumann. I'll contact you here as soon as I know something. But don't just wait around at the hotel. You should use the time to explore Rome. The concierge can give you a guide."

"Are you sure you want to do this?" she asked.

"Yes, I'm sure."

Isabella could read more in his eyes than in his words. He still loved her but was ready to let her go. After all she had endured, he conceded that she deserved this chance at happiness.

"Thank you, Massimo."

****

The next morning, Isabella came down to the lobby to discover that Massimo had arranged for a car and driver for her. She marveled at the status he had already attained, and she imagined that his aspirations would likely be fulfilled with amazing rapidity. She took advantage of the transportation provided and explored the Colosseum and the ruins of the Roman Forum before proceeding on to Saint Peter's Basilica and the museums of the Vatican. She spent hours enthralled by the magnificent paintings and sculptures, awed by the spectacle of wealth and power. Her last stop was the Museo Nazionale, where she examined the vast collection of ancient art. It was late afternoon when she returned to the hotel and anxiously inquired if a message had been left for her. Massimo had indeed left word that he would meet her at the hotel that evening with important news.

When he arrived, he told her he had learned of Günter's internment at a prisoner-of-war camp near Bolzano. He held her hopeful eyes in his gaze as he explained that, although the possibility of a visit was unlikely, he would attempt to exploit his connections to secure her permission to see him.

Two days later, Massimo returned to tell her that he'd obtained official approval for her access to the prison camp.

"This is highly unusual, you understand, and I had to cash in a few favors to get it." Then Massimo added with a hint of displeasure, "Permission is granted for a spousal visit only. You'll have to tell them that you're his wife. I'll contact our comrades in Verona to find someone who speaks English to take you there."

"I don't know how to thank you, Massimo." She threw her arms around him and kissed him on the cheek.

"I do hope you'll be happy, Isabella."

****

On her journey back to Verona, Isabella reflected on the course her life had taken and how she'd arrived in such singular circumstances. A shy provincial girl with the modest ambition of pursuing a degree and a career of her own, she had become a partisan spy who barely escaped with her life. She was proud of her contribution to the Resistance and of finding the courage to follow her own path instead of merely submitting to Massimo's sway.

She dared to envision a life with Günter, certain that he would not try to control her as Massimo had. His love had always been given freely and he respected her as no other man ever had. *If only he will take me back, I know he will not subdue my spirit but encourage me to grow and develop my own interests. But if he still despises me...* She cautioned herself to prepare for the possibility that imprisonment had intensified his bitterness, that her presence would not be welcome.

Chapter 30

Massimo had arranged for Giuseppe, a partisan associate who spoke some English, to drive Isabella to the camp for German prisoners of war. It was located near Bolzano, some eighty miles north of Verona, a journey of nearly three hours.

A dirt road brought them to a chain-link fence crowned with angry coils of barbed wire. Beyond the barrier, Isabella glimpsed clusters of prisoners listlessly moving about under the scrutiny of armed guards.

Giuseppe pulled up near the gate. One of the sentries glanced in their direction, then conferred with his colleagues while pointing toward them.

"Wait in the car, Isabella," Giuseppe advised. "I'll tell them why we're here."

"All right," she replied, her fidgety hands twisting in her lap. Her muscles tensed as she watched him approach the soldiers.

Finally Giuseppe signaled for Isabella to join him, and they were escorted to the guardhouse just inside the fence. She produced her papers for the sergeant in charge, who asked her, through Giuseppe, which prisoner she wished to see and why.

"Tell him I'm here to see Captain Günter Schumann. Tell him I'm his wife," she instructed Giuseppe.

Isabella was shown to a small room with a simple wooden table and three chairs. A tiny barred window high above offered little light. A bare light bulb hung from the ceiling. *This must be an interrogation room.* Horrific memories of her own brutal treatment at the hands of her Nazi captors flashed through her mind as she paced in nervous anticipation, praying that Günter's resentment toward her had diminished.

****

It must have been at least twenty minutes later that an M.P., who remained inside near the door, brought Günter into the room. He was sullen and gaunt. His eyes were glazed but still the brilliant blue she so adored. He looked at Isabella without saying a word.

"How are you, Günter?" she asked hesitantly.

"All right, I suppose. Still alive, anyway," he said without expression.

"How are they treating you? Oh, you're so thin! Do they give you enough to eat?"

"The Americans treat us decently. I can't complain about anything, really."

"When are they going to send you home?"

"I've no idea. For all I know I could be here for months, maybe a year. But I don't know that it matters all that much anymore." He let out a bleak sigh. "I'm not sure I even want to return to Germany. There's probably nothing left of it."

"I don't believe that. I know how you long to see your family, your homeland. The war is over now. It's time to put our lives back together. You mustn't be so despondent. Just think, after all we've been through... We've both survived, we..."

"What is it you want, Isabella?" he asked, cutting her off.

She bowed her head contritely, and then looked up at him. "Can you please ask the guard if he would give us some privacy?"

"The lady would like to speak to me in private. Do you think you could leave us alone for a while?"

267

Günter requested in English.

"How do I know she won't pass you a weapon, Schumann?"

"Isabella, he thinks you're going to pass me a weapon."

"That's ridiculous, Günter! Tell him to search me if he must."

"She doesn't have any weapons. She says you can search her."

The M.P. nodded, then opened the door. "All right, five minutes. I'll be right outside."

She waited until the door closed behind him. "Günter, I don't mean to trouble you by coming here, but I had to see you again."

"Why?"

"Don't you know why? I've thought about you every moment, prayed every day that we could somehow be together. Don't you know it's because I love you?"

He glared at her as he replied, his tone laced with rancor. "You love me? How is it possible that you could love me and then betray me like you did? I believed once that you loved me, that you cared for me, until I found out the truth. You've destroyed me, Isabella!"

"Please, Günter...*please* let me try to explain. I was fighting for my people, for a free Italy. I didn't set out to hurt you, or to love you. When we met, you were my enemy. You weren't even a person to me, just a symbol of what I hated. But now that I've come to know you, I see who you really are—the sweet, wonderful man who could make me happy for the rest of my life!"

"I can't, Isabella. There's just too much pain. I think it would be best to forget that we ever knew each other."

"I could never forget you, even if I spent the rest of my life trying." She began to weep. "*Please* don't turn me away..."

"I...I don't know how I can trust you now," Günter replied haltingly, his voice starting to tremble. "You broke my heart once. Do I...do I let you try again?"

"Believe me, I understand that. But I'm telling you the truth! I love you with all my heart and I will never, *never* deceive you again, if you could just give me one more chance!"

Günter said nothing more; he seemed lost and afraid. In his eyes she saw defeat, as if he had neither the strength nor the will to fight her anymore. She wanted to beseech him, to fall to her knees and beg him to take her back, but she feared it would only add to his misery.

She took his hand in hers, kissed it, and let it go. Soberly she said, "Tell me you don't love me, and I'll leave now. You'll never have to see me again."

"How can things ever be the same between us?"

"Then you don't love me anymore?" She stifled the sob that rose in her throat.

In silence, Günter stared at the ground, and her heart wrenched at his despair. Awkward seconds passed before he looked at her again, his eyes glistening with tears. It tore her apart to confront him, but she had to know if there was any chance of winning him back.

"If you don't love me, just tell me. I won't ask anything more of you."

Neither spoke for several moments. Slowly, he reached out and held her by the shoulders. Then he touched her face, drying her dewy cheeks with his fingers. She looked deeply, longingly into his eyes, silently pleading for the words she ached to hear. At last he replied, as tears rolled down his face, "I do love you, Isabella! I never stopped loving you, even...even when...I hated you!" He pulled her into his arms as he wept, overcome with emotion.

"I know I wounded you deeply. I'll do anything to make it up to you. I never wanted to hurt you—*please believe me!* I'm so sorry. Can you ever forgive me?"

He cradled her face in his hands. Then tilting her head toward him he kissed her. "I forgive you, Liebchen," he murmured.

They clung to each other as the door opened. "I've got to get you back for roll call, Schumann. Sorry, ma'am, you'll have to leave now." The M.P. waited patiently.

Günter squeezed her hand and let go. As she watched the M.P. lead him out of the room, tears of joy and remorse ran down her cheeks.

Chapter 31

For his journey from the repatriation camp,
Günter was given a small sum of money, his release
papers, and a one-way train ticket to Munich. He
had been transferred from Italy to a facility in
occupied Germany where he and his comrades were
re-educated and "denazified" into harmless non-
combatants. Though interned for nearly a year,
Günter considered himself fortunate. Some former
Wehrmacht soldiers were still being held by the
Allies pending war crime investigations. Others
were transferred to countries devastated by German
aggression and put to work rebuilding factories and
roads, their involuntary labor exploited to reduce
Germany's enormous debt of war reparations.

The train ride from the camp in Hesse, far north
of Günter's home in Bavaria, took many hours.
Günter's window seat afforded an unobstructed view
of his shattered homeland, and the monotony of the
trip invited reflection on how these past years had
changed both Germany and himself.

The motley landscape revealed a country still
rich in natural beauty but scarred by manmade
destruction. As the train headed south, the
snowcapped Alps loomed in the distance. Amid
broken relics of civilization—industrial plants,
government buildings, churches, and dwellings—
blades of grass sprouted, and trees were beginning
to bud. Undaunted by catastrophic upheaval, nature
burst through the ruins in a startling declaration of

271

rebirth.

But at various points along Günter's journey the wreckage was laid bare. Countless cities and towns were nearly leveled. When the train stopped, passengers disembarked into open fields or at burned-out shells where train stations once stood. The only sign that a particular spot was a transit depot were the carcasses of railcars strewn beside the tracks, picked clean by scavengers.

Günter reflected with a grief-stricken heart on the films he'd been shown at the repatriation camp, images offered as proof of the unspeakable evil of the Nazi regime. The withered corpses of men, women and children piled high and stacked like cordwood spoke of a virulent hatred molded in the bosom of his beloved Germany. Some of his fellow prisoners had reacted with disbelief, some with anger and horror, others with silence. For Günter, the sickening revelation drew bitter tears. *What did I fight for?* For Germany, he'd always told himself. While rejecting Nazi ideology, he had justified his participation in the war with a staunch devotion to his home and his people. To him, patriotism transcended political beliefs; Germany was still Germany, despite the detested Reich and its vile Führer.

But now he wondered what it even meant to him to be a German. That his own countrymen were capable of committing such hideous atrocities provoked feelings of shame and revulsion. It was as if centuries of German culture—embodied in the works of Beethoven and Goethe, Dürer and Kant— were obliterated by twelve years of madness. At times he became so distraught that he saw no use to his life at all and nearly lost his faith in humanity, even in God. All that sustained him was the thought of seeing his father and sisters again, and the dream of someday reuniting with Isabella.

Günter hadn't heard from his family in many weeks. He imagined the postal system was barely functioning, and it was a certainty his arrival would precede the letter he'd written home when told of his impending release. Günter looked out the window as the train slowed in preparation for its final stop. The battered panorama of Munich was still recognizable. He'd attended university there, a time full of hard work but also the delights of his youth. *What's left of the city I loved so much?*

Günter pressed through the teeming Hauptbahnhof, searching for the train that would finally bring him home. It was nearly evening, and he was frustrated to learn that the next train in the direction of his village would not depart until morning. *Perhaps I can walk around the city a while, then come back to spend the night.*

He headed toward Marienplatz. As a student, he and his friends had relished the outdoor concerts and haunted the beer halls of the charming plaza in the center of the city. When he reached it, the shock of seeing its skeletal remains impelled his anxious retreat to the railway terminal.

Günter surveyed the station for a few square feet of unoccupied floor space where he could settle in for the night. The building was crammed with both travelers and displaced persons; some had a specific destination, while others had no place to go. He spotted a vacant corner and hurried to claim it, careful not to trample the people who sat or lay on the cold marble floor. As he sat down, he nodded politely to his neighbor, a tense young mother trying to soothe her bawling child. He reached into his pocket for his last scrap of bread and offered it to the woman. She thanked him and accepted. Then he drew Isabella's latest letter from his breast pocket and reread it, as he had many times since he'd received it weeks before. Her words of love were a balm to his troubled soul and, eventually, he was able to curl up in his shabby greatcoat, lay his head on his duffle bag, and sleep.

****

Günter's train arrived at the Flüssbaden depot at ten o'clock the next morning. From there it was another fifteen miles to his village, but he hoped to find a taxi at the station. *If not, I'll have to walk.* But when he disembarked at Flüssbaden, there were no taxis in sight, just hordes of ragged refugees.

Flüssbaden was very different from the place he remembered. Before his years at university, this was the only city he had known. Though insignificant compared to Munich, Flüssbaden was the local destination for theater, amusements and shopping. Now, its deteriorating buildings showed the neglect of the war years, and the faces of its citizens were languid and remote. Günter's thoughts drifted back to the festivities of Christmas there when he was a boy. He closed his eyes for a moment, treasuring the memory of sparkling colored lights, the crisp chill in the air and the huge snowflakes he'd brushed off his long, dark eyelashes. *"Your eyes are almost too pretty for a boy," Mama always used to say.* He recalled tugging at her hand, silently begging for a treat, as they passed the wondrous aromas of Lindemann's bakery, and stopping in front of the toyshop, where he marveled at the shiny model train set and the army of tin soldiers. *But now it's spring, and that was a lifetime ago.*

With a sigh, Günter set out on foot. He had walked along the dusty road out of Flüssbaden for almost an hour when he heard the clip-clop of hooves approaching him from behind. He turned to see an elderly farmer atop a dilapidated wagon drawn by a pair of emaciated, mangy horses.

"Young man, do you need a ride?" the farmer called out.

"Yes, thank you. How far are you going?"

"I'm heading toward Kirnberg."

"If you can take me as far as Mitteldorf I'd be grateful."

"Come on, then," offered the old man.

Günter climbed aboard the wagon. "Do you live in Kirnberg?"

The farmer flicked his whip at the team. They snorted in protest but grudgingly obliged. "I've a small farm near there. Are you from Mitteldorf?"

"Yes. It's been two and a half years since I've been there. I can't believe I'm really so close to home now."

The old farmer glanced at Günter's faded, frayed uniform, noting the shadow of darker green fabric in the shape of the national emblem, the eagle and swastika, which Günter had removed. "Where were you stationed?" he asked.

"Italy. Before that, France."

"Well, at least you've returned with all your limbs still attached. Did you see a lot of fighting?"

"Things were pretty much over in France by the time I got there. Italy was worse, but I didn't have it too bad. I was in the supply corps."

"My son was in the infantry. He died in Stalingrad in '42," the old man said after a pause.

"I'm very sorry. Do you have other children?"

"Oh, yes, five more. My other two sons made it home all right. They don't want to be farmers. They haven't told me this, but I know. I know they're only staying because they think I need them around. Well, I guess I do need them around. I mean, there are lots of young men, like you, looking for work, but I can't afford to pay anyone. I can barely feed my own family. Things will never be the way they were before."

Günter sat quietly for a while and savored the warmth of the sun on his face and the scent of wildflowers, drifting on the breeze and caressing his nostrils. His mood brightened as he pictured Else's golden hair and fair blue eyes, eyes that would surely gush with tears when he took her in his arms. *Even Papa will weep with joy,* Günter thought, and felt his own eyes moisten.

He wondered, too, if Klaus would be there ahead of him. The young man was alone, his entire family killed and his home city of Dresden now under Soviet occupation. Germans and Russians harbored a fierce, mutual antipathy and most of Günter's comrades were loath to live under Communist rule. They expected harsh treatment from the Soviets, and many risked their lives to escape to areas controlled by the western Allies. Günter was relieved that Bavaria was now occupied by the Americans, and he trusted that his region would be governed justly. Before being separated from Günter at the prison camp, Klaus had confided his fears of returning to Dresden. When repatriated, prisoners of war were not permitted to travel freely but compelled to return to their home districts. Troubled by Klaus's predicament, Günter had given him his own address to use, making him memorize it well, so that Klaus would be able to stay with Günter's family. Most enlisted men had already been released, and Günter hoped that Klaus wasn't among the unlucky ones retained for forced labor.

Taking in the green rolling hills of the countryside, Günter noticed how the land seemed almost untouched by the war, except when they passed a broken-down farmhouse or deserted pasture. They rode on for another half hour before reaching the outskirts of Mitteldorf.

"You can leave me by that road up ahead. I've just a short way to walk from there." Günter alighted from the wagon after shaking the old man's hand. "Thank you very much, mein Herr. Auf

Wiedersehen."

"Good luck, young man."

****

Günter traveled along back roads, saving himself a few miles. The anticipation of seeing his family quickened his pace. In his mind, he raced to the front door, threw it open, and embraced his father and sister. But his body was weakened by a year of inactivity and the paltry rations of the prison camp, and he had to stop more than once to catch his breath.

As he neared the house he paused. *Just around the next bend and I'll see it.* His heart pounded, and he was lightheaded with exhilaration. This was the moment he'd dreamed of, prayed for, these last six years. He was finally coming home for good.

Günter rounded the bend and saw it, just as he'd remembered. *Well, perhaps a bit run down, and in need of a fresh coat of paint.* As he approached, an old half-bred Alsatian sheepdog came barreling toward him, nearly knocking him over. The dog yelped with exuberance, lashing its tail furiously and propelling its entire body against him as a gyrating mass of fur.

As Günter knelt, the dog slobbered its unrestrained welcome, then rolled onto its back in submission.

"So, you remember me, old boy," Günter said as he rubbed Odin's belly. He wondered how the fifteen-year-old dog had survived so many lean years. Smiling to himself, he realized that Odin had managed to outlast the Nazis.

Hearing the barks, two children came out of the house to investigate. Günter stood and looked at them curiously, while Odin turned his head from Günter to the children and back, as if attempting a mute introduction.

"Come here, Odin," said the boy, who looked to

277

be about seven years old. A girl of about three or four peeked out shyly from behind him. The dog hesitated, looked up at Günter, and then lay down at his feet.

"Hello, my name is Günter. Do you know if the people who live here are home?"

"We live here," the boy responded. "I'm Hans-Jürgen, and this is Lieselotte. You can call her Lilo. Mama isn't home, but Uncle Klaus is looking after us."

The fleeting, irrational thought that perhaps his family no longer lived here had crossed Günter's mind but evaporated upon hearing Klaus's name. "*Uncle* Klaus?" he asked with a smile. "And where is Uncle Klaus?"

"Um...I think he's in the back. I'll get him. Lilo, you stay here," he ordered his little sister.

"That's all right. I'll go find him."

Günter walked around to the back and saw a young man perched high on a ladder, hammering makeshift wooden shingles to cover holes in the roof.

"Klaus!"

Klaus looked down and gasped, then rushed down the ladder, taking the last four rungs in one leap. "Captain Schumann!"

After a half-second of reserve, all distinctions of rank fell away and the two men embraced in a heartfelt expression of friendship.

"It's great to see you, sir! Else and your father will be so happy you're home," Klaus told Günter as he led him inside the house.

"Where are they?"

"They went to visit some of your relatives over in Seitenbach. Matthias and Hilde, I think."

"When will they be back?"

"Oh, probably not until the evening. How are you, sir? When were you released?"

"Just yesterday. And what about you, Klaus?

How long have you been out?"

"A few weeks. Your family is wonderful, Captain Schumann. I can't thank you enough for inviting me to stay here."

Günter gazed around the living room. There was his mother's heirloom china in the cupboard, his father's hunting rifle hung above the fireplace, the overstuffed floral sofa... *Everything is in its place.*

"You must be hungry from your trip. Come into the kitchen, and we'll find something for you to eat."

Günter thought how strange it was that Klaus, the lad he'd taken under his wing, was now serving as host in Günter's own home.

Klaus heated some leftover potato soup for Günter and the two sat in the kitchen for hours, relating experiences of their internment and reminiscing about Italy. Klaus explained that the children Günter had just met were refugees, along with their mother, staying with the Schumanns until they could find a permanent home. Günter anxiously inquired about other members of his family, particularly his sister Maria. Klaus told him all he knew. She and her three young children were living with her mother-in-law in a small apartment outside of Stuttgart. Her husband Helmut, a sergeant in the Army, had been captured by the Soviets during the last days of the war and transported to a work camp in Siberia. Maria feared it might be years before she saw him again.

Later, Günter and Klaus moved to the cozy living room as the children played on the floor in front of them. It had already grown dark when they heard footsteps outside and the front door opened.

For an instant Günter froze, and the two figures at the door stopped in their tracks. A moment later, Else flew into his arms. Günter held his sister's face in his hand and caressed her silken blonde hair. Months of gloom melted away in a rush of tender emotion.

"My son..." exclaimed their father as he joined them in a poignant embrace.

"Oh, Günter, I can't believe you're really home!" Else cried.

"I...I can't believe it myself!" he murmured.

"Come," she beckoned, as she took her father's hand and her brother's and led them into the kitchen. "I'll make us all something to eat. You too, Klaus."

After a quick look around to make sure that the children hadn't followed them, Herr Schumann reached for his precious bottle of schnapps, hidden behind the pots and pans under the sink. He took four small glasses from the cupboard, filled them, and handed one to each of the others.

"God bless you, son. Thanks to the good Lord for your safe return!" he declared as he raised his glass.

Günter was too moved to speak.

"Bless you all," offered Klaus.

"If only Maria and the children were here...and Helmut, too," Else said as she clung to Günter, nestling her head against his shoulder. "Then everyone I love would finally be together."

Günter held his sister tightly around her waist as he thought of Isabella, whom he loved most of all, and wondered when he would see her again.

****

Over the next few weeks, the family caught up on years of separation. The war had left its mark on all of them, but their commitment to each other restored some of the faith that Günter had lost.

He noticed how much Else had matured, both inwardly and out. No longer the little girl he'd helped raise, she'd lost some of her innocence but retained her sweet, loving nature, and for that Günter was grateful. She'd cut off the braids that had hung down to her waist and now wore her hair in a short, simple style. She had swapped her skirts and dresses for trousers, more practical for the work she'd undertaken. She and their father distributed food and clothing to refugees, which involved the strenuous task of hauling fifty-pound sacks of flour and potatoes and the cases of canned food donated by the Allies. Günter admired how Else had come into her own as a resourceful, determined young woman. She ably tended a household of seven people, managing to stretch the scant rations and keep everyone reasonably nourished. Whatever brutality she may have witnessed while nursing soldiers near the front, it hadn't broken her spirit but rather augmented her compassion and competence.

Günter noticed something else, too. Though discreet, the growing bond between Klaus and Else was plain to him. As he sat in the kitchen one evening helping Else prepare supper, Günter carefully broached the subject.

"I think Papa is very fond of Klaus, don't you?" he asked as he took a potato from a bowl on the table and began to cut it into chunks.

"Yes, he's really become part of the family. It was so generous of you to invite him here, Günter," Else replied as she opened the oven to take out a loaf of schwarzbrot.

"Did he tell you what happened to his family?"

"Yes, it's very sad."

"He seems happy here, though. I hope he decides to stay. Do you think he will?"

"I suppose. Well, I don't really know. Why don't you just ask him yourself?" Else turned now and looked directly at Günter. With her posture, she seemed to demand a straightforward response.

He reached for her hand, inviting her to join him at the table. "I think someone has replaced me as your protector. I think you've a new champion, and I couldn't be happier."

"Is it that obvious?"

Günter nodded.

"Do you think Papa knows?"

"Probably, and I'm sure he's happy, too. I'm glad Klaus is here to help him. Maybe they can even re-open the store. I can't stay here forever, you know. I've got to look for some work. In fact, I've decided to head back to Munich very soon. I'm going to inquire about a job with the Americans. They're not so bad, after all. I worked with them at the repatriation camp, and they suggested I apply as a translator at Allied headquarters. Thank God I was stationed in Italy and held by the Americans and not by the Russians. I can only imagine how Helmut must be suffering now."

Else's face paled and she began to shake.

"I'm sorry, I didn't mean to bring up a painful subject. I know Maria is going through a terrible time. I'll try to get to Stuttgart to see her."

"It's not just that, Günter." Else averted her gaze.

"What is it, then?" he asked as he clasped her hand.

"I know something of the Russians myself. I was in Poland when they invaded." She put her hands up to her face and began to weep. "You don't know what it was like."

"Tell me," he entreated.

"I was a prisoner, too. Papa doesn't know, and please don't tell him."

"Mein Gott..."

"They didn't keep us very long, the women, I mean. But some of them...the Russian soldiers... They did things to the German women, horrible things. You know how we treated the Russians, don't you? They wanted revenge."

"Did they...did they hurt you?" he asked in a

quaking voice.

"No. But my friend Gisela..." Else whimpered, and Günter drew her close, rocking her in his arms just as he had when she was a small child. "I was lucky. One of the Russian soldiers...he took pity on me. He got me out of there. But I don't know what happened to Gisela after that. I never saw her again."

They held each other for a long while. Else's sobs alerted Odin, who had been lying in the next room. He came into the kitchen and sat next to Else, laying his muzzle in her lap. As she stroked his head, he looked up at her with devoted concern.

"You see, you don't need me around here at all," Günter said softly. "You've got Klaus *and* Odin to watch over you."

Else's tears subsided, and she managed a faint smile. "I told Klaus about what happened in Poland, and he told me about his family. He's been so understanding. And he's caring and easy to talk to. I think he's falling in love with me."

"And you?"

She blushed. "I...I think that I might be falling in love with him, too."

"You know that no one will ever be good enough for my baby sister, but I suppose Klaus is passable. But if he's going to be my brother-in-law, you'll have to get him to stop calling me 'Captain Schumann'!"

"Wait just a minute. Who mentioned marriage? I'm not even twenty yet!"

Günter laughed, then kissed Else on both cheeks. "You're right. But I'm very, very happy for both of you."

****

A week later, Günter prepared to make his farewells and travel back to Munich in search of work. He hoped to earn enough to support himself and help his father restart his business, as well.

Though Günter was saddened at the thought of leaving home again, Munich was only a couple of hours away by train, and he planned to visit often. In the short time he had spent with his loved ones, he'd observed their strength and resilience and was confident that his family would persevere.

Through Else and Klaus, he saw hope for Germany, too. Despite physical and spiritual desolation, and the agonizing recognition of their guilt in backing a murderous regime, Germans could still believe in the renewing power of love. For himself, Günter knew that his own salvation rested in the love of one woman, so far away but at every moment in his mind and in his heart.

Chapter 32

2 June 1946
Dearest Isabella,
I hope you and your family are well. It was wonderful to spend a little time with Papa and Else before I headed to Munich to look for work. Unfortunately, I haven't been able to get to Stuttgart to visit Maria yet. Her husband Helmut is still being held by the Russians, and we've no idea when he might be released.
As I told you, I got on pretty well with my former captors at the repatriation camp. I guess they appreciated my help, interpreting for the other German prisoners. I decided to follow their suggestion and seek employment at Allied headquarters. In fact, the camp commander even gave me a letter of recommendation. I was lucky enough to secure a position as a translator with the American military administration in Munich. I'm able to supplement my modest salary by instructing some of the Americans in German.
Finally, after many weeks, I can give you a permanent address. I live in a boarding house now and am grateful for adequate food and shelter. I've written the address below, as well as the address where I work.
I miss you terribly and wish I knew how to express how deeply I love you. It's been many weeks since I received your last letter. I can't believe how long we've been apart. Do you realize that in

September it will be a year? I was crushed when I learned that they turned you away the next time you tried to see me at the camp. To think you came all that way, only to discover that you had been granted permission for just one visit. I've cherished every letter you've written to me. It's the one thing that got me through those last dismal months of internment.

Conditions here are grim. From what I've seen and heard, most of Germany is in ruins and hunger is widespread. I wish you could have seen the Germany I remember, before the catastrophe that decimated our land and our people. I don't just mean the appalling loss of life and the destruction of cities. I can't begin to describe the unspeakable horrors that we are now learning about. I only pray that we Germans will someday be forgiven for the atrocities that have taken place.

I cannot ask you to come here now to live in this desolate place. But know that it is my dearest wish that one day you will do me the honor of becoming my wife. I pray that conditions in Germany will improve enough that I might ask you to join me. Though I have little to offer you, I vow to spend every day of my life providing for your welfare and happiness.

Please write to me soon, darling. I long to hear from you and to know that you are all right.

With all of my love,
Günter

As soon as Isabella received Günter's letter, she hurried up to her room, took her suitcase down from the top of the closet, and tried to decide what few possessions she would need for her new life in Germany. That was the easy task; now she would have to explain to her family that she was leaving. She had known for months, since their bittersweet farewell at the prison camp, that her life could not begin again until she joined her beloved in his homeland.

She could conceive of no reason to delay; in her mind she was already planning her journey. When she descended the stairs to the kitchen, she found her mother and Francesca busily preparing lunch for the family. Isabella wanted to blurt out her news but managed to contain her exuberance, realizing that it would be better to explain it to everyone when they were all assembled for the midday meal. She sat alone on the back steps and waited, reflecting on her long-hoped-for dream, now so close to fulfillment. She thought, too, of the sadness this separation would bring to her family. *I'll miss them tremendously. Once I leave for Germany, who knows how long it will be until I see them again?* But she didn't want to think about that now. Instead, she imagined nestling in the loving shelter of Günter's embrace, looking into his deep blue eyes, and caressing the soft, smooth skin of his cheek. It was nearly enough to inspire her to run all the way to Verona, and impatiently await the next train to Munich.

****

"Isabella, you've hardly touched your food. It can't be that you don't like it. I know my minestrone is one of your favorite dishes," her sister Francesca observed.

"What is it? You seem very agitated," Laura added.

Isabella hesitated before beginning. "I have some important news to tell you all." Anxiety knotted inside her, and she tried to steady her nerves. "You know that I've been corresponding with Günter." Her family was aware of their acquaintance, but only Laura knew that they were in love. "He has written to tell me that he's settled in Munich with a job and a place to live. I've decided to join him there as soon as possible."

Leonardo was the first to respond. "What are you saying, Isabella? You're going all the way to Germany?"

"Are you planning to stay there?" inquired Enzo, the next oldest after Leonardo. The others looked on in amazement.

"Günter has asked me to marry him, and nothing in the world would make me happier than to be his wife. I love him more than anything!"

"Oh, Isabella...Isabella..." Her mother could manage to say nothing more as she shook her head and wept.

"I never really understood your friendship with this man," Leonardo stated frankly. "And now you tell us that you're in love with him? Just how does a partisan end up falling in love with a Nazi?"

"He isn't a Nazi. And I don't care to discuss how our romance began, but he's kindhearted, honorable and completely devoted to me." Then Isabella added with a trace of indignation, "I'd like to think that you might be happy for me."

"I'm very happy for you!" Laura interjected. "I know how much you love him." She rose and rushed around the table to embrace Isabella.

"I'm happy for you, too," offered Anna, Leonardo's wife.

"We...we all are, Isabella. It's just that...it's just that the thought of your leaving is breaking our hearts!" Giovanni said as he approached his sister and took her in his arms. The rest of the family tearfully joined in, expressing their affection and wishing her happiness, despite their sorrow.

"I'll miss you all so much!" she told them. *But I must be with the man I love.*

****

A telephone call to Massimo connected Isabella with an official who, when offered reasonable financial incentive, provided the documents required for emigration. Within two weeks of receiving Günter's letter, Isabella was ready to depart. Leonardo drove her to the train station, where they exchanged their last good-byes.

"So, you'll write to us the minute you arrive?"

"Yes, I promise."

Leonardo pressed some money into Isabella's hand. "Here—you might need this."

"You don't have to do that," she responded, moved by her brother's gesture.

"Please take it."

"All right. Thank you."

"If this Günter doesn't take good care of you, I'll have to go to Germany and straighten him out!" His attempt at humor only heightened the sadness of parting.

"Don't worry, Leonardo. Günter is a wonderful, generous man. He loves me very much."

When the last call for boarding was announced, they shared a final embrace before Leonardo lifted her suitcase onto the railcar.

"You be careful now, Isabella."

"I will. And I promise we'll visit as soon as we can. Germany isn't so far away, you know."

As the train pulled out of the station, she waved until first his figure with upraised arm and then the station itself disappeared into the receding horizon.

****

Isabella's taxi passed through the rubble that was once the vibrant city of Munich. Here and there she saw women and old men carting away wheelbarrows of bricks from buildings leveled by Allied assaults. Wan, emaciated citizens with expressionless faces stood in long queues for meager rations. Her heart pounded with apprehension and longing as she considered the life that now lay ahead. As the massive destruction unfolded before her, she tried to turn from these dismal sights to thoughts of Günter. Soon she would see him, after all their anguished months apart. Though she'd written back immediately to tell him she was coming, she realized she might arrive ahead of her letter and surprise him.

The car pulled up in front of the American military headquarters, a solemn gray edifice, pockmarked by machine-gun strafing but one of the few in Munich that had sustained only minor damage. She wanted to race up the steps and call out his name until he came rushing to her arms. But she held back and cautiously ascended to the door, trying to maintain the illusion of a woman in control of her senses.

"Guten Tag. I come here to...uh...to see Herr Schumann. Günter Schumann. You understand, I hope?" she said in German to the man at the front desk.

He raised an eyebrow and asked, "And you are...?"

"Oh, yes. I am Isabella Ricci."

He picked up the telephone, but she could understand little of the conversation since he spoke very quickly, and at a barely audible volume. But she heard him mention her name and inferred from the few words she could decipher that Günter was there and would be right down to meet her. *This man must think I am insane,* she supposed, aware that she trembled with anticipation yet grinned like an enraptured adolescent.

"Isabella! Is it really you?" Günter ran to her and held her face in his hands, gazing in blissful wonder—and then enfolded her in his arms.

A few of his co-workers observed the reunion. Some glanced at them and then looked away, but most smiled, heartened to witness a scene of such absolute joy.

He took her hand and led her out of the building. His fingers caressed her face as he looked into her eyes, and her heart overflowed with love. They kissed, at first slowly, tenderly, relishing the softness of each other's lips, and then with a breathtaking passion that brought tears to their eyes. For several minutes, all they could do was to hold each other, as if they would swoon if they let go.

"I can't believe you're here! Why didn't you let me know you were coming?"

"I did write to you after I got your letter, but I couldn't wait until I heard back from you. I wanted to see you as soon as I could."

"I'm overjoyed to see you, and to hold you in my arms. But, Isabella, things are very bad here, and I hate to think of you living under these conditions."

"I don't care about that, Günter. All I want is to be with you. I couldn't bear our separation any longer."

"But how did you manage to get across the border?"

"My friend Massimo works with American military officials in Rome and has many connections. He helped me get the necessary papers. Fortunately, you live in the American occupation zone."

"Come, let's go someplace where we can be alone." He smiled as he slipped his arm around her waist.

"Don't you have to return to work?"

"When I heard you were here, I asked permission to have a few minutes with you and my supervisor told me to take the rest of the day off. He must have figured I wouldn't be able to get any more work done today!"

****

As they walked to his boarding house, Isabella decided she would confess the many lies she had told him, certain that he would forgive her. *There will be no secrets between us.* They reached the building, once the stately home of an affluent Bavarian family and now in a forlorn condition of decay, disfigured by war and neglect. Günter took her up to his room.

"I don't know what I did in my life to deserve this happiness," he said as he looked at her adoringly.

"Do you really believe that people get what they deserve? I don't. What about the millions of people killed in this war? What about all the victims of the Nazis, of the Fascists? Did they all deserve to die?"

Günter looked down, and then lifted his head to reveal grief-filled eyes. "Of course not. The things my country has done... I can't begin to understand any of it." As he stroked her cheek, a faint smile broke through his melancholy countenance. "I'm just grateful I have you, and I know we can make each other happy."

"Yes, darling. But let's not talk about sad things anymore. Not now. Now, all I want to think about is the life we are starting together." She looked about the humble room. Faded roses on peeling wallpaper hinted at a tranquil, far-distant past. The scarred, mismatched furniture spoke of generations long gone. She wondered about those who had dwelled here before them—and how joys and regrets might have shaped their lives. "So, this will be our first home."

"Our first home as husband and wife. Let's get married right away." His smile broadened and his sapphire eyes blazed with ardor.

"Oh, you want me to marry you? Where's my ring?" She held her left hand out to him and smiled.

"I'm sorry. I don't have a ring for you. I suppose you'll want to return to Italy now."

"I'm afraid I don't have enough money left to get back to Italy. So you're stuck with me."

"Well, we'll just have to get used to each other

then." He sat on the bed and beckoned her to sit beside him. "Come here, Isabella. I'd like to start getting used to you right now."

"Anything you wish, mein Herr." She sat next to him and threw her arms around him. "I love you very much, Günter."

"I love you, too, Liebchen."

A word about the author...

Lisbeth Eng is a native New Yorker whose love of literature, history, and romance led her on the rewarding path to romance writing.

An English major in college, Lisbeth has also studied Italian, German and French. Besides writing, world travel is her passion, and trips to Italy and Germany have lent authenticity to her European-set World War II romance novel.

Lisbeth currently lives on the Upper West Side of Manhattan, a stone's throw from Central Park and Lincoln Center, and loves the fascinating pace of life in the Big Apple.

Lisbeth loves to hear from her readers.

Visit her at
www.lisbetheng.com

Other Vintage Rose stories of World War II

SCHERESADE by Ronit Lèvy: Erika's life is full of promise with her new life in America. So why have nightmares returned? With a passionate young neurologist and an embittered Holocaust survivor, she follows the clues to unravel the mystery of her past and discover true love.

THE TROUBLE WITH PLAYBOYS by Margaret Tanner: A wealthy young Englishman travels to Australia and loses his heart and then the woman who holds it. In the turmoil of war they meet again in Singapore, but in the chaos after the Japanese invasion each believes the other is dead. Prequel WILD OATS gives more background to the story.

A DAUGHTER'S PROMISE by Christine Clemetson: Serene Moneto risks her family and her freedom to give shelter and aid to an injured American soldier. But as he recuperates, Miles finds himself fighting to liberate Serene from a life worse than any death.

SOMEWHERE IN NORTH AFRICA by Lindsay Downs: Algeria had been invaded by the Allies. An Army nurse and a Navy officer are thrown together, then separated by the misfortunes of war, including the horrors of a torpedoed ship.

SOLILOQUY by Janet Fogg: A special birthday present brings more than Erin could ever have asked for as she is swept back in time and into the intrigue of the French Resistance. Will her wishes save her and her lover, or will she lose him forever?

KINDERTRANSPORT by Jennifer Childers: As a nurse, Erika is sworn to nurture and preserve life, but authorities demand she turn over the six young lives that have been entrusted to her. Can she find another way out for them? Will Rickard help or is he one of "them"? Is a life the price of freedom?